ANGEL NICHOLAS

The only girl in the midst of four brothers, I spent my childhood hiding behind romance novels. Now the mother of four overly-energetic children, a Whimsy kitty and slobber-flinging Great Dane, fiction is still my refuge. Excessive caffeine fuels my typing, stiletto heels maintain my sass, and the splendors of Idaho alongside its gregarious people inspire my muse.

You can follow me on Twitter @_AngelNicholas

Sweet Deception

ANGEL NICHOLAS

Harper*Impulse* an imprint of
HarperCollins*Publishers* Ltd
77–85 Fulham Palace Road
Hammersmith, London W6 8JB

www.harpercollins.co.uk

A Paperback Original 2015

First published in Great Britain in ebook format by Harper*Impulse* 2014

Copyright © Angel Nicholas 2014

Cover images © Shutterstock.com

Angel Nicholas asserts the moral right
to be identified as the author of this work

A catalogue record for this book is
available from the British Library

ISBN: 9780008128142

This novel is entirely a work of fiction.
The names, characters and incidents portrayed in it are
the work of the author's imagination. Any resemblance to
actual persons, living or dead, events or localities is
entirely coincidental.

Automatically produced by Atomik ePublisher from Easypress

All rights reserved. No part of this publication may be
reproduced, stored in a retrieval system, or transmitted,
in any form or by any means, electronic, mechanical,
photocopying, recording or otherwise, without the prior
permission of the publishers.

To my darling munchkins, for their tolerance of late dinners, forgotten events, a less than immaculate house, and my general distraction. I love you!

Chapter One

Nausea churned as the Roller Coaster of Death plummeted to the ground.

"I can do this." Ally's short fingernails bit into her palms.

The ride blew past her, blowing her hair back, the screaming of its occupants piercing her tender eardrums. Cold sweat popped up across her skin.

"Why am I doing this?" Oh, right. She'd gotten tired of listening to everyone else on the entire planet, or just her office, talk about the fun they were having while she went home to a glass of wine and a book. An excellent book, but still.

The ginormous roller coaster drew her gaze skyward. Some demented creator had produced a horrific edifice with tracks climbing high into the clouds before dropping to the earth and disappearing inside a concrete building filled with fog and general creepiness. The mechanical roar and screech of the amusement park almost drowned out the heckling of her inner coward.

The line for the ride emerged from the crowd, bringing her hesitant approach to an abrupt halt. People lined up behind her and milled around on either side, boxing her in. The cold sweat from earlier spread and she shivered. Fenced in, blocked, no immediate avenue of escape. She swallowed the saliva pooling in her mouth.

A sweaty hand grabbed her arm and she jumped.

"Hey. You, you and you two come with me. You've been chosen for the best seat on the coaster." The guy's grin about split his pimpled face as he ushered them away from the disappointed crowd.

Ally followed in a daze, misty visions of dashing for the nearest exit tempting her. The best seat? She didn't want any seat, let alone the best.

Arriving at their destination, the guy stopped and turned to face them. Pimple face, aka Mr. Obnoxious, gestured to the side with a flourish worthy of a grand ringmaster. Her jaw dropped. Surely not *that* seat.

Mr. Obnoxious grabbed her arm again.

Gritting her teeth, she yanked free and scrambled in on her own.

A juvenile delinquent, by the look of his saggy clothes and scruffy appearance, climbed in behind her and a blonde sat beside him.

The thump of a sneaker-clad foot on her seat made her swing around. Her gaze traveled up, skating over thick muscles, golden hair and bronzed skin; something clenched deep in her belly.

Ally swallowed thickly and averted her gaze as the leg's owner dropped into the seat with casual grace. His leg grazed hers, the coarse feel of tiny hairs against her smooth skin foreign. Self-consciously trying to make her plump curves smaller, she glanced up through her lashes at the newest addition to the suicide machine. Shaggy blonde hair, the shadow of a beard darkening his square jaw, his raw masculinity short-circuited every one of her nerve endings. He had the kind of good looks guaranteed to bring women by the droves and fit her image of a typical California Surfer Dude. Her lips flat-lined.

"Alright, folks. Let's get you all buckled in, safe and secure."

Safe? Secure? Was this an issue?

Mr. Obnoxious grabbed the seat belts and buckled them around her before she even had a chance to lift a finger.

Narrowing her eyes, she turned to give the jerk a piece of her mind and encountered the amused, blue-green gaze of her surfer neighbor. She clamped her jaw shut and faced forward. What fun.

After instructing everyone on proper safety protocol, Mr. Obnoxious stepped away. The other passengers chatted, clearly looking forward to the ride and all very much insane. Waiting for the rest of the ride to be loaded, Ally glowered out the front of the death-by-idiocy car and eavesdropped on her companions. Apparently, the hot guy to her right belonged with the woman in the rear seat and the juvie was riding solo.

Why had she left the safety of her comfy couch?

The metallic screech of gears made her jump. The roller coaster lurched forward. Their "special" car shuddered before accelerating smoothly down the track. Despite the restraints, the first sharp turn flung her into Surfer Dude's rock-hard body. Apparently, there were a few benefits to a shiftless lifestyle. Pressed against him from shoulder to knee, she met his gaze. A wave of heat surged into her cheeks. Was the guy perpetually amused, or what?

"Sorry." She straightened with effort as the car went into another loop.

Holy crap, he smells good.

They wound in and out of tunnels, faster and faster until the ride slowed, click-clacking up a steep grade. Ally white-knuckled the hem of her shorts.

Crisp masculine hair chased tingles up the side of her arm, distracting her from imminent death. Surfer Dude's golden thigh pressed against her hand. His thigh moved, doing a slow slide over her wrist. She glanced up. The heat in his expression made a mockery of all her internal cracks about easy-going. He was about as relaxed as a hungry lion crouched in tall grass, eyeing the plump lines of a grazing gazelle. Licking her lip, ultra-sensitive to every inch of skin he touched, she tried to scoot away. The ride went into a free fall.

The bottom of her stomach disappeared and she lost her breath. Jerking free of Surfer Dude's gaze, her eyes widened as they screamed down the track, slammed around a corner and into a building. In the dark and shadowy interior, fog machines worked overtime. They shot in and out of clouds of the stuff. Moist air whooshed past her ear; severe claustrophobia kicked in.

She fought to remain calm as she breathed the thick, weird-smelling fog. Squeezing her eyes shut only worsened her panic. She bit her lip, holding in a moan of pure agony.

The girl behind her let out an odd squeak. People yelled. Ally snapped her eyes open. The clinging mist lent a dreamlike quality to the scene as the coaster flew high above the ground. Several cars ahead, two men had removed their seat belts and were wrestling. The fighting men stood and she gasped.

"What the hell?" Surfer Dude leaned forward.

One of the men toppled out and disappeared into the swirling fog. Eyes wide and heart in her throat, Ally gasped. Screams ricocheted off the walls. The second man peered over the side and then sat. Just...sat.

A few heartbeats passed. The ride clattered along the track, the low rumble blending with the muttering of her erstwhile companions; the noises were distant. Surreal. She tightened her grip on her restraints. *No one touches my straps.*

Her brain ceased functioning.

People shouting, demanding the ride be stopped, finally penetrated her fog of shock. Someone must have heard or seen what happened because the cars slowed as they rounded several more loops. At ground level inside the building they came to a stop.

"What's going on?" An uneasy mix of teenage belligerence and anxiety threaded the juvenile delinquent's voice.

The blonde in the rear leaned forward. "That wasn't supposed to happen, was it?"

Ya think?

Surfer Dude twisted around—Ally assumed to comfort his plastic-perfect girlfriend. "It's okay, honey."

Ally started to shake. She could barely see through the shifting gloom. Strange men were talking about stuff she only encountered from the safety of her living room while watching TV and, oh yeah, she'd witnessed a man plummet to his death. Would anyone notice if she covered her ears and cowered on the floor of this thing?

Lights bobbed closer, accompanied by the sound of men's voices. From the fragments she caught, they sounded like the police.

"Hey! Freeze. Police."

Bile rose in Ally's throat.

A scuffle and swearing followed. Running feet slapped against the concrete and the bobbing lights disappeared.

"Okay, let's go." Surfer Dude took charge, instructing everyone on getting out of the car. They all climbed out, the cool concrete floor of the dark building a small jump down from the raised track.

Ally scrambled to unclip the seat belt and get out. She almost wept when her feet touched solid ground. There might be more to Surfer Dude than good looks after all. Even so, she didn't plan on ever getting on another roller coaster. Who knew fears could be so sensible?

Escape was in sight.

Well, not sight exactly. Between the poor lighting and the dense artificial fog, she could barely see her hand in front of her face. She leaned against the cool block wall, letting her heartbeat slow, and gradually realized she was completely alone. Apparently, her fellow passengers managed to keep their wits about them and beat a hasty retreat out of this walking nightmare.

"Hello?" she whispered.

The darkness heightened her other senses. The slow drip of water. Low-wattage bulbs flickered here and there, barely penetrating the shifting gloom. Water condensed on the hard gray walls and the scent of moist earth filled her nose. Which was strange since she stood surrounded on all sides by concrete.

Why didn't someone turn off the fog machines?

More importantly, why was she still standing there?

Hesitant, one hand maintaining contact with the damp wall, she started away from the ride. Some guy had met his maker down here. The last thing she needed was an up-close-and- personal look at death.

Shouts erupted again, commanding yells ordering someone to stop.

Oh, wow. So not good.

The sharp echo of gunshots followed and she dropped to a crouch. Ally wrapped her arms around her bent legs and curled into the smallest ball possible. The scrape of her shoes as she edged closer to the wall seemed overly loud. Huddled against the wall, moisture seeped into her clothes and she shivered.

Gingerly rising to a crouch, she broke into an awkward trot, still hugging the wall. Two heartbeats later, pounding footsteps drew close. Ragged breathing accompanied the thud of shoes on concrete. The hair on her nape rose.

Hand on the wall, she broke into a run. A rough spot tore at her fingers, but she didn't pull away, praying for a doorway. Or a nook. Really, a cranny or crevice would do. Anything she'd be able to duck into and hide. *Please, please, please, please.*

The wall ended and she nearly tumbled into the opening.

Yes! She slid inside, the pitch-blackness of her cranny not nearly as scary as what was coming behind her. The heavy footsteps drew closer. She shrank back farther, dormant instincts screaming. Terror wrapped clawed fingers around her throat. A whimper escaped without her permission. So close…

A broad hand clamped over her mouth and a strong arm yanked her back against a warm, hard body. Eyes wide in the dark, her lungs seized. She almost peed her pants. Footsteps and heavy breathing passed within inches of her not-so-empty hidey-hole.

I am so screwed. She parted her lips.

"Quiet," came a low masculine growl. "Just because he's passed doesn't mean he won't double back."

His palm caught her gasp as the familiar voice clicked into place. Surfer Dude held her tight against his hard body. She sagged with relief but abruptly stiffened again when he didn't release her.

What the heck?

Mumbling into his hand accomplished zilch. He didn't budge. She squirmed in his grasp. Nothing. Out of desperation, she licked his palm.

Soft laughter rumbled in her ear.

She shivered in delicious response. Wait, no. She shivered in revulsion. Yep, revulsion.

"You're gonna have to do better. Licking only brings to mind all sorts of fun games." The hand over her mouth moved down. Slowly. More of a caress, actually. He cupped her chin, skimmed his fingers down her throat and over her collarbone...

Whoa. She smacked his hand away. No way was he hitting second base when she didn't even know his name. Oh, for crying out...No way was he hitting second base period.

He chuckled again. As if he knew *exactly* what she was thinking.

She rolled her eyes. As if. A scuff of sound in the distance grounded her. Was Surfer Dude intentionally trying to distract her from the danger of their situation? Where was his girlfriend?

"I think it's safe now." His whisper reminded her they stood cuddled together like lovers.

She pulled free, her face burning. "Where's your girlfriend?"

"Who?"

"The gorgeous blonde on the ride. You remember her, right?" Okay, that might have sounded more snotty than she intended.

She leaned forward to peer around the wall, but his hand on her abdomen stopped her. All her nerve endings fired in response.

"That was my sister, Celia," he whispered low in her ear. "After I got her out of the building, I came back for you. You went the wrong way." She started to respond, but he cut her off. "Now step back while I see if the coast is clear."

Setting aside the whole girlfriend issue for the moment, she straightened her spine and stood there like a delicate flower of womanhood while the big manly man peered around the wall.

Hey, if he wanted to play hero, far be it for her to stand in his way.

He snagged her hand, dragging her along behind him as he stepped out of their hiding spot and down the tunnel. Did the guy have spidey-sense? How had he unerringly found her hand in the dark?

Returning to the main part of the building brought relief mixed liberally with trepidation. After hanging out in the pitch black, dim light was a drastic improvement. Even so, a deranged psychopath was running around inside with them.

She added a little more enthusiasm to her step. Walking behind Surfer Dude and admiring the broad expanse of his back distracted her from imminent danger. Okay, so the muscle she was admiring was a little farther south.

He stopped and she smacked face-first into his shirt. And lingered. *Good Lord, he smells good.* Voices drifted down the building, rudely distracting her from olfactory bliss.

"You sure you haven't seen anything, MacAfee?"

"Nah, he didn't come my way, Sarge."

Her hormone-induced bubble burst. She peeked around Surfer Dude. Two uniformed police officers stood in a doorway with a man in street clothes. Probably a detective or something. Luxurious, beautiful sunlight shone beyond the door.

Intent on the freedom the swatch of sunshine represented, Ally sidled around Surfer Dude. He pulled her back into his chest and covered her mouth. She sighed into his hand and crossed her arms. This was getting old. Maybe she should stomp on his foot. Kick him in the shin. Elbow him in the ribs. Or just bite him.

"Don't even think about it," he warned, his low voice barely reaching her ears.

Annoying man. He could read minds too?

"See the dark shadow against the wall there? Between us and the door?"

Squinting, she strained to separate the subtle differences in the shadows. A soft sound reached her, like the shift of a foot in dirt. Her eyes widened as the silhouette of a man pressed into the corner became clear.

A reflection glinted, like a deer's eyes in the middle of the night as you flashed by in your car. He was looking their way. She pressed back into her human wall, shaking. She belatedly sensed the alert edge in Surfer Dude's stiffened muscles.

Slow and easy, hugging the wall beside them, he moved backward. The rough block wall scraped her bare arm. She didn't care. The closer they were to something solid, the safer she felt. A sense of impending disaster filled her.

A muffled thump and whoosh of furnace-hot air creased the air beside her face. Surfer Dude jerked her into another dark hole in the wall. Burning pain lit her cheek as a dull thud smacked into the wall, raining chunks of debris on them.

His whisper-soft expletive blistered her ears. He unerringly found her hand again, tugged her out of the hole and jogged into the darkness—away from the door. Left with no choice, she followed. Her other hand crept up to touch a fiery spot on her cheek and her fingers came away damp and sticky. She wiped the thick substance on her khaki shorts.

Could this day get any worse? She should have stayed in bed.

Running up the metal steps, she did her best to keep quiet. The light improved as they climbed. His well-muscled butt distracted her from the burn of her thigh muscles and what felt like a gigantic bull's eye on her backside.

Finally—*thank you, God*—they arrived at the top of the unending staircase. Sucking air, legs shaking like wet noodles, she gratefully sagged against the nearest wall. Oblivious to her state of near-collapse, Surfer Dude leaned over the stairwell, staring down into the inky black below. How he could see anything, she didn't know. Neither did she particularly care.

Eyeing his hunky rear end, she touched her cheek. Wincing, she traced the throbbing, damp line of skin. Surfer Dude straightened and turned. His eyes narrowed on her. Two big steps brought him toe to toe. Sucking in a breath at his nearness, she tried to step back, but there was nowhere to go.

"Damn." His sigh feathered across her skin. With gentle fingers, he pulled her hand away and tilted her face toward the light. "I didn't realize."

His face came closer. Close enough to count eyelashes. Totally unfair; they were longer than hers.

"It's not bad," he murmured. "Just a graze. If I'd realized sooner he had a gun...I'm sorry, Sugar Lips."

She lifted her fingers in a shaft of brilliant sunlight and stared at the glistening blood on the tips. Her vision dimmed.

"Oh no you don't."

His voice came through a tunnel. Everything went dark.

Chapter Two

Bright sunshine penetrated her closed lids. Ally rolled her head away before forcing them open. Squinting, she contemplated the bare leg an inch from her face. Tan and muscled, with a sprinkling of blonde hair. Nice.

"Finally awake, Sleeping Beauty?"

The smooth velvet baritone washed over her, the slight roughness making her hormones sit up and pant. His voice made her think of naughty whispers in the dark, soft sighs when he kissed a special spot and the husky moans of unhurried lovemaking on satin sheets. She yearned toward it and had to fist her hands to resist temptation. No doubt he made the same unspoken offer to every female who crossed his path.

His words registered.

A snort escaped her lips before she could think better of it. His low chuckle heated her cheeks. Braving the sunlight, she turned to look at him. Up a brilliant white T-shirt, over a well-defined jawline, smiling lips and a straight nose, to focus on amused aqua eyes.

Surfer Dude. And apparently her head currently resided in his lap. The heat in her cheeks ratcheted up to a near-burn.

She sat up. They were on a roof, in a narrow spot of shade provided by the rooftop stairway access. Against her will, her gaze flitted back to where Surfer Dude lounged with impressive nonchalance.

"Feeling better?"

Prim dignity came to the rescue as she smoothed her mousy-brown hair, self-consciousness hidden behind a façade of calm reserve. "Yes, thank you."

She ached to tug down her too-short shorts and make sure her lacy tank top still kept everything adequately covered. Pride brought her hand back to her lap and she clasped her fingers tight to prevent unlicensed wandering.

"I take it you don't deal well with blood?"

Tensing, Ally searched his expression for any sign of condescension. Seeing none, she relaxed a little. "Not my own."

"Yeah, I don't know many people fond of seeing their own blood." He shrugged. "No biggie, Sugar Lips. The bullet only nicked you."

"Would you quit calling me Sugar…" The hot irritation faded alongside her voice. She swallowed and managed a single squeaky word. "Bullet?"

Hunky guys calling her mocking names ranked pretty high on her annoyance scale. Bullets? They'd never made it *onto* the scale. His shrewd gaze sharpened. Ally lifted her chin. He didn't intimidate her.

"Yeah. You seem to have a penchant for finding trouble."

"Me?" Her spine stiffened. "What about you? You were there too."

"Sure, but you seem to have a way of attracting attention. Not surprising, I guess, with those big eyes and…" His gaze dropped to her lips, which promptly plumped and tingled. "…truly luscious lips."

"Oh, get real, Surfer Dude."

Oh. My. Word. I did not say that out loud. Fire burned in her cheeks, growing hotter when he chuckled. *So glad I can prove entertaining, at least. Obnoxious jerk.* She turned away and ducked her chin so her long hair fell forward to hide her face until the blasted blush faded.

"Surfer Dude?"

The laughter still coloring his voice made her want to crawl into a hole. Why did she always have to humiliate herself in front of attractive men? No wonder she was still single.

"I don't know your name," she mumbled into her hair. "I didn't know what to call you."

"Hey, whatever works. Name's Greg."

"Ally."

"Sorry?"

He swept aside her hair, long fingers wrapping around her chin to angle her face back toward him. Meeting Surfer...uhm, Greg's sparkling eyes, she swallowed.

"My name is Ally."

He stared at her until her stomach tumbled to the hot roof they sat on. Which was beyond silly. No way on this planet a guy like him would want her.

He leaned closer, the heat in his eyes holding her suspended in breathless anticipation. His lips settled on hers with no hesitation, moving with a confidence she couldn't begin to comprehend. Her lids slid closed against an eruption of butterflies. Deepening the kiss, his tongue glided over the seam of her lips, asking and gaining admission. The taste of him exploded across her tongue like deep, dark chocolate.

Shaken, she jerked back and eyed him. Things like this didn't happen to girls like her. Girls like her led boring, quiet lives in boring, quiet duplexes. Girls like her sat at home on Friday nights watching romantic movies, eating popcorn, wearing warm pajamas and fuzzy slippers. Alone.

Girls like her did not meet gorgeous men on roller-coaster rides, have hair-raising experiences in dark buildings and make out with said gorgeous man on sun-kissed rooftops.

"That's really low." She leapt to her feet.

"Huh?"

At the sound of his footsteps, an unwelcome image of him climbing to his feet with catlike grace filled her mind.

"Did I miss something?"

She spun around, crossing her arms and glaring at all his golden glory shining in the summer sun. Jerk. "What kind of man goes around kissing another woman when he has a girlfriend? A girlfriend I've met! Sort of."

Greg sighed and crossed his arms. "Didn't we already have this conversation?"

Ugh. Even his frown was adorable.

"Well..." Ally snorted and spun away. What kind of idiot did he take her for? Seriously. "Even if she is your *sister*, you shouldn't have kissed me."

His eyes narrowed. "Celia *is* my baby sister. Why shouldn't I kiss you?"

She turned back, worrying her lower lip with her teeth. Baby sister or not, there was absolutely no way a man like Greg would be interested in her. Gullible was so totally *not* her middle name and lack of experience didn't equate stupidity. She had girlfriends. Sort of. Okay, so she eavesdropped while women at work gossiped about the men in their lives.

Ally wrapped her arms around her middle. "Because."

"Because?" He groaned and scrubbed his hand over his face. "Fine. Whatever."

Running a hand through his blonde hair, he turned away. Ally snagged her lip between her teeth again. Maybe she had been a little hard on him. So she wasn't the type of girl to take someone at face value. Sue her.

"Look, I'm sor—"

Several yards away, the rooftop door exploded open. Greg whirled and slammed into her, taking them both down hard on the rough asphalt roofing. The air left her lungs in a gasp. The roof dug into her back. She struggled to suck in air with his heavy weight pinning her in place.

"Shhh," he said.

About the time her lungs started to burn, he seemed to sense her sincere distress and lifted off her a fraction. Fresh oxygen fueled her brain. They lay behind what looked like an air conditioner, hidden from view. More specifically, hidden from whoever had made such a dramatic and noisy entrance into their sky-high haven.

The door crashed open again. This time, anxiety weighed down her diaphragm.

"Freeze!"

Instinctively obeying, her muscles seized up. The sounds of a scuffle followed. She stared into Greg's eyes. He winked and her tension eased. Why, she didn't know.

Footsteps drew near, followed by low laughter. "Off-duty and on top of some woman. Classic Marsing."

Greg's heavy weight rolled off her, but he didn't get up. He lounged on his side, watching her. The plain-clothes detective she'd seen earlier by the building exit stood over them, shaking his head.

Carefully, she sat up, gingerly testing her aching body parts while she eyed the two men. A few yards away, some guy—the deranged psychopath, presumably—was being handcuffed and read his rights.

"Always on top of some woman?" Ally repeated numbly.

Since she'd never been stupid, she easily put together two plus two and came up with a lying jerk. There went her fantasy of believing him about the sister, or believing in a sincere attraction, despite the kiss they'd shared. Acid burning her stomach, Ally crossed her arms and shut her eyes. *I am such an idiot.*

"Marsing?" She glanced at the detective.

"Didn't have time for a proper introduction, huh? That's our Marsing. Quite the ladies' man right, Detective?" The guy smirked, arms crossed and feet shoulder-width apart.

Now nauseated as well, Ally climbed to her feet.

"Shove it up your ass, Hank," Detective Marsing growled. He

smoothly rolled to his feet and offered his hand, which she batted away with sharp irritation. "Don't tell me you believe this laughing hyena. He's full of crap."

Hank hooted with laughter, slapping his thigh. Gritting her teeth, Ally started walking. Several uniformed police officers were escorting a thickly muscled man off the roof. Neck muscles bulging, he turned and met her gaze. His pale-blue eyes sent a shiver down her spine, joined by a river of ice when one side of his thin lips pulled up in a menacing smile. She'd always thought it a dramatic turn of phrase with no basis in reality, but her blood literally ran cold.

A hand on her arm brought her up short. She barely swallowed an undignified screech. Heart racing, she spun to glare at Detective Marsing. "What? Exciting as this has been, I'd like to go home now."

"Ally." He plowed a hand through his hair. "Look, ignore Hank. He's always been an ass. He can't help it."

"Which is so sad for Hank, but I don't see what his being an ass has to do with any of this." Ally sighed and pushed the hair off her forehead. "I don't understand what's going on. I don't even care anymore. I just want to go home."

"Okay. Officer Smith will take you—"

"No."

"Why not?"

He was yelling at her now? Her blood began a slow boil. He could take his offer and...*Deep breath, Ally.* "I'm not your concern." She rolled her eyes. "Stop pretending you care."

"I'm *not* pretending." He stepped closer, invading her space. Again. "It's my job to make sure you get home safe. Are you always such a pain in the ass?"

His words bit into her miniscule self-confidence and she blanched. This day sucked. Who was she kidding? Her life sucked.

She sighed. "Fine, have Officer What's-His-Name escort me home. But I drove, so he'll have to follow me. Is that fine with you?"

So she sounded snippy. So what?

His hand firm on her elbow, he practically frog-marched her over to a massive black man leaning against the stairway access. Warm midnight eyes watched their approach. How they'd even found a uniform large enough to fit him boggled the mind.

"Freddy, Ally. Ally, Officer Freddy Smith." The curt introduction showed his irritation, but she refused to care. "Freddy, follow Ally in your cruiser. I want to make sure she gets home safe. Although, I'm starting to wonder why," he added, just loud enough for her to hear.

She glared at him. Like she'd asked to witness a murder and almost have a bullet lodged in her brain. Yep, good times.

"Sure thing, Detective Marsing." Officer Smith grinned.

Before she could do more than turn away, Detective Marsing spoke again. "One more thing…."

Ally glanced back. He stood in the glaring sun wearing an inscrutable expression. Gone was the good ol' surfer boy and easy sparkling charm.

"Stop by the EMTs on the way out and have them take a look at her cheek."

Unconsciously, her hand headed for her cheek. Detective Marsing intercepted it. His big hand wrapped around hers, making her feel small and petite for the space of several heartbeats. Until her common sense kicked in.

A flicker of humor returned to his eyes. "Let's not go there again, Sugar Lips."

Swallowing a pang of bittersweet longing, regret and any number of other useless feelings, she turned away and followed Officer Smith into the shadowy depths of the building. Memories assailed her and she hesitated before forcing herself to put one foot after the other down the stairs. As if sensing her unease, Officer Smith glanced back.

"How'd a pretty little thing like you get mixed up in today's ugliness?"

"Just going for a ride, Officer Smith. Against my better

judgment, I might add."

"Don't like roller coasters?"

"Yeah, you could say that. What happened, anyway?"

"Well, I don't know that I oughta say. Seeing as how you're friends with ol' Marsing, though, I guess it's okay."

Ally debated setting him straight, but she wanted to know what had happened. Besides, she'd been shot at! Her fingers itched to inspect her little wound and she made a fist, her short, sensible fingernails biting into her palm.

"As you saw, the lowlife shoved some poor SOB outta the coaster. Of course, I doubt he counted on us being here when he did it. Pretty stupid to not take into consideration all the witnesses."

"Who was the, uh." Ally's belly flipped. She'd tried really hard not to think about the man who'd fallen. "Victim?"

"I'm not allowed to say."

Ally shut her mouth and followed him out of the building. The silent amusement park sent a shiver racing over her skin.

The EMTs were more than happy to patch up her little boo-boo. She sat inside the ambulance, a first for her, while they did their thing. Some antiseptic and a couple of butterfly bandages later, she climbed into her shiny pale-green Prius.

Officer Smith tailed her all the way to her semi-attached house in the suburbs. She had never been more excited to see her unexciting, drab little home. A tidal wave of relief swamped her as she pulled into her garage.

The black and white cruiser parked directly behind her. In her rearview mirror, the big officer talked on a cell phone. She swung open her door and scrambled out when he disconnected.

The officer's massive body blocked the fading sunlight as he strolled inside her garage. "You gonna be okay, Miss?"

"Yes. Thank you. I'll be fine. Thank you for seeing me home. I hope it didn't put you too far out of your way."

"Nah. I always enjoy a pleasant ride through the 'burbs. Nice change from the busy city streets."

"Yes, it is."

She shifted uneasily, glancing from him to the door into her house.

"So…" he planted a hand on top of her car. "You live here all alone?"

"Uhm, yes." Ally swallowed, feeling hemmed in. "Were you talking to your wife? On your cell phone?"

"Not exactly."

Where had the charming, talkative man gone? She liked that guy. She wanted him back. "Well," she forced a smile, "thanks again."

He didn't move. Something shifted. The air thickened and she struggled to draw a full breath. His dark, unwavering eyes sent a shiver of ice down her spine. She sidled a few steps away. He no longer seemed friendly and easy-going.

"The boss doesn't like untidy jobs."

"Uhm…boss? As in, the police chief?"

Of course, he was talking about the police chief. She wanted to laugh at her absurdity, but the sound strangled in her throat.

He shook his head. "Not exactly. I do a little work on the side for this other guy."

Her stomach bottomed out.

Beyond him, the garage door stood open, but there wasn't a single person to be seen. The quiet neighborhood where everyone stayed in their houses and bothered no one didn't seem like such a fabulous thing about now. She backed up a few more steps.

"He gave me a call on the way over. Wants you taken care of." He herded her backward toward the door into her house.

No way he was referring to massaging her feet or barbecuing a nice steak for her. She tried to swallow, but her mouth had taken on a keen resemblance to the Sahara. "Uh, why me?"

"That's a need-to-know sorta thing. And you don't."

No, no, no. This can't be happening. This is really bad. I don't do really bad.

The back of her feet hit the step below the door, forcing her up and inside, with Officer Smith's massive bulk following. Ally fought back a whimper. This guy was *so* huge. She didn't stand a chance.

"Nice place."

This stranger, police officer gone rogue, who planned to do... something not good, was admiring her home. She had the ridiculous urge to giggle. Giggling involved breathing and she was pretty sure that function had seized up. Shaking her head, disbelief warred with flat-out terror.

How had a simple outing, an attempt to get a bit of a life, turned into this?

Officer Smith shoved her into a chair in her living room. Detective Marsing had insisted on sending her home with an armed escort. Her soon-to-be killer pawed through her belongings and Ally gritted her teeth. This was all Marsing's fault

Smith picked up a romance novel she'd been reading, snorted and tossed the book over his shoulder. Crossing her trembling arms, she narrowed her eyes. Like it wasn't bad enough he planned to kill...Her thoughts fractured. Panic beat at her. Dragging in a deep breath, she used sheer force of will to bring her emotions under control.

A porcelain figurine shattered on the floor and she snapped her gaze back to the behemoth pawing through her drawers. Clarifying outrage flowed through her.

He turned his back completely, and Ally had a lightbulb moment. Toeing off her sandals, she eased to her feet. He grunted and shifted his impressive weight. She froze, lightheaded with fear. The temptation of escape whispered in her ear. So very close.

When he didn't turn, she walked backward on unsteady feet, slipping around the corner into her beautiful, immaculate kitchen. He was so sure she would sit there like a good little girl while he satisfied his curiosity. Fat chance. Steel slid up her spine. Maybe she *was* boring and terrified of far too many things, but she wasn't going to sit obediently on her hands and wait to die.

She spun on bare feet, raced through her kitchen and into the garage. The police cruiser in the drive fenced in her car. Tearing around the corner, she dashed across the neighbor's side lawn. Heart racing, anticipating discovery any moment, she leapt the waist-height fence into their backyard with the agility of a trained athlete.

Grinning over her small feat, she aimed for the back fence.

A bellow from inside her house made her flinch, pulling the plug on her pride. Remembering an old police show, she hunched and ran in a zigzag pattern. Heart pounding, palms clammy, the six-foot privacy fence loomed before her. A zing, a crunch to her left. She stared at a fresh, neatly splintered hole just to the side of her head.

Oh, God! He was shooting at her. Actually shooting. In broad daylight. In her neighbor's backyard. Didn't they have rules about that sort of stuff?

Nerves shredded, Ally gritted her teeth. Three more feet. Two. Another crunch. She swore the heat of the bullet singed her shoulder. Arms extended, she jumped for all she was worth. Up, braced her arms and pushed off. She landed with an oomph on the other side, followed by another crunch and a hole in the wood fence.

For a split second, she crouched panting, staring in disbelief at the fence towering over her head. Had she really done that?

Cursing from the other side got her up and moving again. Squealing tires and a revving engine brought her head around. A car tore into the alley and raced toward her. More bad guys? Had he called in reinforcements?

Ally froze.

Did I do something horrible in a past life to deserve this?

Truly, I'll help the poor. Serve food at the soup kitchen. Go to church every Sunday. Donate money to the shelter. I'll even babysit my friend's bratty kids.

Just please, please, please get me out of this alive.

The shiny black Camaro careened to a stop with the driver's side door facing her. Heavily tinted windows revealed nothing. In a last desperate bid for freedom, she darted past the door. Strong arms encircled her waist and dragged her back toward the idling car.

Chapter Three

"No!" Ally screamed like a banshee, flinging out her arms and legs, scrabbling for purchase. Hard hands sent her flying across the front seat.

"Ally."

"Let me go!" She dove for the door handle.

"Ally!" He grabbed her elbow and pulled her back, away from the passenger door. "Damn woman, you are way more trouble than you're worth."

Almost blind with panic, she twisted around and crouched on the seat, prepared to draw blood.

Shocked hazel clashed with furious aqua. Her mouth fell open. Muttering under his breath, Detective Marsing threw the car into gear and spun out of the alleyway. She whipped her head around in time to see a blocky head pop up over the privacy fence as they disappeared around the corner. She'd done it. Escaped. Stayed alive. Like an atomic bomb, the events of the past hours and the emotions she'd worked so hard to control mushroomed up, exploding inside. Tears stung.

"Can't you stay out of trouble for five minutes?"

His harsh tone burst the erupting emotional storm. Her tears dried before they fell. She plopped down into the passenger seat, staring at him as the last few minutes replayed. Then she flung herself across the console and wrapped her arms around his neck.

"I am sooo glad to see you. You don't know how glad." She tightened her arms and breathed him in. He smelled incredible; like sunshine and the ocean and relaxation. "Do you have any idea what I've been through?" A thought froze her outpouring of gratitude and she sat back on her heels. "Wait a second. Everything I've been through since getting home is *your* fault!"

"What? I didn't do anything."

Her jaw dropped. "You sent me off with some jerk who tried to kill me, you...you...jerk!"

"Jerk?" Detective Marsing turned incredulous eyes on her. "Someone tries to kill you and *jerk* is the best you can come up with? That's sad, Ally."

Crossing her arms, she sat back. "Just admit it. This whole situation *is* all your fault."

"What is it with women? Look, if I'd known Smith was part of this thing, I never would have sent him with you."

"Confession is good for the soul. Come on, it won't hurt. Much."

He sighed, scrubbing his hand over his face. A smile tipped up the corner of his mouth and he glanced at her. "Fine. If it'll make you feel better, you're right. This entire situation is my fault."

"Thank you." A man like Detective Marsing didn't make such admissions easily. She smiled a little but shifted in her seat, disconcerted. She glanced at his Greek-god profile. He'd drop her off somewhere and she wouldn't have to worry about the way he made her feel again.

The atmosphere in the car settled into an uneasy truce and gradually her smile dissolved. Staring at her dirty toes, she clenched her hands in her lap. Well, nothing ventured, nothing gained.

"I live a very quiet life." She sighed. "Nothing exciting happens to me. I avoid excitement like the plague. So, why would anyone want to, uhm, *off* me?"

"Off you?" Marsing grinned. "I don't know."

"Are you going to find out?"

"Yes."

He pulled into an underground garage beneath a gleaming high-rise.

"Where are we? I thought you were going to, I don't know, drop me off at the police station, I guess."

"Not a good idea. I need some time to figure out what we're facing."

We. Against her better judgment, her heart softened and opened the teensiest bit. "Thank you."

He grinned, an awe shucks sorta smile. Her stomach flipped. All he needed was a cowboy hat to tip.

"Just doing my job."

The walls around her heart slammed shut again and she battled back an ache of disappointment. They idled down neat rows of expensive cars. BMW, Mercedes, Saab, Lexus and Audi. She straightened, for the first time conscious of the high-quality leather under her butt.

"You live here?"

"Sort of."

"Sort of? What kind of answer is 'sort of'? Either you do or you don't live somewhere. You can't 'sort of' live somewhere."

"Sometimes, okay? You could try the patience of a saint, Sugar Lips." His gaze dropped to her lips and a slow, intensely hot smile formed. "And I'm no saint."

"Gee, I hadn't noticed."

Her irritation from the rooftop fiasco returned. Saint, ha, good one. More like the department Don Juan. Wasn't she just the luckiest girl in town?

He steered the car into a spot sandwiched between a Jaguar and a Beemer. She hopped out as soon as he killed the engine. Tapping her feet at the rear of his car, she glared at her toes. Barefoot and dirty. Just the look she dreamt of sporting when going into a ritzy condominium building. Lovely.

"Detective, I can't go in there looking like this."

"You look fine." He grabbed her arm and tugged her along beside him.

She glared at him. "How do you know I look fine when you haven't even looked at me?"

"Believe me, I've looked far too much for my own peace of mind."

She blinked. "What? I don't even have shoes on. I look like some homeless person you dragged in off the street."

His lips tightened. "Hardly. You're far too beautiful to be mistaken for homeless." He glanced at her feet and shrugged. "It's hot. You like going barefoot in the heat. Just go with it, keep your chin up and no one will think twice. Wealthy people are eccentric. Trust me, bare feet are the least of what I've seen around here."

Beautiful? He thought she was beautiful? Struggling to process such a strange new concept, she clipped several bumpers and set off a symphony of car alarms. No one had ever called her beautiful before. *Cute* had come up a few times over the years, *cuddly* more often than she'd like and *attractive* brought out and dusted off on a few occasions.

Beautiful. Huh.

"Move your tush, Sugar Lips." He tugged her at a faster clip across the cool expanse of cement.

In the elevator, he released her and she rubbed her arm. He hadn't hurt her, but still. "Your little habit of grabbing and hauling me around is getting old. Just a little FYI for ya."

He grinned, a baring of teeth attractive enough to make her knees go weak—dratted man. "Just making sure you don't get lost or kidnapped when my back's turned."

She returned his patently false smile as he pushed the button for the top floor. The high-tech LCD display prompted him to enter a code. The penthouse. Of course. And he just stayed here *sometimes*. Poor guy. What a rough life.

After silently whisking them up through the building, the elevator doors slid open. A marble inlaid foyer opened onto a living room that screamed, "I've got more money in my sock drawer than you'll ever see in this lifetime." Frowning, she rubbed her hand over her churning stomach. She didn't belong here.

Ally took a step, then hesitated. Trusting Officer Smith hadn't been the brightest idea, but surely Marsing wouldn't rescue her and bring her to his place just to kill her. Gnawing on her lip, she stared at the back of his golden head as he strode into the condo. Either she trusted him or she didn't. Trusted him to keep her safe, anyway. Time to fish or cut bait.

She sucked in a breath and walked off the elevator. "So…uhm… does your family live here? Parents, siblings?"

His lips tightened. The happy-go-lucky guy disappeared.

Nerves jangling, Ally bit her lip hard. Had she made a mistake after all?

Fingers smoothing over the top of a curved couch, she crossed to a wall of enormous windows framing the city. She cleared her throat and faced Marsing again, clenching her jaw to keep it shut.

His eyes sparkled and the sardonic twist to his too-tempting lips had returned. Heck, even his hair seemed cocky.

"Uhm…" *Pull yourself together, Ally. Sheesh.* "Pretty fancy digs, Detective."

"Thanks."

Oookay. Ignore one question, glaze over the next. So much for polite chitchat. He might as well just tell her to mind her own business. She turned to admire the skyscraper view.

"Make yourself at home."

She glanced back over her shoulder. The room was empty. "Detective?"

Where had he gone? Ally peered through an arched doorway. A massive mahogany table with twenty high-back chairs filled the room, a huge oil painting on one wall and a gilt-framed mirror on the other. The flower arrangement in the center probably cost the same as her monthly mortgage payment.

She wandered back into the living room, taking in the plush

furniture and museum-quality paintings. One in particular caught her eye. Swirls of frothing green and blue swept across the canvas, a vision of serenity with a seaside cottage perched on the edge of a sandy beach.

A door closed somewhere, snapping her out of her trance. She investigated another hallway. Thick silence draped the dark passage and she couldn't help a little shiver. Crossing her arms, she turned in a circle. She'd crawled through dank tunnels, huddled in creepy nooks with who knew what, rolled on a tar pitch roof and run around in the dirt barefoot. No freakin' way was she sitting on any of the furniture in this place. Not until she'd had a long, hot shower. Gnawing on her lower lip, she made a beeline for a closed door near the entry.

"Uhm...Greg?"

A wide expanse of bronzed skin greeted her when the door swung open. A lucky bead of water traveled down over chiseled pecks, ducking in and out of washboard abs before vanishing into a tantalizing trail of dark golden hair. Hair that disappeared into the top of a low-slung towel. Make that a cold shower.

Mouth dry, she forced her gaze away and tightened her arms around her ribcage. *No touching*. She focused on a cream porcelain lamp sitting on a deep mahogany side table. "That's a lovely lamp. An antique?"

His deep chuckle found a whole swarm of poor, defenseless nerve endings. "I wouldn't know."

Of course he wouldn't. He was clearly one of those men who spent every spare minute in the gym or some woman's bed. More than likely he used books as paperweights.

From the look of those bulging biceps, he could probably bench-press her.

That doesn't matter. She wanted more in a man than the number on his weight machine. Like an IQ in the triple digits, the desire for self-improvement and an appreciation of the arts.

Her gaze returned like a homing pigeon. Marsing stood with

a shoulder braced against the doorframe. Indulging her depraved senses, she soaked him in. His muscled calves, strong thighs, the irritating disturbance of a fluffy white towel and—oh, momma—his chest.

More than his gorgeous, underwear-model-perfect physique, the strength and air of calm he exuded made his seem so... capable. The kind of guy you could depend on. A perfect place to rest your weary head, and other, uhm, body parts. Oh, man, she was out of control. Heart pounding, flushed and tingly, she bit her lip and met his eyes.

He raised his eyebrows. "Shall I remove the towel for you?"

"Would you?"

She gasped and slapped a hand over her mouth, heat flooding her cheeks. Marsing laughed. Ally spun away and lit out for the other side of the living room like she had a wild badger on her tail.

Deep breath in, then out. She regained her equilibrium and managed to remember why she was there in the first place. Sadly, it had nothing to do with ogling a detective.

"What's going on?" Spread before her like an exquisite buffet of sensory delight, downtown had begun to light up as night fell outside the windows. "How did you know where I live? Why did you show up like that?"

"We didn't know about Freddy until about ten minutes after you left. The guy we arrested at the park shared that nugget en route to the precinct." He paced the room, his fingers buried in his damp hair, all tense and tough and manly. "I'm sorry I got you mixed up in all this. I don't know why Smith was ordered to..." He cut himself off, glancing at her. "I will find out, though."

"How did you find me?"

"Locator chip in the cruiser. They activated Smith's and sent me his location. I got there as fast as I could, Ally. Smith has been with the department for ten years. He's the last guy I would suspect of doing something like this."

Hating her ill-fated attraction to a man millions of miles out of her league, she turned away and shrugged with a nonchalance she was far from feeling. "Are you planning on wandering around undressed all night?"

His reflection in the glass looked down and grinned. "It's comfortable."

"Go get dressed, for crying out loud."

Still grinning, he disappeared into the room behind him. Ally kept her feet firmly rooted to the floor. Overactive and underused hormones would only get her in trouble.

Something buzzed. An intercom? The low rumble of Detective Marsing's voice drifted from the bedroom. A minute later he emerged, dressed in black slacks and a white Oxford with black and baby-blue stripes. The elevator doors opened and a tall man stepped off, the silver badge glinting on his belt.

"Lucas," Marsing said.

"Marsing."

Lucas focused on her. The urge to hide behind the floor-length drapes tugged at her, but she resisted. His ice-blue gaze traveled down then back up more slowly. On second thought, she'd go with hiding. As her fingers curled into the thick fabric of the curtains, Marsing turned and pinned her to the spot.

"Ally, this is Lucas Jones, a detective with the neighboring precinct. We go way back; playmates from our academy days. Lucas, this is Ally."

To her undying relief, Lucas' gaze flickered away from her. The sardonic twist of his lips must be what passed for a smile. "Only you, Marsing. Only you."

"Whatever. You scare the shit out of most people, but I know your mother. And all your sisters."

"Don't talk about my sisters. Unless you want to get pounded again." Lucas cracked his knuckles. "I still can't believe you snuck off with little Beth-Anne. Necking with my sister. Gross, man."

"I was sixteen. You plan on bringing that up till we're eighty?"

"The trauma lives on." Lucas clutched a hand over his heart.

"Right here."

Greg chuckled. "Yeah, yeah. What've you got?"

Lucas' icy gaze focused on her again. This time, irritation helped her withstand the frigid attention and she lifted her chin. He turned away, dismissing her.

"Not a lot, but word on the street isn't good. The big guns want her taken care of. As of yesterday."

"What the hell for?"

"No one knows and, if they do, they're not saying. All we know for sure is she's in one big pile of shit." Expression grim, Lucas glanced at her.

On one level, Ally understood detectives faced danger, murder and mayhem in general on a daily basis. Still, they could have acted as if they actually *cared*. For all the concern they showed, Marsing and Lucas could have been discussing the weather.

"Kinda cloudy today, Joe."

"Yep, sure 'nough. Mighty hot for this early in the summer."

"Got that right. Wonder if it'll rain?"

"Nah. Should hold off for a while yet, Billy Bob."

She wasn't sure why her imaginary voices were always Southern. Hysteria-tinged laughter bubbled.

The elevator's musical chime announced an arrival. The elevator doors opened and female chatter spilled out. Giggles punctuated every other comment.

Oh, joyous day.

A platinum-blonde fashion plate with an easy smile stepped into the entry, styled within an inch of her life. Painfully aware of every single extra pound she not so gracefully wore, Ally squirmed. The glare she aimed at Detective *Marsing* should have knocked him flat. What was the deal with him and skinny blondes? Strangely familiar skinny, gorgeous blondes.

"Aw, shit," Marsing muttered.

Chapter Four

The guy who exited the elevator behind her was a real conversation piece all on his lonesome. The type of guy more often seen with a rough motorcycle gang than a delicate, upper-crust blonde. The smoothly shaven head, dark menacing eyes and bulging arms covered in dark tattoos weren't real warm and fuzzy. His hooded gaze swept the room, pausing on Ally, and her nerve endings shriveled.

Marsing frowned before turning his attention to the blonde. "Celia, what are you doing here?"

Lucas leaned against the wall, crossing his arms. His narrowed eyes never wavered from the bald guy.

"I wanted you to meet Boner. We met last week at a club when he saved me from this horrid creeper dude, and we haven't left one another's side since."

Her voice scraped against Ally's ears, an irritating combination of vaporized arsenic and elegant old lace. Celia snuggled up to Boner's—*What kind of name is that, anyway?*—muscular arm, smiled adoringly into his expressionless face, and waved a slender hand in Marsing's direction. "Boner, this is my big brother, Greg."

Boner jerked his chin up in one of those weird universal male greetings. "Yo, Greg. What's up?"

"That's Lucas." The whine disappeared when Celia introduced

Lucas, along with her smile.

Marsing's narrowed gaze didn't waver from Boner. "Boner, huh? What is it you do for a living?"

Boner shrugged. "I pick up jobs here and there, man."

"Pick up jobs." Marsing repeated the phrase slowly, his lips thinning.

"Greg." Celia sighed dramatically. "Don't be a bore." Her bright-blue gaze landed on Ally, moving from her messy hair to her dirty bare feet. "Greg, who's that? Another one of the strays you're so fond of?"

Ally curled her toes into the thick carpet, shame and humiliation twisting around her spine.

Celia sniffed, her pert little nose elevated. "I really think it would be more appropriate to confine that sort of activity to your bachelor pad."

Everyone turned to Ally. Fingers twisted in the curtains, she squirmed. Boner's eyes narrowed, more unwelcome attention thickening the dislike coating the cool air.

Marsing stiffened. "My God, you sound just like Grandma, Celia."

Celia's snooty gaze swung back to Marsing. "Thank you."

"That wasn't a compliment. Grandma was an unprecedented snob. Get over yourself." Marsing shook his head, lips pressed into a thin line. "This is Ally, a friend of mine, and you'll treat her with respect."

He didn't say, "Or else," but the words hung in the air. She couldn't believe he'd defended her like that. Some of the tension eased out of her aching shoulders.

"Ally Thompson?" Boner rubbed his bald head and grinned. "Ain't this my lucky day."

He knew her name? Tension returned with a vengeance, closing her throat and sinking tentacles into the floor, freezing her to the spot.

An alert, crackling stillness washed over the room.

"Yeah. Why?"

Marsing stood with his legs spread, weight balanced on the balls of his feet. Ally frowned. Alarm tightened her muscles to the point of snapping, yet Marsing looked calm. Even she knew some tattooed bo-hunk knowing her name spelled trouble with a capital T.

An unpleasant gleam appeared in Boner's eyes. "No reason." One beefy arm reached behind him while the other went for the blonde's slender arm.

Marsing and Lucas moved as smooth as butter on a hot Southern day. Lucas snatched Celia away from Boner, ignoring her shriek of outrage. The snake on Boner's arm flexed and his hand reappeared sporting a big ol' gun.

Before Ally could blink, Marsing had hauled her out of the room. Didn't even pause as they crossed a spacious bedroom, or look back to make sure they weren't being followed. Her heart pounded loud enough for him to hear, but he was too polite to comment. Thankfully.

"Damnit. Leave it to Celia to hook up with another loser. She's always had shit for taste in men."

Her oh-so-special experience with Officer Smith came to mind. Ally bit her lip but couldn't quite hold in a muttered, "Must run in the family."

She didn't know Celia. Or Marsing, for that matter. Even so, she couldn't help a niggle of uncomfortable sympathy for beautiful Celia. The irritation pouring off Marsing could have seared raw meat to a tender well-done.

Gunfire erupted in the other room. Her pulse skyrocketed and she instinctively ducked. Something shattered.

Marsing shook his head. "There goes Grandma's favorite vase."

He pulled her into a cool, white-tiled expanse of a bathroom and locked the door. "I'll give you a choice. Do you want to stay in here or with me?"

She crossed her arms, doing her best to ignore the crashes and gunshots. "Tattoo Man is one room away, armed with a mighty big gun. I'm sticking to you like feathers on a duck."

"What is it with you and nicknames, anyway?"

She flinched and took a step back. Making up nicknames was a stupid habit left over from the trauma of high school and embarrassing as hell. Not to mention a secret. Before she'd so utterly lost her composure with Marsing.

Marsing's hand dove through his sandy hair, his heavy sigh filling the room. Something big slammed into the door and she jumped.

"Damn." Marsing shoved her in the shower, strode across the room and opened an exterior door. Soft sunlight spilled in as he stuck his head out. He turned, eyes narrowed and lips tight with impatience, and snapped his fingers at her.

A frown tugged at her brow. Great, now she was a dog.

Another heavy thud hit the door and she raced across the room like a scared little mouse. Which she supposed fit. A snug hidey hole in the wall and a nice hunk of cheese sounded lovely about now. Grimacing, she followed Marsing outside and down the long terrace that stretched along the entire side of the condo. A door a few feet away swung open and he slammed her into the wall, his body covering hers. Heart pounding in her throat and hands tingling, she forgot to breathe.

"Hell, Jones," Marsing snapped. "Warn a guy next time. I almost took your damn head off."

Lucas snorted, pushed Celia behind him, and waved his hand toward the door. "Get back inside and give me a hand. This guy's like the Hulk."

Marsing steered her through the open door into the dark interior of the condo. Disoriented after the bright sunshine, she moved closer toward the relative safety of Marsing. A meaty hand clamped around her wrist, stopping her retreat. Panic flared, bright and hot. Jerked off her feet into a rock-solid chest, Ally cried out. The sound of guns cocking echoed through the room and froze her captor mid-motion.

"Not the wisest choice you've made in recent times, Boner," Marsing said.

"Back off or I'll snap her neck." Boner's voice rumbled through his barrel chest, his emotionless tone turning her knees to jelly. A soul-deep yearning for life surged in her breast. Sweet, sweet life. She didn't want to die.

Boner clamped her against him like a human shield, one massive arm wrapped around her ribcage. Ally winced at the mental image. Hard metal dug into her temple. Her heart skipped a beat.

Facing Marsing and Lucas did not improve her desperation one iota. They stood to either side of the open doorway, guns drawn and pointed straight at her, despite Boner being the intended target. *What fickle fairy did I tick off this morning?*

The men's voices swirled around her. Fighting to breathe, she forced herself to calm down before she dissolved into hysterics.

Instead of calm, sadness spread like a sedative through her limbs. The hard press of metal to her skin clarified the multitude of insecurities holding her back in life. How they dictated her behavior. Sadness morphed into irritation.

On the horizon, the sun disappeared. Ally took a deep breath and sagged in Boner's tight grip. She surged back up, slamming her heel into his instep. He grunted. His grip loosened. As hard as she could, she jammed her elbow into his solar plexus. Boner's arms fell and she spun, driving the heel of her hand into his nose while smashing her knee into his groin.

Boner crashed to the floor, curled in a fetal position and whimpered like a baby.

Holy crap.

"Ow, ow, ow…" She cradled her hand to her chest. Hitting someone hurt! She hobbled away.

Lucas holstered his gun and handcuffed Boner. Marsing lowered his gun and stared at her like he'd never seen her before.

She ignored him, slipping onto the deck and breathing in the moist evening air. Watching movies proved highly beneficial after all. *Thank you*, Miss Congeniality.

Shivering, she wrapped her arms tight around herself. When she closed her eyes, sensory memory replayed Boner's vice-like arms and the press of steel against her flesh. She snapped her eyes open with a startled whimper.

"You okay, Ally?"

Detective Marsing. She refused to turn around and let him see the tears in her eyes. "I'm fine."

His fingers encircled her arm. She stilled, waiting, but light footsteps sounded on the balcony.

"Greggy, O.M.G. I am *so* sorry. I had no idea. I swear."

Marsing sighed, the puff of breath shifting her hair. "I know, Celia."

He dropped his hand from her arm and Ally turned. Tears streamed down Celia's porcelain cheeks, blue eyes luminous in the deepening night. Even now, her hair hung in a perfect blonde curtain down her slender back. After her brush with death, not even a twinge of envy ruffled Ally.

Marsing crossed to Celia's side. "We need to work on your taste in men."

"That's for sure." Lucas glared at Celia as he joined them on the deck. "Where the hell do you find these losers?"

"I didn't know he was a…a…" Celia trailed off, paling under Lucas' hot glare.

Ally turned all the way around and leaned her backside against the balcony railing. She welcomed the distraction they provided from the lingering terror beating through her. Unwittingly fascinated by this side of ice-cold Lucas, Ally stared. The heat in his eyes and friction of irritation in his voice could set off a forest fire.

"Maybe now you'll show some intelligence with the men you screw."

"Lucas." Marsing's low growl of warning sent a hot shiver down her spine. Irritation, she told herself firmly.

"Someone needs to save her from herself," Lucas said.

Marsing crossed his arms. "Are you volunteering?"

Staring into Celia's eyes, Lucas opened his mouth. His gaze drifted lower and he snapped his mouth shut. Ally's eyebrows climbed. He shrugged a shoulder and strolled back into the condo, his cool nonchalance fooling no one. Except Celia. Ally took in her rounded shoulders and arms wrapped tight around her waist.

In a previous lifetime, Ally would have just stood there feeling sorry for her. Not now. Not after everything she'd been through today. "Why don't we take a little walk down the balcony while the boys take care of our uninvited guest?"

She slid an arm around Celia's shoulders and a vision sprang to mind, showcasing Ally as fat and ungainly beside Marsing's Barbie-doll-perfect sister. Her mother had tried her hardest to mold her into a plastic-perfect image with rigid diets and ruthless exercise regimes. Utter misery and zero self-esteem was all she'd managed to achieve. Ally pushed the painful image away.

"I didn't know he was a bad guy," Celia murmured, head down. "I'm so sorry. Are you okay?"

"Everyone's fine. There was no way you could have known. Don't beat yourself up over something completely out of your control."

Celia sniffed a little. "You're sweet."

Ally snorted. Their eyes met and they started giggling.

"Good grief." Marsing muttered. "My condo isn't *fine*."

Celia's giggles died and a dull flush stained her cheeks. "I know. I'm so stupid."

Ally swung around, the unfairness of his accusation stinging. Her stomach knotted. She hated confrontation, but she wasn't going to let Marsing's selfishness pass. Maybe Celia did have bad taste in guys, but she wasn't psychic.

"It's not her fault your condo's messed up." Her voice trembled and she paused to take a deep breath. "It's the fault of the creep in the other room."

"True. It's your fault too."

"What?" Her eyes narrowed.

"How is any of this Ally's fault?" Celia placed her delicate hand on Ally's forearm. "That's not fair, Greg. I'm the one who brought him here, like the stupid airhead blonde everybody thinks I am."

"Or maybe…" Ally's voice was low and silky. "The fault lies directly at the feet of a certain well-trained, armed detective."

He spun on his heel and disappeared inside.

Ally glared after him, for the first time understanding the term "seeing red". What a jerk.

"Don't pay any attention to him." Celia smiled. "I'm sorry, I'm not very good with names and I don't remember yours."

"Ally Thompson."

"Celia Marsing. Suppose we should go see what the boys are up to?"

Ally glanced toward the open doorway.

"It's okay. As irritable as he gets, Greg won't bite. Lucas, on the other hand…"

"I don't think biting you is what Lucas has in mind." Ally flushed at her boldness.

"What?" Celia's eyes widened. "You think Lucas is into me?"

"Definitely." The steamy looks Lucas kept throwing Celia's way were a fire hazard. "The man has the hots for you."

Light from the kitchen showed hectic color flooding Celia's cheeks. Her wide eyes were hazy and unfocused, as if the very idea of Lucas desiring her got her all hot and bothered. With a small smile, Ally left her to her thoughts and headed for the kitchen.

She paused in the open doorway. Uniformed police officers hauled Boner to his feet and dragged him out, moaning. He shuffled between them like a ninety-year-old woman without her walker. A few feet away, Lucas and Marsing were having an intense conference with an older man in a suit. His bushy eyebrows furrowed impressively as they talked, though their voices were too low to overhear. She hesitated in the doorway.

"Ma'am?" Apprehension clear in his brown eyes, an officer stood a safe distance from her. Was he worried she'd knee him in the balls too? "I need to get a brief statement from you, if you have a few minutes."

She moved to follow him into the dining room but paused. A shiver of awareness touched her and she turned to meet Marsing's gaze. Lucas lounged beside him and the older man had vanished.

"Lucas," she said. "Celia is still out on the patio. Alone."

A spark lit Lucas' chilly eyes. He didn't hesitate to head for the patio. Marsing stared after him, a stunned expression on his face. Ally turned back to the officer waiting for her.

A short time later, she set aside the finished statement with a tired sigh. Lucas strolled through the room, Celia at his side, their heads bent together in quiet conversation. Neither one seemed to notice her sitting alone at the large mahogany table as they passed. Invisibility was nothing new, but no one seemed to need her. Should she just leave now or what?

Going home didn't seem like an option. Didn't criminals stake out people's homes and lie in wait for them? Then there was her lack of shoes. Lack of clothes.

Heaving a sigh, she rose and wandered into the living room. The beautiful room was demolished. Bullet holes in the walls, lamps knocked over and broken, furniture scattered, pictures askew. Ugly reality swept through her, making her head throb, pulse pound and skin go clammy. The room had been stunning when she arrived. An entirely different sort of stunning came to mind now.

Head spinning, she made a beeline for the elevator.

"Where you headed, Sugar Lips?"

She glanced back. Detective Marsing leaned against the doorframe, all rippling nonchalance as he stared at her with the familiar curl of amusement on his lips, total Surfer Dude mode.

"Well, I have no shoes and only the clothes on my back. I was thinking I'd take a taxi home."

"I don't think so." Despite his lazy stance, the intensity of his stare made her twitchy.

Feeling sick, she flicked her wrist at the room. Destroyed because of her. She couldn't hold onto her self-righteous irritation enough to keep referring to him as *Detective*. "I'm so sorry about your home, Greg. I feel awful. I really do. I clearly can't stay here and I'm not your responsibility."

"You think you'd fare better on your own? In your home, which is no doubt staked out?"

All the blood pooled in her feet, leaving her lightheaded and feeling like she'd fallen into some sort of alternative reality. What had happened to her boring, predictable, safe little bubble of existence?

"What am I supposed to do?"

"Guess you'll have to learn how to relax and hang loose."

"What?"

"You know, chill."

Was this guy for real? Intense, rude, Super-Cop personified one minute, totally unhelpful Surfer Dude the next. She didn't need this aggravation. "What kind of advice is that? I have no way to get anywhere, I've witnessed a murder, men keep trying to kill me, and all you can say is I need to *chill*?"

She spun on her bare foot to leave. Pain shot through her. Gasping, she looked down at the pool of shattered porcelain all around her. Based on the limp flowers scattered across the floor, the pieces had formed a vase in a previous life. One more thing to feel guilty about. Fortunately, she had the agonizing pain caused by glass shards in the bottom of her foot to distract her. Lovely.

Greg lifted her in strong arms and swung her against his hard chest.

"What are you doing?" she gasped. "I'm too heavy. Put me down."

"I'm helping." He said it with the angelic innocence of a five-year-old boy caught putting a bug in a girl's hair. "You're injured. And you are *not* too heavy."

Disarmed by the close proximity, she clamped her lips shut and shot him a skeptical look. The amused sparkle in his eyes was at odds with the intensity of his gaze. Confusing man.

He juggled her slightly to get through the arched doorway into the dining room and scorching heat suffused her face. She could just hear the gears working in his head, evaluating her weight. He probably thought she sat around eating donuts, bags of chips and fried food. Drowning in embarrassment, she shut her eyes.

In another lifetime, in a different body, she'd love a hunky guy carting her around. Since she was still in this one, she didn't.

He set her on one of the elegant chairs. "Be right back."

Probably wanted to run into the other room to catch his breath. Seconds later, he returned with a first-aid kit and knelt at her feet. He pulled out a pair of ginormous tweezers and she flinched.

"Easy, sweetheart."

Her foolish heart clenched over the casual endearment. *Department Don Juan*, she reminded herself fiercely. His eyes locked on hers and the helpful little reminder fled the building.

"I'll be gentle, I promise." Imprudent or not, the fatal combination of his solemn gaze and low voice caused a hairline crack in her defensive wall.

He carefully placed her foot on his bent knee, angling it to the side so he could see what he was doing. She focused on the wall over his head, unwilling to watch him pick bloody pieces of porcelain from her foot.

She sucked in a breath when he pulled out the first piece.

He held it up. "Yep, Grandma's antique vase died a brutal death."

Ally winced. Despite his crooked grin, the pain of the loss shone in his eyes. He removed more shards, his gentleness soothing even though it didn't mitigate the pain. He set down the tweezers and took out a bottle of antiseptic. She tensed. The cold antiseptic burned inside the cuts and she swallowed a sob. A few wraps of light gauze he secured with medical tape and he set her foot down and looked up.

"As to your other issues, my sister keeps a room here with clothes and stuff in it. I'm sure she won't mind if you borrow some of it."

"Seriously?" Half-laughing, half-groaning, mortified beyond belief to be having this discussion with a ridiculously attractive stranger, she closed her eyes. "Nothing that belongs to your sister would fit me."

"Why not?"

Good grief. Surely, he wasn't that clueless. No way on God's green earth was she explaining. She could only take so much humiliation. "They just won't, okay?"

He shrugged and rose. "Whatever. At least see if Celia has a pair of shoes you can wear."

"Fine." Gracefulness be damned. She surged out of the chair and hobbled from the room, ignoring her throbbing feet.

"Her room is the first one on the left down the hallway."

Chapter Five

Celia's room was an oasis of soft pink and cream, a girl's paradise filled with gilt furniture. A massive canopied bed rested dead center. Ally swallowed a wistful sigh.

Double doors opened into a jaw-dropping closet.

A few clothes? By whose standards? She shook her head. Row upon row of beautiful clothes filled the walk-in closet. At the far end, slanted shelves displayed a dazzling array of shoes.

In a green-tinted haze of envy, she limped forward, trailing fingertips along the shelves.

She might live in a bubble, but she still recognized the designers. Prada, Valentino, Dolce & Gabbana, Fendi, Gucci, Manolo Blahnik, Miu Miu, Versace and more.

What kind of man left a life of luxury and became a cop making diddly squat?

Someone with an amazing story to tell. Someone who's probably a great guy underneath all his posing and blustering. Gnawing on her lower lip, she focused on the shoes. She didn't like the idea of borrowing designer shoes but she couldn't very well walk around barefoot.

Donna Karan sandals caught her eye. Gorgeous cork platforms with gold crisscrossing straps and gold chunky heels. They were nothing like the boring flats filling her closet at home.

She slid them on. Absolute bliss, despite the pain in her foot, and a perfect fit. Biting her lip, she stared at the clothes. Maybe a loose-fitting dress would work.

A blue-and-white print caught her eye and she pulled it out. The fabric fell in tiers from a standing collar to an A-line skirt. She checked the tag. A size eight by Proenza Schouler. She'd never heard of the designer. A size eight over her size sixteen curves. She cringed. Better than a size two, but still.

Chucking her dirty clothes, she pulled the silk dress over her head. The fabric caressed her arms, hugged her breasts and skimmed her hips. She hummed her pleasure. Feeling a bit like Sleeping Beauty approaching the Evil Queen's enchanted mirror, she tiptoed over to a full-length mirror. She stared at the floor, stomach knotted painfully. Taking a deep breath, she lifted her gaze. Her eyes widened and she forgot to breathe.

The dress bared her shoulders and the hem stopped at mid-thigh.

She looked...she looked...different. She bit her lip. Her shorts and tank top had revealed just as much skin, but the dress accentuated the things she liked about her body. The shoes did amazing things for her legs.

Gathering up her clothes, she tugged a simple linen bag off a shelf and stuffed them inside. With a final wistful glance, she closed the closet doors. Spying an attached bathroom, she detoured to wash up, only to draw up short inside. The bathroom was lined with mirrors. There was even a mirror in the shower stall. She had zero desire to see that much of her self naked, so a thorough scrub in the sink would have to suffice.

She left Celia's bedroom freshly groomed and feeling light-years away from the girl who'd set out from her town house that morning. Feminine contentment curled through her. She was determined to enjoy every minute of this singular experience. She'd never be able to afford these kinds of clothes on her salary. Not unless she spent an entire paycheck on one outfit. Then she'd be homeless, and what would be the point of beautiful clothes when she had to cuddle up to a smelly old man in an alleyway for warmth?

Ally winced anew at the destruction when she passed through the living room. Greg worked at the sleek granite counter in the kitchen. He turned when she entered the room, her shoes clicking across the tiled floor. His eyes widened, his jaw went slack and irrational pleasure flooded her.

His mouth snapped shut and he cleared his throat. Twice. "I see you found something to wear."

A slow smile grew, but she remained silent.

He returned to his work on the counter.

She crossed the kitchen to stand beside him. He was making sandwiches of dense bread piled high with turkey, lettuce, tomato, avocado, mushrooms and some sort of sauce. Her mouth watered. The food smelled amazing.

"Hungry?" His voice was husky.

"Starving."

For once, she wasn't self-conscious. Maybe the trauma of having a gun held to her head was to blame, or the amazing clothes. Then again, she hadn't eaten since her grapefruit, egg-white omelet and yogurt breakfast eight hours ago. Her stomach rumbled.

Greg handed her the laden plates and she carried them into the dining room. She set them down and glanced over her shoulder, catching him staring at her rear end. She could get used to that. Maybe. Okay, so give her five minutes and she'd start worrying about her butt again.

He scooted her chair in as she sat. Ally swallowed. She hadn't been on a date in so long his behavior felt foreign. Not that they were on a date. She stared at her plate. "Is there really some guy out there who wants me dead?"

"'Fraid so."

Her ears rang and her pulse pounded like a whole section of drummers partying in her head. "Why?"

"That's the million-dollar question." His eyes narrowed, the hard-boiled cop banishing Surfer Dude. "Run into any suspicious-looking characters lately? Cross any homicidal maniacs? Borrow money from a loan shark?"

"Funny."

"You seriously have no idea what's going on?" He leaned forward, crowding into her space, none of the attraction from two minutes ago in his hard eyes.

Like she was hiding a violent criminal past. Sheesh. He was the policeman. Wasn't it his job to know these things?

"Yes, I seriously have no idea what's going on." She resisted adding, *you big jerk*. He was trying to help her. "I'm a claims processor for an independent health-insurance company. Trust me, I lead a very ordinary, very boring life. No homicidal maniacs and no loan sharks. Do I look stupid to you?" She rolled her eyes, muttering, "Never mind."

"You aren't, Ally. That's not what I meant." He rolled a crumb between his fingers, contemplating her. "A claims processor. Huh."

"What's that supposed to mean?" She leaned back and crossed her arms.

"Nothing." He grinned. "Testy, aren't you? And not hungry, apparently."

Ally looked down at her untouched plate of food. She should eat something. Her stomach twisted. She shrugged and rose. They cleared the table and stuck the dishes inside the dishwasher.

"Let's head out, Sugar Lips."

"Where are we going?"

Greg winked. "It's a surprise."

She made a quick trip to Celia's room and grabbed a soft sweater. Greg met her in the foyer with a cheerful grin, a black duffel bag slung over his shoulder.

How he could be so carefree was beyond her. Glass and broken china crunched beneath his feet in his trashed living room and he had a naïve, frightened woman to protect—namely her. He clearly had issues. Serious, thrill-seeking issues.

They stepped into the elevator and his spicy cologne snaked around her, making her eyes cross and thighs tremble. She slid a little farther away. She didn't need this stupid attraction. Especially now. Figuring out what was going on took priority. Not to mention getting away from Mr. Super-Cop before she did something stupid, like fling herself at him. Queasy self-consciousness crept in and she tugged at the too-short hemline of the slinky dress.

The doors opened onto the garage, but Greg held her back. She leaned on the brass paneling of the elevator and stared at the ceiling panel while Greg did his thing. Deep breathing slowed her racing pulse. Fear and attraction were a toxic combination.

Hopefully, there weren't any hit men, mobsters or otherwise criminally inclined individuals lying in wait to kill her. How many times could a girl be threatened in one day? She'd surely surpassed her lifetime limit.

Greg hauled her out of the elevator. The He-Man tactics didn't exactly warm her heart. She stumbled along behind, desperately trying to keep up and maintain her balance. Years of flats and sandals hadn't happened by accident.

He held the passenger door open, scanning the garage. She climbed in and buckled her seat belt, trying to swallow around the lump of fear in her throat. Greg slammed the door shut. On the driver's side, he dropped down beneath the window then climbed in without a word.

"Well?"

"Well, what?" He buckled up and started the car.

For the love of... "Do you always crawl around on the ground before leaving?"

"Just making sure nobody attached a little surprise to the bottom of my car. Considering how badly this guy seems to want you out of the picture..." He shrugged.

The dull throb in her head exploded into life with vicious enthusiasm.

The engine rumbled as he pulled out of the garage. He glanced at her, a little frown between his brows. "We're fine, Ally. We just have to be careful. I'm sure my name has come up with these guys by now. Whatever you know, or they think you know, they'll figure you've told me. Which means keeping either one of us around isn't safe."

She moaned, leaning her head against the seat. Her life had become an episode of *Southland*.

"Relax. We'll talk more later."

Tension had crept into his voice and she glanced at him. "What's wrong?"

"We have a tail."

"A tail?" Like a cat? That didn't make any sense. Oh. Duh.

"Someone's following us?" She threw off her seat belt and spun around to stare out the back of the Camaro, but she didn't see anything beyond ordinary traffic. "How do you know?"

"Training and experience."

She shivered, plopping back down in her seat.

"Buckle up, Sugar Lips."

Chapter Six

Ally latched the seat belt, grabbed the door handle with one hand and the seat with the other. Greg swerved around a car. Glancing back, she spotted a dark sedan maneuvering to stay behind them. Her heart leapt into her throat as Greg narrowly avoided the rear bumper of a delivery truck. They roared down the block, taking the next corner so fast Ally's shoulder slammed into the door with bruising force.

Before she could catch her breath, he whipped them around another corner. The hard right flung her the other way. They tore down a quiet alley and onto a sleepy residential street. He slowed, taking the next corner at a more sedate pace. Kept all four tires on the pavement even.

Ally's racing pulse didn't care.

His gaze locked on the rearview mirror and she turned to peer out the back window. Towering maple and oak trees filtered weak moonlight through their full branches to shine on stately homes. The street remained empty. She straightened, her stomach quivering like unset Jell-O.

"I don't know how much more of this I can take."

Greg smiled. "Too much excitement for you?"

"Yes."

He laughed. She sank low in her seat, longing for a steaming hot bath to ease the tension from her muscles. Ha. If this was excitement, she needed it about as much as she needed a hole in the head. She winced and rubbed the sore spot on her temple where Boner had pressed the muzzle of his gun. Poor word choice.

Greg pulled into the parking lot of a dumpy motel, the flashing sign illuminating the dilapidated puke-green and pink exterior. The place probably rented rooms by the hour.

Greg disappeared inside the tiny lobby. A few minutes later, he dropped a key in her lap, complete with a key ring in the shape of a miniature rubber…dildo? No way. She leaned closer, gaze tracing the outline of ridges and what definitely looked like the head of a, err, phallus.

"We were in luck. They had one room left."

"Great." She stared at the thing resting between her clenched thighs. No way was she touching that key ring. Someone could have used it in desperate times.

"What?"

"Nothing." She tossed him a polite smile then yanked open the door and scrambled out. She had no business being ungrateful. He was keeping her safe. A sleazy motel, complete with gross key ring, was the least of her worries.

Meticulously avoiding the swinging plastic penis, she fit the key into the thin door. The dim interior wasn't encouraging. Greg shut the door and curtains before hitting the overhead lights. She cringed.

Two beds covered with gray and red shiny comforters squatted over stained gray carpet and were flanked by black lacquer nightstands where large lamps with brilliant-red lampshades perched precariously. Even the walls were a dull shade of gray. Heavy drapes in eye-straining swirls of red, gray and black finished off the décor.

His surprises were certainly…surprising.

"This isn't so bad."

She turned and stared. Was he insane?

"I have to admit, I was a little worried when I first spotted this place." He switched on one of the monstrous lamps and mystery stains on the bed's shiny cover leapt into high relief. "Yeah, this'll work great. Which bed do you want, Sugar Lips?"

She flinched and took a step back, her skin crawling. His smile slipped a few notches.

"Come on. This place is perfect. No one will look for us here. Considering my family's money, they'll expect me to check into a fancy hotel, not some dive." Strolling past her, he stuck his head in the bathroom. "There's even a bathtub. I'll flip you for it."

He held out a quarter and cocked an eyebrow. She managed to unglue her feet, cross the room and peer into the tiny bathroom. A healthy assortment of chips dotted an avocado-green bathtub. Rust stains circled the drain—not what she had in mind when envisioning a hot bath.

"You're going to fit in there how?" She glanced at Greg. Barely an inch separated them. Startled to find him so close, her mouth dried.

His gaze dropped to her lips. "I suppose it'll have to be a shower, then."

His voice lowered, husky and intense. Awareness rippled through her. He stepped back and pressed a towel into her arms while he maneuvered her into the tiny room. She blinked at the glaring fluorescent lightbulb, her nose twitching at the bathroom's musty smell.

He gave a mocking bow. "Ladies first."

Ally stuck her tongue out at the closed door. The childish gesture made her grin as she started the water and took off her clothes, feeling lighter than she had all day.

She eased into the hot water and squeezed the contents of the microscopic "complimentary" shampoo/conditioner into her hand, thinking about Greg. Pictured him leaning against the doorframe in his condo, minus the towel. Imagined licking all his golden skin. Groaning, she rinsed and climbed out of the worn bathtub.

She contemplated the clothes carefully draped over the sink as she dried off. No way could she sleep in those. Talk about sacrilege. Lips pursed, she looked from the clothes to the door to the solitary towel in her hands. Cursing tiny towels to hell and back, she maneuvered the scrap of fabric to cover her important bits.

Ally gathered her clothes, took a deep breath, sent up a quick prayer and stepped out of the steamy bathroom. The cooler air raised goose bumps. She peeked around the corner. Greg lounged on the far bed, his eyes glued to a couple of sportscasters arguing on TV. White-knuckling the towel, borrowed clothes pressed to her chest, she sidled around the corner toward the empty bed. She gingerly peeled back the coverlet, while trying to keep the towel in place.

"Nice outfit."

Her head snapped up. Deep-blue eyes leisurely surveyed her. Heat flashed across her skin and she dove for the sheets. Covered in scratchy cotton, she dropped the wet towel over the side, then carefully arranged the dress on a spare pillow. Ally grimaced and tossed the coverlet to the bottom of the bed. Top sheet securely tucked under her chin, she didn't dare look at Greg.

"No worries, Princess." Amusement dripped from his voice. "I doubt anything's contagious."

She sniffed. "Have I said a word?"

"Your expression says it all. I know this place sucks, but a trashy motel is heaven compared to being six feet under."

Her skin prickled. She closed her eyes and saw again the man tumbling from the roller coaster and Officer Smith's massive bulk herding her into her house. The thud of bullets into Greg's walls. Big beefy arms tightening around her ribcage. The cold press of a steel barrel against her skin. Burrowing deeper beneath the thin covers, trembling spread along her limbs.

"So you admit this place is trashy." Despite her attempt at a teasing tone, her voice shook. "What happened to 'not so bad,' 'perfect' and 'great'?"

Embarrassed by her lack of control, she rolled away from him.

She wrapped her arms around herself to try and still the shaking and dried her tears on the stiff pillowcase.

The bed dipped. Greg's arm slipped around her waist as he lay down behind her. "It's okay," his deep voice whispered across her ear. "You've had a rough day. Let it out."

Deep, wrenching sobs stole the remainder of her self-respect. He held her tight, his heat soaking into her, not even a shiver of revulsion stirring him over her blotchy cheeks or snotty nose.

Drained, sleep dragged at her. She used the last of her energy to wriggle closer, until she could feel him from head to toe along her back. Surrounded by him, soothed, feeling as safe as a diamond in a dark vault, Ally fell asleep.

Golden light filtered through the curtains when she woke the next morning. The sunshine did the dismal room no favors. Memories of sleeping snuggled against Greg brought her fully awake. She shivered, glanced down and groaned. The covers had slipped enough to reveal the pale globe of one entire breast.

A full-body flush warmed her. She yanked the covers up. The sound of the shower running penetrated and she relaxed. If she had an ounce of luck left, he'd gotten into the shower *before* the blanket slipped.

The water shut off. Her heart leapt into her throat and she went from languid sprawl to sitting up in zero point two seconds, yanking the borrowed dress over her head. She jumped out of bed, feverishly tugged on her panties and smoothed the skirt down. The bathroom door opened. A silent prayer of thanks winged its way heavenward.

Greg glanced at her as he rounded the bottom of the bed. "Morning."

"Good morning." She ducked her head, using her hair as a shield between them.

Oh, man. Her hair. She probably looked like a scarecrow. Thick and wavy, it needed no incentive to go wild. Going to bed with wet hair? A guaranteed wild-and-woolly look. Not like she'd had a choice, since this top-notch motel didn't provide a hair dryer.

She gathered her tangled hair into an impromptu ponytail as she looked around for a rubber band. Movement on the other side of the room caught her eye. She went still, holding her hair in place with one hand and the other going to the wall for support.

Grayish towel dangerously low on his hips, the muscles of Greg's back rippled as he bent down.

I should look away.

The towel fell.

Her eyes widened and her heart sped up. *That has to be the finest butt this side of the Mississippi.* In one of those glorious moments when time slowed, he pulled a pair of jeans up muscled legs, pausing for a full heartbeat before dragging them up to cover his butt. She swallowed the excess saliva pooling in her mouth and fought the urge to fan her hot face.

Dragging her gaze up his bare torso, her blush fired up another notch when she met his knowing stare. *At this rate, I'm gonna have a sunburn.* And that grin.

"I figured fair is fair." He shrugged, a fluid shift of muscles beneath bronzed skin.

Her hands tingled with the desire to touch and explore.

He'd said something. About…fairness?

She blinked. "What?"

He winked.

Oh, Lord. He'd seen her breast. Ally sank onto the bed with a groan and buried her face in her hands. Of course.

"I don't know what you're upset about. I'm the one who had to take a cold shower."

"Oh, shut up."

Men like him dated beautiful models and the most sought-after debutantes. He had his choice of women. A chubby, boring claims processor who couldn't afford designer clothes, highlights or manicures would hold no interest for him.

Even so...she snuck another peak between her fingers. A girl could at least enjoy the view. He pulled a black T-shirt over his head. Another hot flash washed over her. Probably a hormonal imbalance.

Sighing, she stuffed her feet into the gorgeous platform sandals. They would make for a harrowing experience if she had to run for her life. Again. Maybe if she started praying now, she wouldn't twist her ankle or break a leg.

Luck sure as heck wasn't going to help her out.

"Ready?"

"I don't suppose you have a hairbrush in that mysterious black bag of yours?"

"Nope. No worries. It's a real turn-on when a woman looks like she just crawled out of bed after a night of hot sex. Guys dig it."

"Well, gee," she drawled, giving him a wide berth as she headed for the door. "As long as y'all dig it."

"No need to get snippy." His eyes crinkled at the corners. "We can pick up a hairbrush, if it's such a big deal."

Exasperation and arousal made an odd mix. Ally yanked open the door. Brilliant sunshine blinded her. Greg hollered to wait. Bright spots dancing before her eyes, she glanced over her shoulder into the room as she stepped onto the sidewalk.

Right into the arms of a man with a gun. She whimpered. Seriously?

His gun-free arm looped around her waist, pulling her tight against him. Noxious body odor gagged her.

Desperate for fresh air, she turned her head. Greg stood silhouetted in the doorway of their room, the steely glint in his eyes at odds with his relaxed stance.

"This is a career change for you, Weasel."

"Don't call me that." The tremor in the guy's voice bode ill. The cocky way he pointed the gun at Greg was even worse. Whether his anxiety stemmed from Greg's attitude, his nerves or fear, she didn't care to find out. "Just back off and no one gets hurt."

"Really? Is that what your boss-man said?" Greg cocked his head to the side. "Funny, I heard the orders were to kill Miss Thompson. Makes it a little hard to buy the whole 'No one will get hurt' bit."

Did he have to say it so casually? In sync, she and Stink Boy swallowed audibly. The trembling, the odor, the shaking voice; the guy was a mess. Not a good thing considering the gun in his sweaty hand. Its twin pressed the thin material of her dress over her abdomen, sweating through the fabric and making her skin crawl.

"I'm not gonna let you screw up my first big job, Detective." His damp hand crept up the front of her dress and cupped her breast. "She don't seem your type."

Her skin shriveled. She bit her tongue on a scream and shrank from his hand, bringing her flush up against him. Ally flinched, straightened sharply and held her breath.

Greg's hands fisted. Stink Boy jerked back, his gun wavering. His hand clenched her breast so tight she yelped.

Greg's eyes flashed, a muscle jumping in his cheek. "I'll say this one time. Get. Your. Hands. Off. Her."

Stink Boy pinched her nipple and Ally ran out of patience. Anger and fear coalesced in a hard knot and she slammed her elbow into his scrawny ribs. He shrieked like a girl, released her and staggered to the side.

Greg flattened Stink Boy on the hard pavement, stuffed his gun in the back waistband of Greg's pants and cuffed him.

Ally took a step back.

Yanking the guy to his feet, Greg shook him. Ally was pretty sure Stink Boy's loose teeth rattled. "You and I are going to have a little chat."

"No! Wait!" Sweat beaded on his forehead. "All I know is my boss wants her. That's it. I swear."

Greg stuck his hand in his pocket. The car lights flashed and the door locks clicked open. He glanced at her.

"Wait in the car. Lock the doors."

He shoved Stink Boy into the motel room and slammed the

door. Silence descended. She stared blindly at the motel room's pink door. He'd been armed. Likely high on something. And she decided to act like it's *Mission Impossible*. She pressed trembling fingers to her lips and stumbled to the car, obediently locking the doors.

She closed her eyes and let her head fall back against the headrest. The city seemed to hold an innumerable number of thugs willing to hunt her down. Stink Boy's palpable nerves and gun had put her on edge, but he hadn't been the worst. Officer Jones held that dubious honor. So far.

Ally lifted her head as Greg emerged, glancing around as he shut the door firmly. The DO NOT DISTURB sign swung from the doorknob. Maybe she should borrow the sign and hang it around her neck.

She could start a new jewelry trend.

Greg climbed into the car, while tapping on his cell phone, then pressed it to his ear and spit out a succession of rapid-fire instructions. He clicked it off and wrapped his hands around the steering wheel. The atmosphere in the car was charged. Ally stared out the window at the paint peeling off the motel's grimy exterior, twisting her fingers in the dress. She nibbled on her lower lip, tucked her leg beneath her and untangled her fingers from the fabric. She settled both feet on the floorboards again. Greg still didn't start the car. He sat staring at her, freaking her out.

"You okay?"

She started when he spoke. The trembling she thought she had under control returned and a few stupid tears trickled down her cheeks.

"Aw, baby." He gathered her in his arms and held her tight, rubbing her back, murmuring unintelligible reassurances in her hair. In general, it made her feel warm and safe. She closed her eyes, took a deep Greg-scented breath and nestled a little bit closer.

Ally swallowed a sigh of regret when he released her. But, he didn't move back. He brushed the tears off her cheeks. Her heart clutched. Twice he'd held her while she sobbed out her stress and fear and adrenaline overdose against his chest.

She lowered her gaze and sat back. "Sorry about your shirt."

The engine rumbled to life. He backed out of the parking space and she glanced at the motel room.

"What were you doing in there, anyway?"

"Uh, handcuffing him to the bed so the locals can pick him up."

Her eyebrows climbed. His shoulders were hunched and he didn't meet her eyes. He was rubbing his knuckles, a few of which looked scraped and red.

"Okay."

His cheekbones darkened with a flush. "Weasel is pretty low on the totem pole. Guess they don't realize you're with me."

"You know his, err, boss?"

"Yeah. These guys define the term 'underbelly of society'."

She eyed the tree-lined neighborhood. "So, where are we going? What do we do now? Do you have any leads on who's after me? I mean us. Whatever. What's the plan?"

"Whoa. Slow down, Sugar Lips." He grinned. "First things first. Breakfast. Women get real irritable when they go too long without eating. There's this little place I know with the best omelets."

Just what she needed. A reminder about his vast experience with women. And omelets.

Settling deeper in the seat, she crossed her legs and stared at the scenery whipping past. Speed limits obviously didn't apply to police officers. Must be nice. Not like she'd speed even if she could.

One maddening hour later, they climbed back into the burnt-orange leather-upholstered interior of the Camaro. She had to admit, she felt better after eating. More in control.

"Do I get any hints about where we're going?"

Greg shot her an amused glance. "I told you—"

"Yes, I know. It's not something I need to worry about. The big strong police detective will take care of everything. Well, forgive me if I'm not willing to take a back seat when this all revolves around me and something I may or may not know about some mysterious criminal mastermind."

"Well, that was dramatic," he drawled in true Surfer Dude fashion.

Ally rolled her eyes. "Keep it up and criminals won't be the only ones after your blood."

"Threatening an officer of the law?" He shook his head. "If I weren't so turned-on right now, I'd read you your rights and handcuff you. Actually, we can try that later. In private."

Face on fire, she crossed her arms. Turn her on and give her hot flashes to distract her from the fact he wasn't telling her a flippin' thing. Great plan. So what if it worked.

He guided the car to the curb, put it into neutral and applied the brake. She blinked. Here? No way. She'd never been to this part of the city. Neither had she suffered any overwhelming desire to.

Garbage littered the sidewalks, ancient cars unmoved in the past decade occupied the gutters and crumbling brick buildings loomed over them all. Sinking her teeth into her lip, she turned to Greg.

"It'll be okay." He patted her thigh. "I'm going to have a quick conversation with a man about a horse. Wait here. I'll be right back. Promise."

A horse?

He climbed out, ducking down to make eye contact again. "Sit tight."

The door slammed shut. Always with the orders. She eyed the building squatting on the block amongst the other ramshackle brick structures, an ugly ogre waiting for an innocent victim to stroll close enough to grab.

Four men materialized out of the shadows at Greg's approach. Ally gnawed on her lip and wished for a cell phone. What if she needed to call 9-1-1? The men stopped a few feet from Greg, speaking in voices too low to carry. Their gazes strayed in her direction. Chewing harder on her lip, she sank in her seat.

The four men backed off and Greg vanished into the gloomy

depths of the building.

Five of the longest minutes of her life later, he reappeared. She did a quick scan for injuries, ridiculously relieved when she didn't spot any. The lopsided grin he shot her belied the tense lines around his eyes. He nodded at the lounging men as he passed, climbed into the car and pulled away from the curb. Several minutes and numerous turns later, he broke the heavy silence.

"It's not good, Ally." His use of her given name tightened her nerves more than his tone. Surfer Dude had vanished.

"This guy is so high up in the food chain, no one knows who he is. I don't know what the hell you've gotten yourself messed up in, but it's big." He met her eyes. For a split second, his gaze dropped to the spot where her teeth clamped down on her lip before returning to the road. "Normally, I'd be thrilled to have something like this drop in my lap. This could make my career. But your involvement..." He looked away.

Ally didn't say anything as she watched him, worrying her lip.

He was quiet for a minute. "The guy killed at the amusement park was Michael Smith. Do you—"

The air left her lungs in a rush. Michael Smith. Her friend. Coworker. Dead. Her head spun.

Greg's lips thinned and he pulled to the side of the road.

"Michael was the man who fell off the ride? I mean..." She waved a limp hand, unable to say the words. To make the entire situation more real. Beyond Michael's death, one thought loomed large. "Is it strange we were both at the park on the same day, on the same ride, at the same time?"

"It's a very convenient coincidence."

"Especially since I hate roller coasters. The odds of me going on one were extremely slim."

"So why did you? Why were you even at the park?"

"Because!" She threw her hands up in the air, exasperated with herself and the situation. "Everyone at work is always going somewhere and doing something. They return on Monday gushing about a new restaurant, some hip downtown dance club, a weekend get-a-way, the amusement park... My contribution is always, 'I read a good book.' Or I could mention my hot 'date,'" she made air quotes with fingers, "with my therapist. Wouldn't that impress everyone!"

"Therapist?"

"Yeah." She shifted uncomfortably. "I've seen one for the past two years."

"Dare I ask why you were seeing a shrink?"

Ally shrugged, studying a microscopic smudge on the windshield. "A few years ago, a drunk driver killed my family. My mom, dad, grandma and little brother were coming home from the Olympics." Despite the grief weighing down her soul, a small smile tipped the corners of her mouth. "My brother had just won the gold medal in snowboarding."

Greg snapped his fingers, startling her. "Nicholas Thompson. I heard about that. The gold medal, the accident..."

"The surviving sister, too terrified of flying to accompany her family, therefore missing out on sharing Nick's greatest moment."

"And missing out on dying."

Her shoulders hunched and she wrapped her arms around her ribcage. Survivor's guilt. For the most part conquered, but sometimes the ugliness crept up and blindsided her. "Actually, I was driving. I picked them up from the airport." Enough about her life. "I don't get why anyone would...Michael is...was a sweet guy. He wouldn't hurt a fly. It doesn't make sense."

He frowned at her but let the subject change stand, to her relief. "Maybe he was involved in something, and whoever had him killed thinks he told you about it. Were you two dating?"

His voice sounded odd. She glanced at him. His hands were tight around the steering wheel and the skin around his eyes and mouth was tight.

Huh. "No, we weren't dating. We were just friends."

He nodded, shoulders relaxing.

Too bizarre.

"What about any mutual friends, then? Someone he could have offended."

"Michael and I worked together. We didn't socialize outside of that. I don't know anything about his personal life."

Greg steered the car back into traffic. Several blocks later, he pulled into a parking spot outside a police station.

"What are we doing here?"

"I need to see if they've gotten anything out of the guy we brought in yesterday or if Weasel became chatty."

She trailed along behind him, like a forlorn puppy, into the stuffy interior of the building. Scuffed and scarred floors, gray walls, and old desks set a mundane backdrop for the bustling activity. Uniformed officers and men in uninspired suits mingled with tattooed women and grungy males with bitter eyes.

Greg ushered her past the front security and down a hall while she gaped at the scene. She swallowed a sigh of disappointment when he led her into a sedate room, minus the criminal element. He pointed her toward a desk with his favorite order, "Stay put."

Glaring mutinously, she sat and refused to dwell on his broad back. Nor did she notice the easy way he wove through the desks before disappearing down the hallway.

She crossed her legs, brushed lint off her dress and looked around. All heads faced her. Conversation ceased. Ally swallowed thickly, tummy tightening painfully.

She pasted on a smile, doing her best to ignore the onset of nausea.

The man seated at the desk nearest her had his eyes glued to her bare legs. Despite the admiration on his handsome face, she longed for a pair of blue jeans. She shifted her legs to the side and kept him in her peripheral vision. His gaze made its way to her face.

Appreciation warmed his baby-blues. "Why's a fine-looking woman like you hanging out with Marsing? You have way too much class for him."

She reluctantly faced him. Under normal circumstances, she'd appreciate his attention. Well-dressed in a mocha suit and red power tie, his smile a flash of white in his tan face, emphasizing a dimpled chin and strong cheekbones, surrounded by neatly cropped golden curls. Today? Detective Goldilocks' over-the-top flattery fell flat.

Her smile stretched tight. "Thanks."

"So," he leaned back in his squeaky chair, hooking his thumbs through his belt loops, "You're ol' Marsing's flavor of the month."

She flinched. Her lack of experience in handling overt rudeness sucked. Eyeing his badge and gun, she opted for placid agreement. "Apparently."

"You don't seem like his type. You'd be a lot better off with someone like…" He glanced around the room then looked back at her with a smug grin. "Me."

Is he for real? As if. Good looks didn't compensate for totally corny lines. Okay, so amazing looks. Still.

"Can I get you a drink while you're waiting?"

"That would be nice." Anything to get rid of him.

"What would you like?"

"Uhm, what are my choices?"

"Maybe you should come along, so you can pick out whatever you want."

Ally glanced toward the doorway where Greg had disappeared. A police officer had tried to kill her yesterday. Going for a walk with Goldilocks didn't seem like a brilliant idea.

"Come on. It'll be fine. We'll be back before Marsing. He can't have every second of your day. Besides, you're surrounded by cops. Safe as a baby in a buggy."

With a mental shrug, she rose. She *was* in a police station. The detective clearly didn't know who she was. Just—how had he put it?—Greg's flavor of the month. She so adored that description.

Goldilocks whipped around a corner and she broke into a trot. Why did men have to walk so darn fast? She'd like to see how well they walked in four-inch heels. A mental picture of Goldilocks in a dress and stilettos flashed and she grinned as she rounded the corner.

Detective Goldilocks grabbed her elbow. Tight. Alarm bells went off. She tried to wrench her arm free and stomp on his foot as she opened her mouth to scream.

Chapter Seven

"Oh no, you don't." He slapped a damp palm over her mouth and yanked her close. "I heard about that move."

How many dirty cops did this department have, anyway?

"That's right, just stay calm and everything will be fine."

"Do I look stupid?" she mumbled into his hand, glaring at him.

He held her tight to his side and started walking. Tension radiated off him like too much cheap cologne.

Sticking close to the wall, he half-walked, half-carried her down the deserted hallway. The deserted hallway in a police station. Her quiet life had become a black comedy of errors. Or this police department was really that inept. Seriously, were all the other cops sipping coffee and inhaling donuts in the break room?

A red exit sign glowed above the metal door ahead. She wriggled harder. If only she'd thought to grease herself down earlier, 'cause no way was she going outside with him.

The door loomed. She whimpered, searching desperately for rescue. He reached for the door and Ally went limp. Goldilocks staggered and her head bounced off the wall. Sharp pain shot through her skull and down her neck. She moaned into the hand clamped over her mouth.

Spots danced across her vision and she drove the heel of her shoe backward, aiming for his shin. The wedge met with solid muscle. His hold loosened and she jerked free, stumbling as she turned to run.

Goldilocks swore. His solid weight punched into her side, slamming her against the opposite wall. Her head bounced off the wall again, hazing her vision. He hauled her through the door. Pain exploded at the bright sunshine and forced her eyes closed.

Bright spots flickered against her closed eyelids. His arms banded tight around her diaphragm. She struggled to draw a full breath.

He let go and she collapsed. Not in a lovely, graceful swoon, either. Just dropped like a stone, her legs rubbery from the wild spinning in her head.

The smack of flesh meeting flesh and blistering curses roused her. She rolled her head to the side and opened her eyes.

Greg had Goldilocks on the ground, pummeling him. Other men ran up, grabbed Greg and dragged him off Goldilocks. Several more men helped Goldilocks to his feet and into handcuffs. Greg shook off the restraining hands and stalked toward her, furious color high in his cheeks and an unholy gleam in his eyes.

Ally struggled to her feet, narrowing her eyes when the world tilted and pain crashed through her head. She didn't dare take her gaze off the six feet plus of angry male approaching.

"Are you okay?" he growled, toe-to-toe with her.

She nodded, resisting the urge to back up, instinctively knowing doing so would be a mistake.

"What the hell is so hard to understand about 'stay put'?"

Man, he was hot.

Before she could respond, or kiss him senseless, the same older man who'd been at Greg's condo came up and laid his hand on Greg's arm. "Greg, this isn't the time or place. I don't see how this is Miss Thompson's fault. We didn't know Scott was dirty. How was she supposed to?"

Greg glared at her, obviously hoping to sear his message of complete, unquestioning obedience into her brain telepathically.

After everything she'd been through, his dominating, insufferable attitude was too much. Even if she *was* twisted enough to find him unbearably sexy, attitude and all. Issues. Serious issues. She blamed her family.

Crossing her arms, she glared back. "I'm not a dog, Greg. Lose the attitude."

"Greg." The older man had more steel in the word this time, his impressive white eyebrows lowering over his eyes.

Greg stepped back and ran a hand through his hair. "Sorry, Captain. Guess I got a little carried away."

"The stress of the job getting to you, son? You've earned a few days off. We can assign Miss Thompson to another detective."

Greg went rigid. "I'm fine, sir. I don't like to leave a job unfinished."

Ally frowned. He was forever amused or annoyed with her. Surely he'd welcome getting rid of her. Except…he'd said this case could make his career. Her tummy flipped and she lowered her gaze. Whatever the cause, she was glad he wasn't going to hand her off to some other guy. He'd proven he could keep her safe. Well, safer than every other guy she'd spent more than two minutes with, at least.

"If you're sure. We can't have you cracking on the job." At Greg's nod, the captain turned to watch Scott disappear inside the building with his escort and shook his head. "I don't know what the hell is going on with this department. Pardon the language, Miss. Scott's been with us since he graduated from the police academy thirteen years ago. And Smith…" Tension lined his mouth and eyes.

Empathy welled, but what could she say? She didn't know the police captain.

"I can't say, sir," Greg said. "I guess we should be glad we're finding the holes."

"Maybe, but I'd prefer there weren't any holes to find. There'd damn well better not be more. Especially since we don't have Smith in custody." His sharp gray eyes focused on Ally. She fidgeted.

"Miss Thompson. It's been a rough couple of days for you. You okay? Does your head hurt?"

Grimacing, she rubbed her throbbing temples. "You could say that. Nothing half a dozen Tylenol won't take care of."

"Greg, take care of her. And find whoever's behind this mess. I want him brought in a.s.a.p."

"Yes, sir."

With a nod at Greg and a fatherly smile at her, the captain disappeared into the station behind the last of the stragglers. The door swung closed. A sudden fascination with the blacktop overtook her.

Greg sighed. "Look, I'm sorry I lost my temper. I could blame it on adrenaline, but the truth is…"

She glanced up through her lashes.

He scrubbed a hand over his face. "I lost it when I saw an empty chair. Every time I turn around someone's grabbing you. I assumed the worst. And I was right, damnit."

Ally shrugged. She didn't know how to take his comment. Did he care about her as a person, a woman or was he just doing his job? Did he care at all?

He pulled her against him, smothering her surprised yelp as he enfolded her in his arms. He rubbed the back of her neck, easing her headache. His other arm wound around her waist, clasping her tight. He surrounded her so thoroughly her brain short-circuited.

The same couldn't be said for her body. Her nipples pebbled against his hard chest, her stomach quivered, her womb clenched and she grew damp between her thighs. The warm scent she already associated with him infused her every nook and cranny like a high-grade aphrodisiac. One tiny, still-operating brain cell buzzed, "Danger! Heartbreak ahead!" but she was too drunk on sensation, on Greg, to care.

He drew in a deep breath and squeezed her, shooting off mini fireworks. As abruptly as he'd pulled her close, he released her and took a step back. He rubbed a long strand of her dark hair between his thumb and forefinger. Her silly romantic heart saw the gesture as symbolic of his struggle with his longing for her and his subsequent inability to bridge the distance.

The hair slipped free and he sighed. "We'd better head out."

She nodded and brushed off her dress. When she looked back up, Surfer Dude had returned. Relaxed, loose posture, a slight grin, green eyes warm and amused; carefree persona restored in full. After five seconds of full-frontal contact, her composure evaporated like a wisp of smoke on a brisk fall day.

He held the door open and she slid into the passenger seat. The low rumble of the engine was the only sound as they wove through the city streets. Gradually, her brain reordered itself. She stared out the window, trying to make sense of the last day and a half over the dull throb in her head.

There had to be something she was missing. Maybe she'd been mistaken for someone else. Had she seen something she didn't realize was important? She sighed.

"We'll figure it out, Ally." The annoying man was reading her mind again. "Maybe we should sit down and go over your last week. There must be something."

"I was thinking the same thing. I can't figure it out. It's so frustrating."

"Sometimes all it takes is fresh eyes. Or ears."

"That would be great." Ally bit her lip, but what the heck? "Sooo, where are we going to have this conversation? Driving down the road? Another motel?"

He chuckled. "Nah. I thought we'd go somewhere out of the way and peaceful."

"Sounds like heaven."

Greg pulled into a drive-thru coffee shop and glanced at her. "What's your poison, Sugar Lips?"

"Nonfat chai tea latte, please."

The buildings grew fewer and farther between as they left the city behind. He turned onto a dirt lane, babying his Camaro down the road. Around a curve, the trees thinned to reveal a beautiful, sparkling lake framed by thick pine trees and a sweeping shoreline dotted sporadically with houses.

"Wow," she breathed.

"Yeah. This is my favorite place to get away."

"Really? You need to get away from things?" For the first time in two days, she felt light-hearted enough to tease. She fought giddiness. Freedom.

He laughed, steering the car down the twisting hillside to the lake below. She threw open the Camaro's door before he'd come to a complete stop.

Fresh, cool air poured over her, soothing overwrought nerves. Breathing the pine-scented air, she surveyed the surrounding scenery. The lake water shone, drawing her down a path.

Two days ago, the wobbly dock would have sent her scurrying for shore. Now, she didn't pause until she'd reached the very end. Closing her eyes, she tilted her face to the warmth of the sun and smiled.

"This place never gets old."

He walked up beside her, his nearness deepening her contentment. Beauty surrounded her—he pulse of life in the water gently lapping against the boat dock beneath her feet, the rustling of leaves, the gentle breeze caressing her skin and the trill of birds. All of it more effective than any sedative.

"Okay, I'm officially jealous. If I had a place like this, I don't think you could drag me away." She turned and caught an odd expression on Greg's face. His mouth opened then snapped shut.

The look fled, replaced by the casual happy-go-lucky attitude she now recognized. An attitude remarkably similar to a carefully erected shield. The buffer provided Greg with distance and minimized the risk of getting too close.

Not that she had room to talk. Her walls were thick and miles high. She protected them by keeping a safe, familiar and admittedly boring environment wrapped around her like a blanket. Never taking any risks, any chances.

The two of them made quite a pair. She shook her head and looked beyond Greg to the home on the rise.

A massive wall of windows faced the lake, framed by Victorian cottage accents of white wood siding, curled cornices and a gabled roof. Rooms jutted in every direction, giving the house the rambling air of an absentminded professor. Sprawling rose bushes and masses of flowers mingled sociably with the natural bushes and trees. Breathtaking.

"Come on. I'll show you the inside, Sugar Lips."

She followed him back up the narrow path and onto the whitewashed wrap-around porch. He unlocked the door and gestured her inside with a bow. Rolling her eyes, she swept past Sir Galahad.

High ceilings with ornate treatments and spacious architectural design mixed with dignified paneling, rim and wide-planked floors. The grace and beauty touched a musty, unused corner of her soul.

She turned in a slow circle, vowing to savor every second she spent in this lakeside dream. Assorted gorgeous rugs sprinkled the floor and the furnishings and décor combined to create a cozy cottage. Oh yeah, she could hide out here forever.

Hiding. Her bubble of euphoria burst. If only she were on vacation. If only Greg wasn't a wealthy detective only doing his duty.

"You can use this room." Greg gestured toward an open door. "It has an attached bath. Celia uses this bedroom, so hopefully you'll be able to find some more clothes to use."

"I'd rather not borrow more of your sister's clothes."

"You're welcome to…" He grinned. "Anything you like." His lecherous perusal left little room to mistake his offer.

"I might take you up on that, smart aleck."

"Please?"

Turning away to hide her smile, she wandered into the bedroom. Rose prints, lace and ruffles were everywhere; the exact opposite of the cool elegance of the condo. She loved it. The bathroom screamed 1950s. Pink tile with cream accents, a pink sink and bathtub. Even the toilet was pink. Smiling, she turned and about jumped out of her skin. Greg lounged against the bathroom doorjamb, a foot away.

"You approve."

"It's charming, like the rest of the house. I don't know how you ever leave."

He shrugged. "It's been in the family since before I was born."

"Along with the penthouse?"

"Yeah." He grinned, the warmth in his eyes doing funny things to her tummy. "Look who's the detective now."

Cheeks warm with pleasure, she squeezed past him into the bedroom, nerve endings firing off pheromones when she brushed against him. The room's windows overlooked the side of the house. Manicured lawn gave way to a pine needle-scattered forest floor several yards away.

"Dinner in half an hour." His footsteps faded.

Sighing, she plopped on the bed. Resisting her attraction to Greg was exhausting. She didn't fit in his world and she had the distinct impression—helped along by all the cracks of his fellow cops—he didn't do relationships.

Dropping back to lay flat on the bed, she stared at the Swiss dotted-lace canopy. These people had more money than a mule could pack. How many houses did they have? What kind of family dynamics had Greg grown up with?

Her parents had left her alone for the most part. She lacked courage and had zero interest in adventure—so different from the rest of her family. An embarrassment. Grandma Thompson held the gold medal in downhill skiing, Mom had silvered in luge, and Dad had been a member of the gold-medal hockey team before they'd married. Nicholas had happily carried on the tradition with his gold medal in snowboarding, while Ally lived the exciting life of a claims processor, sans any mildly interesting hobbies or extra-curricular activities.

She rolled over. The windows were draped in the same

Swiss-dotted fabric. Maples and pine trees swayed outside. Birds chirped. A puffy-cheeked squirrel scampered into sight. Her lids grew heavy.

The room was dark when she opened her eyes. Moonlight lent a dreamlike quality to the woods outside the window. She sat up and rubbed her eyes, covering a big yawn with her hand.

"Thought you were going to sleep through the night, Sugar Lips." Greg stood silhouetted by the moonlight in the doorway.

"Holy crap." She pressed a hand over her galloping heart. "You should wear a cowbell or something."

"A what?"

"Never mind. Sorry. I didn't mean to fall asleep."

"No harm, no foul."

"Why do men always talk in sports terminology?" She ran a hand through her tangled hair as she stood. Her toes curled against the cold hardwood. She'd had shoes on earlier...Her shoes were now neatly lined up in front of the closet. She raised her eyebrows at Greg.

He rubbed the back of his neck, distracting her with his bulging bicep. "I came to check on you when you didn't show up for dinner. When I found you asleep, I thought you'd be more comfortable without shoes." A shiver of awareness arrowed through her body. "Guess it's part of having a sister."

A sister. Well, that neatly took the wind out of her sails. She was envisioning his hot, oiled, naked body and he thought of her like a sister. Wonderful. Perfect.

"Something wrong?"

"Nope." She pasted on a big smile. "Not a thing."

"Are you sure—"

"I'm starving. Did you say something about food?" Ally winced, but desperate times and all that. She never, ever talked about eating around men. Or food in general. Anything drawing attention to her or her weight.

He stared at her, the room too much in shadow for her to make out his expression.

Nibbling on her lower lip, she laced her fingers and waited semi-patiently until he led the way out of the room. She padded barefoot down the hallway and her gaze slid over to take in his large, bare feet and denim, worn low on his hips.

Settled at the big kitchen table with a bowl of steaming chili and the wonderful aroma of cornbread tantalizing her taste buds, she tried to resist the intimate picture; just the two of them in a big kitchen eating food he'd prepared for her. Her hair mussed from napping and no shoes. *He thinks of me as a sister.*

"I hope I didn't ruin the meal."

"Nope. I left the food to simmer while you slept and warmed the cornbread. No big deal."

What woman wouldn't be flinging off her clothes and crawling across the table when the guy was sweet, considerate *and* could cook? Not even taking into account the sexy hunk of man part. He sucked her in so easily.

Breathe. She would not let her hormones make a fool out of her. He was only here because her life was in danger, playing the hero to the boring claims processor. He had no interest in her personally, beyond a mild brotherly affection. Maybe if she repeated it enough times she'd stop caring.

The delicious chili and melt-in-your-mouth cornbread helped. She even managed not to fantasize about dragging Greg's naked body onto the sturdy table, climbing on top of him and doing things that were illegal in three states. Of course, in the fantasies she *did not* have, she was a perfect size six.

She helped Greg clear the dishes then shoved him out of the kitchen so she could clean. Anything to get some breathing space. Burying her arms elbow deep in suds calmed her.

When she finished, she draped the kitchen towel over the big farmhouse sink and walked into the living room. Greg stood gazing out the windows. Just like that, all her hormones went into happy dance mode again.

"I've already said it, but some things bear repeating. This house is amazing."

He turned and smiled. Those dimples of his were lethal. "I appreciate this place a little more every time I come. Must be getting old."

Ally crossed the room to stand beside him. Peace seeped into her bones. They both sighed at the same time and exchanged quick grins.

"I suppose we should have that talk now."

The reluctance in his deep voice gave her courage. Putting a face to her nemesis scared her.

She got comfy on the overstuffed couch facing the massive stone fireplace. Even resting dormant, the hearth was beautiful.

"Let's start a week before yesterday. We can go back further if necessary."

He sketched out the timeline before handing her the notepad and pencil. Looking at all the events of the past few weeks on paper organized her thoughts. Her simple life made the timeline easy to fill in and emphasized how incredibly dull her life was.

Early to work, late to arrive home, a video under her arm half the time, a romance novel the other half. If she wanted to have some fun, she went to the library or a bookstore. Sometimes, she even went to the movies. Alone.

She hid from life. A ball of shame grew bigger with each stroke of her pencil. Her fingers and her brain cramped. She collapsed back against the couch.

"Well," she muttered, "that was a complete waste of time and energy."

"Nah. I've learned a lot. You live for routines. And your kitchen is scary clean."

"No, it's not."

"Yeah, 'cause every Tom, Dick and Harry scrub counters and floors Tuesday and Thursday then do top to bottom cleaning

Saturday. Yup, totally normal."

Ally flushed. "Ha-ha. You're sooo funny." She caught his teasing grin and dropped her gaze. It *was* pretty lame. "Yeah, my life is beyond pathetic."

"I wouldn't go that far."

She looked up at his tone. His gaze traveled down her body. Her cheeks, toes, and everything in between heated. She surreptitiously peeked at herself. The position she'd adopted thrust her breasts out, accentuating them and making her tummy look almost toned. Heck, even her thighs didn't look half bad from this angle.

Heat darkened Greg's sea-green eyes. He stared at her lips and she licked them. His eyes narrowed. Her pulse ratcheted up. Was spontaneous combustion possible?

Still staring at her lips, he slid down the couch next to her, draped his arm along the back of the couch behind her and leaned closer. Anticipation hummed. His lips settled over hers with the sweetness of a Lindt truffle. He nibbled at her mouth and whispered his firm lips across hers, the pressure so light she chased after him for more. She moaned her satisfaction when he deepened the kiss, the slide of his tongue along hers unleashing passion. She buried her fingers in his thick hair and gave her newfound sensuality free rein.

Greg pulled back, breathing heavily. Along with a healthy dose of oxygen came the realization that she lay draped across his lap, all wanton and uninhibited. She wouldn't mind being wanton and uninhibited. Would, in fact, love it—in another lifetime. Insecurity battered back arousal and she scrambled off him.

Greg grabbed her back. She opened her mouth to protest and his lips covered hers again. Insecurity fell by the wayside. Her mind wanted to analyze his motivation, while her heart relished the sensations pouring over her nerve endings.

Desire simmered in his eyes, tempting her more than Godiva chocolates in the throes of PMS. Regardless, she knew better and she didn't dare test her limits. Not with a guy like Greg.

Aching to be wild just once in her life, she drew back. He let her go this time. Scooting to the far corner of the big couch, she stared into the dark grate of the empty fireplace. Unsettled by Greg's gaze on her, she fidgeted with the pillow fringe. She had no desire to scratch an itch for him. What did she want?

"So…" he murmured.

She flicked a glance at him, itchy and irritable with unsatisfied desire and confusion. His endearing lopsided grin didn't help.

"What?" Her voice came out a little sharper than she intended.

His eyebrows climbed skyward, and she squeezed her eyes closed in embarrassment.

Way to show class and worldly experience, Ally. Snap the guy's head off, which is ever so reasonable when you're the one applying the emergency brake. Sheesh.

"I don't imagine you're tired after your nap. What do you want to do?" The husky invitation in his voice was unmistakable.

She clenched her hands and thighs against temptation. Going to bed with him would surpass her other experiences by a mile. Granted, beating the awkward fumbling of a college dorm room or an unsatisfying two-minute interlude in a pitch-black bedroom wouldn't take much.

She smiled sweetly. "I love Scrabble."

His grin slipped.

"Do you have it?"

"Uh, probably."

"Want me to grab it?"

He shook his head and ran his fingers through his tousled hair.

Her fingers itched to help. Ally sat on her hands. Why, oh why, did she have to be such a stick-in-the-mud? She leapt up and paced to the windows. The stars reflected on the glassy surface of the lake. Greg's footsteps left the room and she bounced lightly on her toes.

It was her fault they weren't naked and satisfying all her fantasies right now. His willingness for a roll in the hay had throbbed against her hip, rampantly apparent.

In the window's reflection, Greg returned. Why did she have to be such a freakin' coward?

Scrabble box in hand, he settled on the floor in front of a big square coffee table and pulled out the game pieces. "Well?" He glanced up. "Are we going to play?"

"Yep." She sat on the plush rug and rested her elbows on the low coffee table.

Greg pulled an A and went first, spelling out B-I-G in the center of the board.

"Gee, make it easy, why don't you?"

He sat back and patiently waited, clearly unfazed by her whining. She stared at her tiles. Finally, she went with G-I-Z-M-O.

"Gizmo, huh? Do you have a favorite?"

Why did she think he was referring to something sexual? Could be the heat in his eyes, the daring look he gave her or the memory of the kiss they'd shared.

"My rolling muscle massager."

"Is that what they call it in your circle?" His thoughtful expression didn't fool her. Especially when he laid D-I-L-D-O on the board. "We use another name where I come from."

He smiled angelically and fished more tiles out of the bag.

Oh, so that's how it was going to be. Well, two could play his little game. She smiled just as sweetly and put down three letters after his. L-U-B-E.

Challenge lit his aqua eyes. "Game on, Sugar Lips."

Thirty minutes later, a fascinating array of very naughty words filled the board. Greg grinned and added C-U-F-F-S after H-A-N-D.

Ally stared at the board. The spirit of competition riding her hard, she narrowed her eyes. Gleeful exhilaration filled her and an evil smile grew. Using the N in N-I-P-P-L-E, she spelled out S-P-A-N-K.

Greg choked. She glanced at him through her lashes. Color rode high in his cheeks and his eyes glittered dangerously.

"Sooo...."

A crooked smile tipped his lips. "You want a spanking while handcuffed to my bed?"

The image whipped through her like a lash, setting all her nerve endings on fire and dampening her panties. Holy crap. In about five seconds she'd lunge across the table and rip his clothes off. She cleared her throat.

"Why did you become a police officer?" She selected fresh tiles from the velvet bag.

She looked up when he didn't answer. His expression was perfectly, utterly blank. The teasing light extinguished, his smile nothing but a memory.

"Freshman year of college, I came home for Thanksgiving." His low monotone slid dread down her arms, tingling her fingertips. "Place was silent, which never happened with a teenage girl in the house. Or my parents either."

The dread congealed in the pit of her stomach.

"Then the smell hit me. Sharp, metallic." Greg fiddled with a small tile, his eyes glazed. "I called for them, but I think I already knew. You know how in a bad dream everything feels muffled? Searching was like that, like moving through soupy fog. Until I walked down the hallway into their bedroom."

Ally bit down hard on her lip, wanting to beg him to stop, wishing she could take back her question. She'd only wanted to know more. A small nugget of information about the man who turned her inside out.

"I've never seen anything like it. The walls, the ceiling, every piece of furniture splattered with blood." He lifted his head and stared out the windows behind her. Ally fisted her hands against the urge to touch him. Comfort him. Instinctively, she knew he wouldn't want her sympathy. "The killer, or maybe killers, I don't know, had arranged them on their bed, post mortem, their hands linked across the silk comforter."

Her head swam with the images—gruesome, horrifying. She

couldn't begin to imagine how much worse it had been for him. To find his parents murdered. They must have been elegant, refined; devoted to one another and their children.

"Fortunately, my sister had left for school before the killer got there." Greg blinked and his gaze focused again, returning him to their game and her. Emotion flitted across his eyes. Shock over what he'd told her, maybe.

"Anyway, their death changed everything. I finished out my degree at the local college and got a bachelors in criminal science instead of law."

"I'm so sorry, Greg." She couldn't hold in the words, or the aching sympathy.

He merely nodded, staring at his tiles.

"What happened to your sister?"

"We didn't have grandparents or any of the aunts and uncles so many families are riddled with. I switched schools. Someone had to raise her. Celia had just turned fifteen."

That set her back on her heels. She didn't know why the thought of him raising a teenage girl shocked her so much. He seemed so lackadaisical and uncaring. A lothario who'd raised his sister. Going through a traumatic experience like that, just the two of them; Greg and Celia must be super-close.

Greg glanced at the clock on the fireplace mantle. "One more game?"

She followed his gaze and her lips parted. "I had no idea it was so late. I didn't mean to keep you up. You must be tired."

"Nah, I'm used to irregular hours. And I don't need a lot of sleep."

"It's two. I'm never up this late." *How lame is that?* Honest to God, though, she couldn't remember ever having been up so late. Stifling a yawn, she packed up the game pieces.

"Where does this go?"

"I'll take it."

He disappeared down the hallway with the game, and Ally

strolled toward her assigned bedroom. She didn't know how to handle Greg, which likely explained why she avoided men like him. Too self-confident, too good looking, too sexy, too muscular, too good a kisser…

Ally tapped her fingernail on the window. A possum scampered away.

A shiver of hot awareness trickled down her spine. She turned and drank in the gorgeous, willing man standing in the bedroom doorway. Why was she holding out? An opportunity like this wouldn't arise again. Having sex had nothing to do with falling in love, right?

"Well, night." He stepped back.

Guess she'd thought for too long. As usual. "Good night."

He left her with an empty room and an even emptier feeling deep inside. When was she going to stop being such a coward? She needed to grab hold of life with both hands. Then again, changing how you handled life couldn't be done overnight. Maybe she should cut herself some slack. Not something she was real good at.

Sighing, she shucked her clothes and climbed into the plush, soft bed. Rough life. She winced. The things he'd been through were rough. The sacrifices Greg had made to raise his sister awed her.

Chapter Eight

Groaning in frustration, Ally rolled over and glowered at the ceiling. Tossing and turning was accomplishing nothing. Throwing off the covers, she climbed out of bed and walked to the door. The deep stillness of night lay over the house like a blanket. Tiptoeing down the hall, her hand brushed a doorknob and she paused.

Normally, she wouldn't dream of snooping, but Greg didn't seem like a stranger anymore and she was bored spitless. Biting her lip, she opened the door and ducked inside. Moonlight streamed across the huge room, falling over a big bed and mirrored dresser. The fractured reflection drew her. Dozens of photographs in ornate frames were scattered across the dresser's marble top.

She held the largest frame to the light. An elegant couple sat in the middle of the beautiful family shot. The man bore a striking resemblance to Greg, right down to the smile. The woman had Greg's aqua-colored eyes. A college-aged Greg stood behind them with a careless grin and Celia rested her hand on her mother's chair.

Tears stung her eyes. She couldn't imagine the pain of Greg's loss or what he'd seen. Beautiful people were supposed to lead blessed lives.

A photo of Greg in a tux caught her eye. His arm was draped around a stunning brunette, who gazed up at him in adoration. A homecoming or prom photo, maybe.

Her stomach clenched.

The bright moonlight flickered and she guiltily jerked her head up. Large, dark shapes glided past the large windows—men dressed in dark clothes that merged with the night. The rush of blood in her ears was deafening.

Grateful she hadn't turned on the light, she spun on her heel and hurried from the room. She froze at the threshold of the great room and her heart sank. For the life of her, she couldn't remember where Greg had said his room was. Panic chewed a hole in her composure. *Damn, damn and double damn.*

"What are you doing up?"

She jumped a foot and pressed a palm over her pounding heart. "You scared the crap out of me. Why are you sitting in the dark?"

"It's not all that dark."

He lounged on the long living-room couch, his wrist draped over an upraised knee and looking every inch the spoiled son of bazillionaire parents. No wonder the chief of police ignored his less-than-deferential attitude. Greg's family probably owned the City Council and donated obscene amounts of money to the city.

"I couldn't sleep. What's your excuse for walking around in the middle of the night in a T-shirt?"

Oh, freak! Ally shrank back. Her lace-covered butt smacked against the cool wall.

"I'm not objecting." Greg's voice did that rough, husky thing that turned her brain to mush. "You look…edible."

A muffled thud from the front of the house shattered the moment as effectively as a slap across the face.

"Someone's outside," she blurted in a panicked rush. "Several someones. I saw them pass…uh, my window."

Ally sucked a breath into fear-tightened lungs.

Before she could exhale, Greg was across the room and flattened her against the smooth wood-paneled wall. All his glorious heat pressed against her. Her head reeled. She might have gone cross-eyed.

She shook her head to clear the lust fogging her brain.

"You chose an inopportune time to flaunt your luscious body." His breath whispered across her ear. She shivered.

"Uhm-hmm." Speech deserted her. Great. Another thirty seconds and she'd be incapable of breathing too.

Another muffled thud. Right, she should be freaking out. Running. Hiding. She shoved against Greg.

He didn't budge.

"Stick close. We're going into my room so you can put on some clothes, unless you were planning on providing a distraction."

"No," she squeaked.

They moved across the living room toward the other wing of the house, hugging the shadows. Down a long hallway, around a corner and into a big bedroom, where he tossed her sweatpants and a sweatshirt. As quickly as her shaking fingers allowed, she pulled them on and stuffed her feet into the too-big sneakers he set on the floor in front of her.

He knelt to tie the shoelaces, and the protective wall around her heart nearly shattered. How was she supposed to maintain her defenses? How could an obnoxious playboy, hard-nosed cop, protective gentleman and brother, willing to sacrifice his dreams and future for his sister, all be wrapped up in one guy?

Gently, he pushed her into a chair in a dark corner of the room. He leaned down and caged her in with his arms. Her pulse tap-danced. "Stay here while I deal with our visitors. Got it?"

By himself? But…he could get hurt. Ally tamped down her alarm. Greg was a trained police officer. He could handle the situation without any assistance from the amateur hour. She nodded.

With her defenses down around her ankles, he leaned in and pressed a hard, fast kiss to her lips.

Her lips sang from the contact as he disappeared out the doorway, melting into the shadows with disturbing ease. Her stomach tied itself in painful knots. Just him against at least two men. Big men.

A grunt and thump sounded in the hall. She clutched the chair arms and her pulse galloped out of control.

A whisper of air across her skin made the hair on her nape rise.

A shadow crossed the doorway and she shrank down in the chair. *Think invisible.* Another thud. She shivered. What if that was Greg's head thudding on the hard floor? The thought of him injured, bleeding, possibly unconscious…she leaned forward and dug her nails into the chair arms.

Oh, man, don't let anything happen to him. And not just because she would be on her own, trying to fend off men intent on doing her bodily harm. Something much, much worse drove her fear. She *cared* about him. Deep down to the bottom of her cowardly soul, cared. Holy crap, she was in *so* much trouble.

A big shadow appeared in the doorway. She released her breath, swearing silently. Despite the dark, despite her fear, she instantly recognized Greg. His broad shoulders, narrow hips, the tilt of his head, his scent.

"You okay?"

"Fine. You?" Her voice didn't quaver. Don't be silly. She had nerves of granite, innards of copper, a backbone lined with steel. Rather like a house.

"Fine."

He crossed the room, rummaged inside a closet, shut the door with his foot and disappeared into the hallway again. Several thumps, muttered curses and low groans later, he returned.

"That takes care of Larry and Moe. Thankfully, they left Curly at home." The white of his grin flashed in the darkness. "I'm going to call the captain and get a cruiser out here with some guys we trust to pick 'em up. In the meantime," he cracked his knuckles and she winced. "I'm going to have a little conversation with them."

Ally drew her legs up in front of her and wrapped her arms around her knees. Danger followed her everywhere. World-weary in a way she hadn't expected to ever feel, she leaned back while Greg did his thing.

Numb and emotionless, she went through the motions of answering the police questions when they arrived. By the time the morning sunrise filtered across the sky, the police left with Dumb and Dumber in tow. One cruiser stayed behind to play watch-dog. An entire night passed without any more sleep than the nap she'd caught before dinner. Exhaustion dragged like an anchor and coffee did little to boost her energy level.

The shower running in Greg's room piqued enough interest to give her a brief surge. Hormones, good to the last drop. She wandered out to the deck overlooking the lake. The cool morning air shot another rush along her veins.

A walk would get the blood pumping and clear her head. She set her coffee cup on the railing. Maybe even rid her of the pointless affection for Greg clogging her arteries.

The early morning sunlight barely breached the treetops as she climbed the hill opposite the lake. At the top, she turned. Smoke drifted lazily from the chimney of Greg's house, wrapping the nearby trees in haze like a scene from a fairy tale. A little pang ricocheted across her heart. She loved this place too much and she couldn't stay.

Ignoring the pinch of her borrowed hiking boots, she started walking. At least Greg's oversized clothing helped keep out the cool mountain air. As she traipsed along, the bird chirps and trills combined with the sway of the trees, a soft rustling backdrop to the quiet noises of nature waking. Crunching pine needles beneath her feet filled the air with a pungent scent, and the trees enveloped her in their protective embrace.

Misery choked off her pleasure. Head down, arms wrapped tight, she mulled over her situation. Nowhere to go and not the slightest flippin' idea what was going on. She still couldn't quite wrap her brain around Michael's death.

Why on God's green earth would someone kill him? A geek to the core and almost as boring as her. He had often helped with her workload. Just a few weeks ago, he'd taken a thick pile of folders off her desk and had them completed and returned within a freakishly fast two hours.

He had no social life that she knew of. No extended family to pull him into the real world on a periodic, painful basis. His parents were elderly and lived in a retirement village in Florida.

She tripped over an exposed tree root. The trees thickened, the forest becoming deeper and more mysterious. Strange noises had her nerves leaping and snapping. She paused, spinning in a slow circle.

Where was she? More important, which direction was Greg's cottage?

She wracked her brain. She watched the nature channel avidly; travel documentaries fascinated her in the way fairy tales enthralled eight-year-old girls and HGTV starred in her DTV recordings.

Something about moss and trees?

She circled a thick tree trunk. One side seemed furry. What did that mean? Screwing her eyes shut, she tapped her forehead. Something about the direction of the sunset?

Her lips twisted. For all she knew, she was walking through a narrow strip of trees alongside a mall or golf course. She was no Eagle Scout. Or whatever the girl equivalent would be. If there was a girl equivalent.

She stopped, tilting her head and listening intently for some sign of humanity. Traffic noises, the hum of electricity, the sound of children playing.

A twig snapped and she spun around.

Nothing moved in the dappled sunshine. The ground rose and fell in gently rolling hills as far as she could see. Nothing seemed out of place. She rubbed her arms and put a hand to the nape of her neck to soothe the hair standing on end. A shiver snaked up her spine as she started walking again. Toward the cottage, she hoped.

She tried to attribute her quickened pace to over-taxed nerves. Numerous animals played in the surrounding woods. Deer, possum, squirrels, bears...wait, bears? She wrapped her arms tight around her middle. Were there bears out here?

She ignored the next twig snap. Sure, it sounded closer. Coincidence. She'd probably disturbed a napping bunny.

Down the next hillside, a darkly shaded spot caught her eye. No longer able to ignore her screaming instincts, she squeezed into the little grove of trees. Hunkering down amidst the tree trunks and large boulders, she waited in breathless silence. Minutes passed, counted off by the anxious beats of her heart. Her nerves grew taut, leaping and quivering at every wing flap overheard and rasp of scraping branches.

A shadow passed, too tall, lean and two-legged to be mistaken for anything but a man. There was no reason for anyone to be out here in the middle of nowhere, unless he was following her. Could be Greg, but just as easily could *not* be Greg.

She felt like smacking her head against the moss-covered rock she crouched behind. Instead, she hefted a sizable branch and waited. Another twig snapped, this one right behind her.

She jerked to her feet with all the grace of a marionette in the hands of a three-year-old and spun, swinging the branch in a wide arc. She caught nothing but air. The branch slipped from her hand and went sailing into the dirt yards away. She gasped. Heart racing, she fisted her hands and turned to face him.

Greg leaned a broad shoulder against a nearby tree trunk, arms crossed. The glitter of green fire in his eyes transmitted the depth of his irritation.

Giddy relief bubbled. "Hey." She smiled, adding a little wave for good measure. "Imagine running into you out here."

"Yeah, imagine."

"What brings you to this neck of the woods?" She arched a brow, lounging against a boulder and crossing her arms.

"Funny. If you've finished your little hike, we should head back. I haven't eaten."

The tight smile accompanying his words brightened her mood even more. She was thrilled to discover exactly how contrary she could be and her smile broadened.

"Oh, but I was just getting warmed up," she said with a moue of distress. "It's so peaceful. I could just get *lost* out here."

His eyes narrowed. He took a step forward, all pretense of relaxed and casual gone with the wind. A strange zing of anticipation shot through her. Effortlessly stepping over the surrounding rocks, he closed the distance until he loomed over her, invading her personal space.

"I do not find any of this amusing." His warm breath feathered across her cheeks. "I did not wake up this morning anticipating saving you from yourself."

The fact that he was right didn't help. Still, his condescension grated. Too much fear, too much uncertainty, too many emotions had run rampant in the last forty-eight hours, and she threw caution to the wind.

"I certainly do *not* need you to save me from myself, you... you...caveman!"

"Caveman, huh?"

He pressed his lips to hers. She wrapped her arms around his neck and sank her fingers into the too-long hair covering his neck. A low groan reverberated from him. He angled his head, deepening the kiss. His arms went around her and his rough hands found her bottom, lifting her off the boulder to align their bodies. The hard throb of his arousal against her pelvis brought to life an answering ache.

She wriggled, needing closer. The slide of his tongue and his masculine taste drove her desire higher. He nudged her legs apart and braced his foot against the rock behind them so she straddled his hard thigh.

She gasped and he sucked on her tongue in a move so suggestive her hips twitched. Arms firmly wrapped around her, he swung around and sat on the boulder with her astride him. She was too busy freeing buttons to give it much thought.

Shoving the shirt off his shoulders, they both moaned when her hands smoothed over his tightly muscled shoulders. She pulled her mouth from his to latch onto the skin between his neck and shoulder, lightly raking her fingernails over his back. He lifted her sweatshirt.

Licking, nibbling and kissing every square inch of his bare skin went straight to her head like a finely aged brandy, traveling down her spine to increase the urgent throbbing between her legs.

An owl screeched overhead. Ally glanced up and caught sight of the big-bodied bird gliding away. She looked at Greg. Awareness replaced passion and heat stung her cheeks.

"I'm too heavy." She slid off his lap.

Greg did nothing to stop her. Muscles flexed as he reached for his shirt. What had she been thinking? She'd responded to him like a desperate woman. Her face heated and she turned away, crossing her arms. It wasn't like he shoved her off, after all. He'd meticulously located each one of her tonsils with his tongue.

"Let's go, Snow White. Before we get any unexpected company. A guy with one eye and a walker could follow the trail you left."

"Ha-ha." She kicked a rock and hurried to catch up with his long-legged stride.

"You should be thanking me." He glanced over his shoulder. "If I hadn't found you, someone else would have. You wouldn't enjoy meeting any of the sweet fellas who've been following you."

"Thank you," she said, sticky sweet, baring her teeth at his broad back.

He glanced back and chuckled.

She glanced down at the baggy, unflattering sweat pants she'd wandered off in. They had accumulated a healthy collection of pine needles and dirt. Like she didn't already feel as attractive as a hog lying in manure. In August.

Okay, so maybe that was a teensy exaggeration. Still...not one of her better days. She hadn't even bothered to glance in a mirror when she dragged her hair into a ponytail earlier. Not a stitch of makeup, her teeth felt fuzzy and her borrowed clothes were sagging down her butt. Not in a flattering, look-how-skinny-I-am, kind of way, either.

"You coming?"

Greg stood at the top of a hill, waiting for her to catch up. Sharply lit, he looked big and tough, capable of fending off any number of bad guys. Which he was. Raw masculine appeal vibrated off him. Her heart skipped a beat or three, intimidation mingling with attraction as she trudged up beside him.

Face averted and arms defensively crossed, she glared down at the valley. Greg's black Camaro shone in the sunshine beside the black-and-white cruiser she'd slipped past earlier. Fat lot of help the policeman was, snoring like a chainsaw in the driver's seat.

"Not your best idea."

Her muscles tightened and her teeth sank into her lower lip.

"Anything could have happened. One of the goons who showed up last night might have caught up with you out here. What would you have done then?"

She turned, helpless anger churning in her belly. "All I did was go for a walk."

"There are no solo walks, strolls or meandering in your immediate future." He closed the gap until a scant inch separated them. "I'm sticking so close to you, pretty soon you won't know where I leave off and you begin."

Ally shivered, nipples tightening. She snapped her spine straight and sniffed. Caveman.

"As if." She stomped down the hillside. Not an easy thing to do in too-small shoes and soft dirt that muffled her footsteps. The aggravating man stayed right beside her.

Had she really said "As if" like some big-haired, bubble-gum-chewing eighties throw-back?

He snagged her arm just inside the door of the cottage.

She sighed and faced him. "What?"

His eyes narrowed and darkened. He traced her lower lip with a fingertip then leaned down and replaced his finger with his mouth. Too confused to smother her response, she wrapped her arms around his neck and parted her lips. She'd give as good as she got and damn the consequences. Desire as wild and reckless as his kiss surged. She rocked against the ridge of his erection.

She slid her foot up his leg, tugging him closer. His mouth kissed a trail of fire along her jaw and down her neck. He cupped and squeezed her breasts. Rising to her tiptoes, she aligned their bodies, grabbed hold of his butt and pulled him into her.

"Damn, baby." He went back to nibbling the sensitive skin along her neck. Her eyes slid closed. Her hips found a desperate rhythm against the hard ridge of his erection. She needed… oh, yeah. Right there.

"You like that?"

"Uhm…"

"Tell me what you need."

He wanted to talk? Now?

The air left her lungs when he palmed her butt and rubbed against her. The pleasure made her sob, "Please…"

"Tell me."

"I need…" Everything. Now. Articulation was beyond her.

Cool air wafted across her pebbled nipples. Anticipation tightened her belly. He lowered his head, nibbled and sucked. Her back bowed. Pleasure shot straight to her core. She dug her fingers into his shoulders, rocking her hips.

Obviously an equal-opportunity lover, he moved to the other nipple. Her head thumped back against the wall, but nothing registered beyond his mouth and his body against hers. His hand slid down her thigh and pulled her leg up over his hip. Happy to accommodate, she tilted her pelvis forward. Mini fireworks exploded behind her closed eyelids.

He released her nipple and blew hot breath across it. "What do you need, baby?"

"Ung…"

The tug of her pants heading south, followed by his rough

fingers, fried her synapse. She dropped her feet to the floor. The pants and her panties dropped. The pleasure of his big hands on her bare skin blurred her vision. Her pulse pounded in her head.

"Damn," he said.

His hands squeezed her bare bottom. Impatient, she tugged at the button of his jeans. She needed him inside her. Now.

His hand pressed over hers, stilling her anxious yanking. The pounding grew louder.

"Marsing! Open the damn door. I know you're in there."

Greg dropped his head to the crook of her neck and sighed.

"No," she moaned, arching into him.

He stroked her skin, sending shivers racing along her nerve endings. "I know, baby."

His low voice soothed, his touch no longer arousing so much as attempting to ease her back down. Impossible. She had never been so aroused in her life. A vicious twist of cruel fate to be interrupted.

The pounding at the door resumed.

Closing her eyes, she dropped her hands and leaned against the wall. The slide of her pants as he pulled them back up was almost enough to send her flying over the edge.

"What the hell, Marsing?"

"I'm coming," he growled.

No. Neither one of them would be coming. She opened her eyes. Hands braced on either side of her head, he leaned in until she could make out shots of green in his eyes.

"Hold my place, hot lips." His gaze dropped to her mouth, and the empty ache low in her belly intensified. He stepped back and handed her the oversized sweatshirt.

She held the material over her breasts and frowned. When did he take it off?

Shaken by her lack of control, she yanked the sweatshirt over her head. As she tumbled through the doorway into her temporary bedroom, Greg pulled open the front door. She leaned against the closed door and stared at the big bed.

What could have been swam before her eyes. Her body throbbed. She took a deep breath, determined to shake it off.

She couldn't become dependent on Greg. The quick release of a tumble in bed would have a steep price. The realization that he desired her shocked her to the tips of her sedate pink toenails.

Still, they were two consenting adults. No reason she couldn't enjoy what he did for her libido. She should be able to have great sex at least once before settling back into the staid life she'd created.

"Ally, let's go," Greg hollered.

Chapter Nine

"Gee, how charming." She stomped into the attached bath. No way was she going back to town looking like yesterday's road kill. She had *some* pride, after all.

Liberal use of a hairbrush, a light covering of powder, a few coats of mascara and some coppery lip gloss later, she at least *felt* better. Trying to be objective, she examined her reflection.

Objectivity was overrated.

A fist pounded on the bedroom door for the third time. Sighing at her reflection, she left the bathroom and opened the door. She smiled with acidic sweetness at Greg, who sported an odd pinched expression, and ignored the butterflies in her stomach. She refused to delve any further into the man's psyche while toeing the slippery slope of soul-deep attraction. They'd end up married with five kids in her imagination.

She arched her brow.

Greg cleared his throat. "My sister doesn't do blue jeans, so…"

He thrust his hand out. A pair of jeans dangled in his grasp. He was loaning her a pair of his pants? Huh. Nonplussed, she met his gaze.

He waved the pants impatiently. "Look, you want 'em or not? I just thought they'd be comfortable."

"Sure. Thanks." She snagged them and put her hand on the

door, intent on closing it.

"Look, about earlier…." He ran a hand through his hair. "I don't think it'd be a good idea to get involved. You're not a casual sex kinda girl, and I don't do relationships."

Her stomach twisted and she pressed her lips together. Who did he think he was, telling her who she was? Her little crush was her problem.

She narrowed her eyes and planted her hands on her hips. "What makes you think I'd want a relationship with you? Maybe all I *want* from you is sex, even if you are a presumptuous jackass."

Heat flared in his eyes.

She flicked her fingers in the air. "Whatever. Don't worry about it."

She shoved the door closed. Or tried.

His palm flattened against the door, his face hardened and he narrowed his eyes. "I just don't think it's a great time to start something, okay? We've got enough to deal with right now."

Ally glared. "Gee, I hadn't noticed."

"What's your problem? I'm trying to be considerate."

"Yeah, you're a real swell guy. We should all aspire to be so self-sacrificing." She jerked the door back, then slammed it closed.

Irritation helped her through the motions of dressing and kept her mind off self-flagellation. She tossed the pants on the bed and dug through the contents of the dresser drawers. Skimpy thong panties did not even remotely appeal. Why would a woman volunteer for torture?

Commando it was. She pulled on Greg's blue jeans, relieved to discover they were a bit too big. If they'd fit, or worse, been tight, she may have seriously contemplated drowning herself. She tugged on a silk T-shirt she'd uncovered in another drawer and glanced in the dresser mirror. She winced. The silk left nothing to the imagination. Every detail of her breasts revealed, nipples clearly outlined by the delicate material.

Perfect. Lips pressed together, she walked into the massive closet and scrutinized the huge assortment of clothes. Ah-ha. She yanked a dark-blue cashmere sweater off a hanger and stuffed her arms into it. Avoiding the mirror, she shoved her feet into the too-small boots again and stomped out of the room.

"Trying to be considerate, my ass," she muttered.

Greg was in the kitchen, throwing stuff into a small cooler. He glanced her way and froze. Eyes boring into her, he examined her from head to toe. She frowned and tugged the cardigan closed. Or as closed as she could get it. Without a word, he turned away. Slamming the lid shut, he hefted the cooler and strode past her.

"Nice," she mumbled. "Now he's going to ignore me. As if this situation weren't already just oh-so-special."

And now she was talking to herself.

She followed him out the front door, feeling about as useful as a week-old infant while he stuffed the cooler in the trunk. Swallowing a sigh, she climbed into the car and buckled up. He joined her and turned the key. The engine rumbled to life. The car jolted and lurched over the ruts in the dirt road until it smoothed into blacktop. The silent tension ate at her reserve.

"I already said I didn't want to get involved either, okay?" *Nice, Ally. Blurting things like a high-school sophomore. Real smooth and disinterested.* She winced and shrugged lamely. "You're not my type."

"Really?" His voice did the low, rumbly thing again.

She crossed her arms and tried to relax. Her throbbing center didn't help. She pressed her thighs together, frustrated sexually and emotionally. She couldn't deal with this right now. Then again, she didn't think she could *ever* deal with Greg.

"We'll be in town in about an hour. That was Lucas banging on the door at the cottage. He's going to meet us back at his place."

"Why?"

"He wants to walk you through the last few weeks."

"We did that last night."

"No, we talked about your normal routine and this past week.

Lucas wants to go further back."

"Fine." Just what she wanted to do. Hang out with the personable Lucas.

All these years, she'd thought she had her life figured out. Herself figured out. Everything had been so simple. Her calm, quiet existence suited her. She'd been perfectly happy a few days ago. Well, maybe not happy. Content.

Greg had to go and introduce her to designer clothes, car chases, beating up bad guys, luxury cars and the exclusive, unattainable life of the rich and famous. Not to mention Greg. Ally straightened in the seat, stress bubbling and roiling. She'd never met a guy like him. All bossy and domineering, yet willing to make huge sacrifices for loved ones. Held her while she cried and beat her at Scrabble. If she let herself…

"What are you thinking about so hard?"

"You." She crossed her arms and scowled. The whole freakin' mess was all his fault.

"Uhm, what about me?" He tossed her wary glances between maneuvering through the busy streets, as if sensing she wasn't flattering him. Clever boy.

Knowing it wouldn't be a pleasant expression, she smiled. "All of the lovely experiences you've shared with me, of course. You've opened my eyes to the world around me and shown me what I've been missing out on. I should thank you. A lot." If those last few words sounded more like a threat, forced out through gritted teeth…well, some things just couldn't be helped.

"Oookay. I don't have a clue what you're talking about."

"Really?" She spun in her seat to face him. "I can't go home, can't go to work, can't do anything except follow you around like a stupid dog." Note to self; shrieking hurt her ears. "And that isn't even going into your on-again, off-again sex issues."

"Sex issues?" His hands tightened on the steering wheel. The muscles in his arms bulged. "I don't have any issues in the bedroom. If you'd keep your act together long enough to actually get there with me, you'd know that."

Ally's vision went black as she sucked in a breath. "Of all the…"

"We're here."

She snapped her teeth together.

Greg shoved the gearshift into park and she glanced out the window at the middle-class collection of homes. Quiet and peaceful. The simple act of walking up the sidewalk, surrounded by suburban domesticity drained some of her irrational anger.

She blinked at the classic A-frame in front of her. Not for a fraction of a second would she have imagined Lucas Jones living in a place like this. The house was far too…conventional for a man of his intensity.

Greg pressed the doorbell and she crossed her arms. The bells chimed through the house and quieted. He pressed the button again. Nothing. He frowned at her and then his watch.

"Lucas left the cottage thirty minutes before we did. He should be here."

Turning, he surveyed the street.

She was no expert, but she didn't see anything weird. The street was quiet, the majority of residents at work. Heck, she should be at work. "What are we going to do?"

Greg's gaze shifted from the street, to the house, to the street, to the house again. "Wait here. I'm going to check around back."

Five minutes passed. Ally started to fidget. How long did it take to check around back, anyway? She stared down the street, tapping her foot and chewing on her fingernail. The door behind her creaked open and she spun around, heart racing.

"It's just me." Greg held the door open for her.

Very traditional furniture and décor greeted her inside. Like the exterior, not what she expected. "Are you sure this is Lucas' house?"

Despite his obvious concern, his lips twitched. "Not what you expected from ol' Lucas, huh?"

"Not exactly."

He left her to explore the living room. She assumed he was

searching the rest of the house. Looking for signs of foul play. Detecting.

There wasn't a whole lot to look at. Traditional landscapes hung on the walls. There were no nick-knacks out. No candid pictures. She sighed and crossed her arms.

"Nothing." Greg returned to the living room. "No sign of him anywhere."

"Really?"

"Yep." He shoved his hands in his pockets, staring hard at the floor, like the answer could be found inscribed in the hardwood.

She chewed on her lip, hesitant to voice the thought going through her head. "You don't suppose…"

Greg's gaze flew up, its intensity making her pause and swallow hard.

"You don't think Lucas could be one of them, do you?"

"Not a chance."

"It seems kinda suspicious though." She'd jumped in headfirst. Might as well push. "I mean, we keep getting found. You said you've known him for years, so he knows a lot about you. Your habits, your homes."

Greg shook his head. "No way. The homes my family own aren't exactly a secret. And my car is distinctive."

"Okay." He knew the guy a lot better than she did. To her, everybody was a suspect. Except Greg.

Speaking of…she admired the snug fit of the jeans over his muscular thighs and the stretch of his T-shirt across his shoulders. Desire tightened her belly and she sucked her lower lip between her teeth. She did *not* want to go there. Especially after the conversation in the car.

She noted the spark in his eyes and dropped her gaze, embarrassed he'd been aware of her perusal.

"So…what now?"

"I don't know."

"You don't know?"

"You have any bright ideas?"

"Not really my department." His tension leached into her. She smiled tightly. "You're the brilliant strategist."

"You're still in one piece, aren't you?"

"Yes, I am."

He'd quickly and efficiently dealt with Boner, Weasel and the two guys from the cottage. She knew he was a hero—her hero, and she appreciated everything about him more than she could say. Stress and fear were making her snippy. She tried hard to swallow her attitude.

She turned away. The window overlooked the peaceful street. A little niggle of envy wormed into her. Lucas' home was in a great neighborhood. The charm of the area appealed to her on a deep level, much more so than her current residence.

An older model sedan idled down the street. She imagined an elderly, white-haired lady, barely able to peer over the large steering wheel and smiled. As the car drew closer, she noted the dull paint, dark-tinted windows and missing license plate. Her amusement died a brutal death. She meant to whisper his name, but a wordless squeak emerged. Didn't matter, because Greg was there. Hand hard on her arm, he pulled her down to one side of the large window. The car came to a gentle stop a few feet behind Greg's Camaro. The doors remained closed.

"Damn it."

Flash-frozen to the spot, she managed to turn her head. Hunched down beside her, Greg stared at the car through the window.

"They're not going to stay out there forever. Come on." He pulled her toward the rear of the house.

"Where are we going?" she whispered, as if the bad guys camouflaged behind the dark car windows might hear.

"Out the back."

She rolled her eyes. "I figured that."

He glanced back, a flash of amusement lighting his grim

expression. "Lucas keeps a car stashed in his garage. We're going to borrow it."

Greg opened a kitchen drawer and snagged a set of keys. He went out the back door, finger pressed to his lips and gestured her after him. She followed him to the detached garage.

They slipped through the side door and Ally stopped in her tracks.

"Are you kidding me?"

He grinned. Pulling open the passenger door, he swept a bow. "Your chariot awaits, madam."

"Funny." But she climbed in with a smile tugging at her mouth.

He started the car and she laughed. "Seriously? Lucas pulls off this whole badass image, black-leather jacket and all. The whole time, he lives in a sedate suburban neighborhood, in an immaculate 1940s Cape Cod with very conventional, almost stuffy furnishings and drives…this."

"What have you got against the car?"

He hit the remote control and the garage door rose with the quiet liquidity of well-oiled tracks. Ally's lips parted in disbelief. Greg drove a hot-rod Camaro, for crying out loud. She wasn't buying his casual attitude for a second.

"This car is Lucas' pride and joy. It's six months old. He'll skin me alive if I smudge a window."

"It's a Taurus, Greg. Give it up."

The car rolled down the driveway. "Okay, so it's not exciting, but this Taurus suits our needs." He applied the brake just before the front bumper nudged out into the open. "Get down."

"What?" Alarm tightened her muscles. "Why?"

"I don't want them to see you. If they think it's just me, or better yet, Lucas, they may not follow."

She slouched down in the seat.

"More."

"Oh, for crying out loud." She slid down onto the floorboards. The tight fit reminded her of every millimeter of extra flesh squishing together beneath the dashboard. "Happy?"

"As a matter of fact…" He grinned at her then assumed a bored expression and allowed the car to roll forward.

The jolt of the car bouncing over the curb slammed her knees into her chest and her head against the dashboard. She gritted her teeth. Being on the run with a very hot cop wasn't nearly as exciting and romantic as the movies made it seem.

Especially when a girl couldn't even enjoy a few of her inalienable rights. Like wearing her own clothes. *And chocolate.*

"Doing okay down there?"

Ally glanced up, caught Greg's lips twitching and narrowed her eyes. "Enjoying yourself?"

His grin about split his face. Torn between annoyance and unwittingly charmed, she settled on grumbling. "I take it I can sit in my seat now?"

"Yeah."

"Probably could have five minutes ago." She grimaced as she eased out of her cramped position and into the seat.

"Hey, I'm just trying to be cautious," Greg said with the innocence of a six-year-old choir boy.

"Uh-huh."

She straightened her legs and wriggled her toes, circulation returning with painful tingles, and indulged in a luxurious full-body stretch. A moan escaped as her muscles relaxed and tendons loosened. Settling back into the seat, she glanced at the road and shrieked.

"Watch the road!" She slapped her hands over her eyes then peeked through her fingers.

Greg barely avoided plowing into the side of a parked pickup.

"Real smooth."

"At least I'm not flaunting myself and moaning." He glared out the windshield.

Her eyebrows shot up. "I was stretching."

"Stretching?" Disbelief coated his words thick as molasses in

January. "Sticking out your breasts and moaning is stretching?"

"Sticking out my...Look, Surfer Dude, you're the one who left me pretzeled on the floor for fifteen minutes. Don't blame me if all you can think about is sex."

Bickering over whether or not her stretching was *sexual*. Seriously, how ridiculous could two adults get?

"Sorry," he muttered.

"What?"

"I said, I'm sorry." He all but shouted.

"Fine."

"Fine."

Crossing her arms, she glared out the window. What was the deal with men, anyway? One minute they were all over you, the next yelling at you. Like she needed more antagonism in her life. No, thank you.

She glanced out the side window, just in time to see a car's front fender up close and personal before it slammed into them. The screech of metal against metal, the squeal of tires and the smell of hot steel and exploded gunpowder from the airbags filled the air. The force of the impact sent her flying across the car into Greg— she'd forgotten her seat belt. Wilting against his solid warmth, she stared at the side of the car where she'd been sitting.

Twisted metal, torn fabric and a limp airbag dangled from the dashboard. Beyond the mangled door, two men sat in the front seat of an old behemoth car. The same car parked outside Lucas' house five minutes ago. Their expressions weren't pleasant.

Their doors swung open.

Greg swore, wrenched the steering wheel to the side and stomped hard on the accelerator. With a loud metallic shriek, their sedan separated from the bumper of the other car and pulled away. Shouts, slamming doors and the rev of an engine followed as they sped down the road.

"You okay?" he asked.

Something warm trickled down the side of her face. Her vision did a weird tunnel effect.

"Ally?" He sounded so far away.

His eyes narrowed and his brow crinkled with concern. Worry, even. She should say something to let him know she was alright. In a minute. A dull roar filled her ears and everything went black.

Chapter Ten

Ally opened her eyes to pale-gray ceiling panels, white walls and a television mounted high in the corner. The tiny room had a dark-gray curtain drawn over one wall. Very unattractive. She struggled into a sitting position. Her head swam. She groaned and bent forward to rest her forehead on her upraised knees, wincing when her hand hit a bandage.

The curtain squeaked as it slid open. "What are you doing? You shouldn't be up yet."

Slowly this time, she lifted her head. Nurses and orderlies in scrubs bustled behind Greg. Her gaze dropped to the cup of strong-smelling coffee in his hand and her stomach rolled. He took a sip from the cup. What had he said? Oh...

"Why not?" Wow, her throat was really dry. Croaking-frog dry.

"Here." Greg pushed a plastic cup of ice water into her hand. She gulped it.

The moisture soothed her throat. Her stomach? Not so much. Bile rose. She handed the cup back and concentrated on breathing. No way was she throwing up in front of Greg.

"Okay?"

She cautiously nodded. A few more minutes of deep breathing and her stomach finally relaxed.

She swallowed to be sure and glanced at Greg. "How 'bout a

recap, since my memory of the last few hours is fuzzy at best?"

"We didn't make a clean exit from Lucas' house. I lost the assholes following us, but you got pretty banged-up. The doctor said you might have a blank in your memory, thanks to a concussion." He grimaced. "You have some colorful bruises on your face and the cut on your forehead needed a few stitches. You'll be pretty sore in the morning."

Ally was sore now and she was positive there was nothing pretty about it. Spying a small mirror over the sink, she gingerly stood.

He frowned. "Sit down."

"I'm fine."

She waited a second for her land legs to kick in before crossing to the sink. Oh, lovely. The monstrous bandage stopped just short of covering her right eye and spanned her forehead. Her cheek was a beautiful shade of purple. The mascara smudged below her eyes wasn't helping anything. Her hair was a disaster and her nose shiny. If the aches and tightness were any indication, she had more colorful spots under her clothes. Dampening a paper towel, hyper-aware of Greg behind her, she did her best to clean up.

"I'm sorry, Ally."

She met his gaze in the mirror. "For what? It's not your fault those lunatics wanted to play bumper cars with thirty-thousand pound cars."

"I should have been paying more attention."

He really did look like he felt bad, poor guy. Must be tough playing Super Man. "I don't blame you. None of this is your fault."

"It's not exactly your fault, either, Sugar Lips." His smile didn't quite manage to reach his eyes.

She shrugged and instantly regretted it. Tightening her lips against a gasp of pain, she sighed. "So it's not your fault and it's not my fault. Since we're in this situation together, let's not assign blame or assume guilt for the crap happening. 'Kay?"

"Sure."

Yeah. He didn't buy it. Must be the He-Man macho-guy thing.

She tried to relax her muscles. They'd suffered enough abuse already. She appreciated that he wanted to protect her and took the responsibility seriously. He didn't need to beat himself up when the bad guys got in a lick or two of their own.

Carefully lowering her aching body onto the narrow bed, Ally bit her lip and leaned back with a sigh. She hurt everywhere.

"The doctor left these pills for you. They'll help with the pain and swelling."

She swallowed the little pills, washing them down with a minimal amount of ice water.

When they finally walked out of the hospital, warm sunshine greeted them. She squinted and swayed.

"Why did you have to be stubborn and refuse the wheelchair?" Irritation and amusement colored Greg's voice. He wrapped an arm around her waist, tucking her against his side as they navigated the parking lot.

"We aren't driving Lucas' poor car, are we?"

"I rented a car and had it delivered."

"Busy boy."

Very relaxed and uber-mellow, she smiled up at him and leaned closer. Greg had a strange expression on his too-handsome face, but she didn't care.

A giant yawn caught her by surprise. She slapped a hand over her mouth in a belated attempt at politeness, giggling. Tripping over her feet, she stumbled against him and giggled some more. She wrapped both arms around his hard abdomen.

He smelled good.

"The pain medication has obviously taken effect."

The thumping of his heart under her ear and the heat of his body relaxed her further.

"Probably not a good thing to take on an empty stomach."

Yawning, she turned her face into his shirt. He smelled *really* good. "Mmm. You smell yummy. Like hot, sexy man. I wanna lick you all over."

He stopped walking and his chest expanded with a deep breath. She pressed against him from thigh to shoulder, like two halves of bread making a sandwich. All they lacked was some salami. Oh, wait. He had the salami. She giggled into his pec.

His muscles shifted and he pried her off his lovely chest. Which wasn't very nice of him. Ignoring her mumbled protest, he pushed her into a seat. Ally yawned and closed her eyes. She couldn't seem to find the energy or interest to open them.

That lovely, muscular arm went around her again. She draped her arms around his neck and tugged him closer. His face landed in the crook of her neck. She didn't mind. Being in an accommodating sort of mood, she even tilted her head. He nibbled her sensitive skin and she sighed. Lovely.

A click and he pulled away, dropping a too-light kiss on her lips. She attempted to tighten her arms to hold him in place but failed miserably. So she pried open her heavy lids and attempted a glare as he backed out of the car. Putting a leg out to follow, she discovered he'd buckled her in like a recalcitrant child and went into full-pout mode.

He chuckled and closed the door.

"You look adorable when you pout." He climbed into the driver's seat. "Especially," he leaned over the console, "the way your lower lip sticks out so invitingly," and licked along said lip before capturing her mouth with his.

Ally went from mildly irritated to hot and itchy in 3.2 seconds. His hand slid into her hair, angling her head. The stroke of his tongue woke her nerve endings to screaming attention like an F-15 doing a fly-by. She moaned into his mouth, clutching him tight so he couldn't escape.

Too soon, he did exactly that and sank back into his seat.

Note to self—death grip needs work. "You keep doing that. It's pissing me off."

Her eyes widened. She didn't talk like that. It kinda rocked.

He shot her an amused glance. "Doing what?"

"Getting me all turned-on then leaving me hanging. Not very gentlemanly to play like that, ya know." Satisfied when his amused look fled, she crossed her arms. His hands flexed on the steering wheel, the play of muscles down his tanned arms momentarily distracting her.

"I haven't been playing with you. I didn't want to take advantage."

She sniffed. "Yeah, I know. I'm not your type. Guys like you want perfect, slim, beach-bunny types. Not boring, chubby, unattractive girls." Limbs and eyelids heavy, tongue way too loose, Ally settled deeper into the seat.

"That's not..." He broke off and shook his head. "We need to get some food in you to counteract the medicine."

"I feel fine." She yawned, melting deeper into the soft seat like ice cream on a hot summer day.

"Uh-huh." He sighed. "You're a beautiful, sexy woman, Ally."

"It's okay. You don't have to lie. My mother warned me what would happen if I stayed fat. I accepted a long time ago I'd haft'a settle for a steady, reliable, average kinda guy if I wanted to get married and have a family." Nestled in her seat, eyes closed, warmth suffused her body, too safe and languid to screen her words. "I just thought for once, maybe I could have the hot guy who seemed too incredible for words. Just one time, I could be that girl." Sleep tugged hard, making it difficult to talk. "Is'okay," she mumbled. "Don' worry 'bout it."

Someone jiggled her shoulder. She pushed the hand off, but it returned and shook harder. Cracking open her eyes, Ally glared at the obnoxious man disturbing her. "What?"

"You need to eat."

"Not hungry." Curling into a tight ball, she closed her eyes.

"Ally, you have to eat." He sounded very firm.

Sighing, she opened her eyes again. "Why?"

"Because." Greg's voice slowed, adult explaining a basic principle to a five-year-old. "You took heavy painkillers on an empty stomach. You need to dilute all those pills in your system."

Grudgingly conceding his point, she sat up and accepted the cheeseburger. And the cup of soda. Ice-cold Diet Coke went a long way toward clearing the rest of the cobwebs. Halfway through the burger, the memory of their conversation before she'd fallen asleep slapped her fully awake . Clear and sharp, painful in recollection.

Cheeks warming, she stared out the window. Anywhere but at him. "Uhm, about what I said earlier? You can just forget... well, all of it."

"Oh, yeah?" he drawled.

Her face burned hotter and she shook her hair forward to cover it. "Please? Prescription painkillers and I don't coexist real well. They make me...well, loopy."

"So I'm not a hot stud? And you don't want to find out how good we'd be together in bed?"

Melting into a puddle of embarrassed goo held definite appeal. Anything to escape. Heck, she'd even welcome the interruption of some homicidal criminal about now. Well, no. That was going too far.

Greg seemed oblivious to her suffering. "Because I sure as hell would."

Oh, wonderful. A whole new pinnacle of previously undiscovered mortification breached. "Greg, I have no intention of being some sympathy case for you. A mercy..." No matter how hard she tried, she couldn't force the word out.

"Fuck?"

She winced and nodded.

"You really have no idea how gorgeous you are, do you?"

Gorgeous? Forgetting her scorching cheeks, she looked up.

Greg captured her gaze, his deep voice flowing around her like molten lava. "You are a sensuous, beautiful, incredible woman, Ally. I don't know what happened to screw up your self-perception, but it's not easy keeping my hands off you. Your sweet curves scream hot and sweaty sex. I've thought so since the first time I saw you."

She could barely breathe. Her hearing must have gone on the fritz. Or the painkillers had scrambled her brains. Men like him didn't say things like that to her. Yet, staring into his eyes, she couldn't doubt his sincerity.

The harsh ring of a cell phone shattered the moment.

"Marsing." A thundercloud slowly spread across his face. "Yeah. We'll be there."

He tapped the phone off, focused his gaze out the windshield, a muscle ticking in his jaw, and his eyes narrowed. The fraught silence stretched her nerves. She had a right to know what was going on. Odds were it involved her.

"What?"

His gaze flicked to her and away again. A shutter had dropped. She couldn't read his expression. He didn't want to tell her. Her muscles tensed, her belly tightened, and her appetite fled.

"That was Lucas." Greg's lips pressed into a tight, hard line. "Some thugs showed up at his house this morning, said they had Celia and if he wanted to see her alive again, he had to go with them. Now they've got both of them."

His fist tightened around the steering wheel.

"They want to trade," he said in a low voice. "You for Celia and Lucas."

"Wow." Lightheaded and numb, she attempted a smile. "A two-fer."

"This isn't a joke, Ally."

"I know that." She sighed. "I also know you don't have a choice."

His jaw hardened. "There's always a choice. No way in hell am I handing you over."

"I don't see any other option."

"You don't know these people. Victor, the slimeball in charge, is involved in drugs, prostitution, you name it, he's probably got a finger in the pie. The things he does to his girls, allows his Johns to do…you don't want to know."

And this Victor guy wanted her? "Why is he not locked up?

Why does he want me?"

"We've never been able to catch him with his pants down. As to why he wants you...we know he isn't behind all this—he doesn't have the kind of money being offered. I'd say it's directly related to the healthy paycheck for your death."

Well, alrighty then. She could almost feel the blood draining from her head. And she thought she was lightheaded before.

Spitting expletives, he slammed his palm against the steering wheel.

Ally flinched.

"I'll come up with something, some way to get Celia and Lucas from them without giving you up. 'Cause, babe, that'll happen over my dead body."

Ally's stomach knotted, his expression and voice far too serious with the whole dead- body thing.

With vicious motions, he shoved the car into gear and pulled out of the parking lot. They drove in silence for a long time. Different scenarios, each more unpleasant and painful than the last, stretched Ally's nerves to the breaking point. Someone, somewhere, found her continued existence infuriating. Her boring, no-social-life, introverted, wouldn't-harm-a-fly existence. It boggled the mind.

Greg pulled into a deserted park. He shut off the ignition, tension filling the quiet car. Ally twisted her hands in her lap. She didn't know what to say. Because of her, his sister and friend were in danger. The enormity of the situation rushed over her like a tsunami, blurring her vision and choking her. She leapt out of the car.

Greg shouted after her, but she didn't pause. Space. She just needed some space. A few minutes to beat back the panic. Darting into the shade of a familiar hiking path, she ran. She knew this park, had played here as a child with her cousins. The path wound down to a little lake, a spot she'd hidden from over-opinionated relatives.

Deftly avoiding tree roots and divots, she flew down the path.

The lake opened in front of her and she slowed, following the trail around the side at a gentle jog. All the exercise of the last few days had left her energetic and feeling better, at least physically, than she had in a long while.

She glanced back. Unbelievable. She'd actually lost Greg. Tendrils of guilt tried to grow roots, but she ignored them. A few moments of quiet, some time for introspection was all she needed before heading back and graciously accepting whatever plan Greg offered.

Ally climbed inside a tight grove of trees growing in a clump above the water. The hidden niche was a tighter fit than she remembered. Then again, she'd been much younger the last time. Thankful the moss was dry and she sat down. The scent of the lake, dirt, and wildflowers filled her nose. She lifted her face to the warm sunshine, letting the breeze caress her anxiety attack away.

She was in no rush to die, but neither could she allow Greg to sacrifice people he cared about. His sister had nothing to do with any of this. Lucas had nothing to do with any of this. Their biggest mistake had been coming in contact with her. She blinked back the flash of tears, crossed her fingers, and prayed he'd come up with a brilliant plan to save everyone.

She could see most of the lake from her well-concealed spot. Her cousins had searched forever trying to find her when they played here. Eventually, they gave up and found someone else to torment.

Male voices drifted on the light wind. Concealed in the shadows, she wriggled forward. Several men stood in the shade on the other side of the lake, unaware or uncaring how well voices carried over water.

"We need to have a few guys hidden, back-up in case Marsing tries anything. I wouldn't put anything past the guy. He's always had a hero complex."

The man sounded vaguely familiar. Swallowing hard, Ally struggled to match the voice to a face.

"All I care about is the girl," another man growled.

She shivered and hugged herself. Marsing and some girl. They had to be talking about her.

"Just spread 'em out. I intend to walk out of here afterward."

"He's just one guy. Quit being so paranoid, Smith."

Jerking back, she smacked her freshly stitched forehead on a low branch and gasped. Tears stung her eyes at the sharp pain. Abrupt silence fell. Even the birds' cheerful chorus stopped.

Ally hunched down, wishing she'd stayed with Greg, pulled on her big-girl panties and dealt with the panic like an adult. She had to get back. No way would she repay Greg by skipping out when he needed her to save his sister and Lucas.

She'd been lucky the men hadn't spotted her when she arrived. They must have heard her gasp. Now they'd be looking for her. Well, looking for someone anyway.

Oh, God, she was too stupid to live.

A hand closed over her shoulder and she choked on a scream. Greg's head appeared between the tree trunks. She sagged with relief. His blue eyes glittered, promising retribution. She couldn't recall ever being so happy to see someone.

He pressed a finger to his lips and she nodded, relieved he knew they had company. He gestured for her to follow. Quietly, she edged out of her spot, wondering how he'd found her little nook. Thankful he had.

Keeping a firm grip on her hand, he led her through the brush and paused alongside a big tree. He scanned the trail in front of them. Nothing moved. They darted across into the cover on the other side.

Easy movement was next to impossible with the thick ground cover and she tripped. Greg didn't slow or glance back. Yep, he was ticked. She brushed her hands off and glanced down. A foot stuck out of the brush where she'd stumbled. The rest of the body was covered by a thick pile of bushes and tree trunks.

She stared at Greg's back. The leg had to belong to one of the guys they had talked about placing in strategic locations. Greg must have *disposed* of him. Maybe even killed him. Her head swam. Overwhelmed and suddenly terrified, she clamped her lips tight and followed him.

The forest opened up into the parking lot. The unguarded parking lot, thankfully. Greg stuffed her into the passenger seat and drilled her in place with a glare, his lips a thin line of fury.

He circled the hood of the car and climbed in, clenching his hands around the steering wheel as a muscle ticked in his jaw. Reining in his temper, she hoped.

"Why did you run off like that?" he finally ground out.

"I needed some space."

"Space? Space!"

Ally winced. "There's no need to shout."

"What the hell were you thinking?"

"It's not like I knew this was the meeting place. You could've told me we weren't here just to admire the view or waste time or whatever."

"You've got men trying to kill you. I have to *tell* you not to run off into the woods by yourself? How stupid are you?"

Jaw dropping, she sputtered. Nobody called her *stupid*. Wimp, coward, boring, prissy, nerd, dork; the list seemed endless. *Stupid* had never come up.

At least she wasn't boring. Running for her life with a hunky police detective playing hero to her damsel in distress—such things didn't happen to cowardly, boring, prissy nerds. She smiled.

"Your smile terrifies me, Ally."

Her smile grew.

"Look, I'm sorry. You're not stupid and you're right. I should have told you more about what was going on."

He shifted in his seat, fiddled with the gear shift and shot glances her way. Greg Marsing. Nervous. Because of her. Cool. And educating, considering the way he started apologizing in the face of her silence.

She filed that tidbit away for future reference. Her smile faded.

If she had a future.

"I'm sorry too. I shouldn't have run off like that. I just… freaked." She glanced at the woods lining the parking lot. "It's all a trap, you know."

"Yeah, I know."

She'd almost messed up everything. They could have captured her without letting Lucas and Celia go. They probably would have killed all three of them.

"I'm really sorry." Hunching her shoulders, Ally curled her legs up on the seat and rested her forehead on the door's window.

"It's not your fault." Greg sounded calmer. "Did they say anything else?"

"They talked about sticking men in a couple of places to surround the area. Their main interest is me. Oh, and Smith is with them."

"Interesting."

A trickle of sweat rolled down Ally's hairline. Dark clouds rolled in, obscuring the sun. Thunder rumbled through the humid air. The electricity of the storm buzzed along her damp skin.

Fat raindrops fell, splatting against the windshield. Greg grinned. The storm grew in intensity, until the rain hitting the car became a dull roar.

Greg laughed out loud. "Perfect."

Had he lost his mind? Probably to be expected, what with the pressure and all. Poor guy.

He grabbed her by the upper arms, tugging her close. "Don't you see? We're supposed to meet out in the open, in the park. Now that it's pouring rain, we have the advantage. You can barely see in this stuff."

He kissed her, his lips firm and warm on hers. Sighing into his mouth, she opened to him. Every time he touched her, she melted. His lips on hers revved her up and turned her insides to liquid heat.

He wrapped her in his arms, freeing her to grab fistfuls of his silky hair. Determined to enjoy every second, she pushed back the desperation. The kiss spiraled out of control. Heaven.

Under her shirt, his hands smoothed up her back. His thumbs brushed the undersides of her breasts and her nipples pebbled. She pressed them into his chest, moaned into his mouth and basically behaved like all the easy girls she'd envied back in high school. Groaning, Greg broke the kiss and sat panting, eyes glazed, color high.

"We have to stop. I have to think, make a few phone calls."

She nodded but didn't move. He groaned again and pulled her in for another desperate kiss, all tangling tongues and shared breath. Cupping her breast in his palm, he kneaded it. He pinched her nipple. She almost came.

Chapter Eleven

Thunder boomed overhead and they jumped like teenagers making out in the parking lot after Homecoming. Ally giggled and dropped back into her seat, belatedly realizing he'd pulled her into his lap. No grunting and groaning had been involved either. She would have noticed. Maybe there was hope for her, after all.

Ally straightened her clothes and cleared her throat. "So... what's the plan?"

He didn't answer and she glanced up. His cell phone was pressed to his ear and he held up a finger.

"That's right. Thirty minutes ought to do it. Yeah." Greg snorted. "Funny. It's my butt on the line here."

He thumbed the phone off and met her eyes. "We have backup, but they're gonna be five minutes behind us. We'll be on our own initially. You okay with that?"

Like she had a choice. She swallowed to moisten her suddenly dry mouth. "Sure."

Reaching across the console, he snagged her hand. "It'll be okay. I won't let anything happen to you. I promise."

It was a sweet sentiment, but she was too much of a realist to believe him. He would do everything in his power to keep her safe. She knew that, but fate had a way of royally screwing her over lately.

"I'm going to get another look at the lay of the land, maybe take care of another one of their back-up. There's too many entrances to this place for them to watch them all, but it won't hurt to give Lady Luck a helping hand. I'll be back in fifteen."

He dropped a kiss on her knuckles and climbed out of the car. The sheeting rain provided such good cover, Ally lost sight of him well before he reached the tree line.

She twirled a few strands of hair around her finger. For the life of her, she still couldn't figure out who wanted her dead. Searching her brain until no dusty corner was left unexplored hadn't helped. A bizarre, terrifying case of mistaken identity was all she could come up with.

Normal, mundane routine had filled her life. Grocery shopping, work and quiet evenings at home. Alone. Her solitary existence had started to chafe, but nothing remotely interesting had happened.

The only exception was the amusement park. Could she have seen something there? The park had been busy; families and groups of teenagers everywhere, standing in line for rides, eating greasy park food, toddlers fussing and babies crying. No cruel-looking men in business suits, no muscle-bound dudes with unidentified bulges under out-of-place jackets and nobody roughed anyone up.

The only dramatic thing happened on the ride, but numerous other people witnessed the same thing. Other people had sat closer to the action, a fact she was eternally thankful for. She doubted any of the other people knew Michael, but she didn't see how being acquainted with a murder victim made her a target.

Ally wrapped her hair so tightly around her finger the tip turned blue and she quickly freed the abused digit. She hoped Greg was having some luck. If he eliminated the threat of somebody coming up behind them, she would feel a little better.

Heck, would they even have Lucas and Celia with them? Criminals didn't seem the type to use an honest playbook.

Greg appeared out of the rain. He slammed the door shut behind him, splattering rain everywhere as he flung his arm into the backseat. When he brought it forward again, he held a big gun. She fidgeted, watching him check it, slip an extra clip in his pocket, turn his phone on and off, until she couldn't hold her tongue any longer.

"Well?"

"I found another guy. Trussed him up like a turkey. So long as none of his friends decide to check on him, we're good."

"What if they don't bring Lucas and Celia?"

"That's a possibility."

"What will we do?"

He sighed, running a hand through his damp hair. "I'm trying to think positive thoughts right now, Ally. We'll deal with it if it happens, okay?"

"I'm sorry." Her stomach twisted. She kept forgetting they were talking about his sister and best friend. This was so much worse for him.

"I know you're nervous, but I'll keep you safe. Ready?"

His grim expression did little to bolster her confidence, but she nodded.

"As I'll ever be."

"Stick close." Hand on the doorknob, he paused. "Ally? Don't try to be brave, okay? Let me handle this."

He was worried about her being stupid again and she couldn't blame him. "I promise."

Hand wrapped around the back of her neck, Greg pulled her close for a quick, searing kiss. Tears stung the back of her eyes, but Ally blinked them away. She refused to be a weepy, wimpy girl. Not when he needed her to be strong.

Greg tucked his gun in the back of his pants, took her hand and led the way to the path. Five steps and her clothes were soaked through. Rain pelted her, gathered her eyelashes into clumps and obscured everything more than a foot away. She had to blindly trust Greg to lead her.

And she did, she realized with a start. She trusted him with her life. In essence, she had for several days now. But this felt different.

The deep silver of the small lake appeared through the myriad tree trunks. The protective canopy of tall pine trees sheltered them from the full brunt of the storm. Ally wiped the rain from her eyes. As they passed the tight grove where she'd hidden earlier, Greg tugged her close behind, offering the protection of his body. Her heart clenched. The man standing between her and harm could so easily claim every part of her.

He slowed and she peeked over his shoulder. A group of men stood on the path with an array of guns on display. A quiet air of menace sucked the peace and serenity out of the rain-saturated forest.

Greg released her hand and patted her thigh. She understood the unspoken command to stay put and curled her fingers into his shirt. She didn't want him getting hurt on her behalf. Tears flashed to her eyes.

"None o' your tricks now, Marsing," a man said, an odd lisp to his words.

Greg spread his hands. "It's your show, Victor."

"Yeah, jus' remember tha'."

Ally stared at the reed-thin man, his reptilian eyes glued to Greg. Something was wrong with his lips. They drooped oddly. And what was with the way he talked? He spit a stream of brown sludge onto an innocent fern on the side of the path.

"Tha' her?" Victor jerked his chin in her direction.

Greg laughed. "Seriously? You've been hired to kill her and you don't even know what she looks like? Sloppy." He shook his head and Victor's eyes narrowed. Not a man who took ridicule well. "Sure wish I'd known that earlier."

Victor spat again then nodded toward the man beside him. "Go ge' them, before I shoot this moron jus' for the hell of it."

"About time you quit with the chew, don't ya think, Victor? Before long you won't have any teeth left, what with your gums rotting out of your skull."

Ally fisted the back of his shirt, biting her tongue. Why was

Greg egging the guy on? He might be a scrawny, sickly twig of a man, but he still scared the bejeebies out of her.

"Wha' the hell do you care?"

Greg shrugged. "I don't care if your whole face falls off. Just making conversation. You seem nervous."

Between one breath and the next, Victor's laugh became a hacking cough. His face turned red and his whole body convulsed. Not a healthy specimen.

The compact, wiry man Victor had sent off returned with Lucas and Celia in tow. Some of the tension seeped out of Ally's muscles. Greg's muscles hardened beneath her hands and as the small group drew closer, she understood his reaction.

A brilliant bruise colored Celia's porcelain cheek. Lucas looked like he'd fought with a bus. And lost. Multiple cuts and bruises covered his face, his shirt was torn, his hair stood on end and he was limping. Quite the change from his prior GQ perfection. Ally flinched, guilt choking her.

Lucas and Celia were handcuffed together and the guy led them forward like animals on a lead. Lucas' expression did not bode well. When his gaze focused on her, his face darkened even more. The accusing look he turned on Greg confused her.

"There they are," Victor said. "Safe and sound."

"Hardly." Even from behind him, Ally could tell Greg had forced the words through clenched teeth.

"Well, they may be a little more … colorful." Victor grinned.

Ally shivered, shifting more of her body behind Greg. Please, God in heaven, she did not want to go with that man. His slimy gaze touched her and she had an urgent need to bathe. With really, really hot water.

"I don' have all day, Marsing. We're all getting soaked. You want these two or no'?"

"Well, I don't know. That all you got, Vicky?"

The men behind Victor chuckled. Victor whirled and they jumped back like frightened children, smoothing their expressions.

With Victor's back to them, Greg shoved her behind a thin sapling and pulled out the big gun he'd stuck in the rear waistband of his pants.

Lucas moved at the same time, delivering a hard kick to the wiry guy holding his and Celia's cuffs. The guy doubled over but came back up fighting. Lucas unleashed a blurred flurry of vicious kicks and the man collapsed, out cold.

"Hey!" One of the other guys rushed to take the downed man's place. Ally gasped. Officer Smith. His was the voice she'd recognized.

Greg fired his gun and Freddy Smith dropped in his tracks.

The gunshot galvanized everyone. Victor and his men darted for cover. Greg followed hot on their trail, the hard look on his face unmistakable.

Ally wiped rain out of her eyes and hunched down behind the young tree. More gunshots rang out. She braved a glance in Greg's direction. The rain picked up, isolating her in a world only a few feet wide.

The solid thwack of a bullet hit her tree. She ran. Her feet slipped on the slimy pathway and she went down hard in the mud. The earthy smell filled her nose and the metallic taste of blood filled her mouth. Lovely.

She wiped her face off. She'd fallen in a group of massive ferns. They'd grown tall in the shade of the pine trees and their broad leaves covered her completely. Ally couldn't see anything beyond the deep-green canopy. Hopefully no one could see her.

Shouts and gunfire sucked away her minor victory. The slap of feet on mud came close and she huddled farther back. Holding her breath, straining to hear beyond the pound of her heartbeat thrumming through her ears, she held still and crossed her fingers. Please let the new arrivals be Greg's back-up.

The rain, forest and protective ferns distanced her from the sounds of violence, lending a surreal feeling to her misty cocoon. She shivered in her damp clothes. Please let Greg be safe. Lucas and Celia too.

The gunfire stopped. There was no sound at all beyond the quiet fall of rain on leaves. A light breeze rustled the ferns. Closing her eyes, Ally strained to hear something. Anything.

Was it over?

Who won?

Did she dare crawl out?

Minutes ticked by slowly. She couldn't stand the suspense and opened her eyes. Pant legs directly in front of her face obscured everything else. Her heart beat as slow as sludge in her chest and her gaze traveled up the pant legs.

"Well, hello, doll-face."

Bile rose. This couldn't be happening. She stared into the muzzle of a very large, very ugly gun, not daring to blink to see if she was hallucinating.

"Get up. Not a sound."

Outside of the ferns, there was rustling of men in the forest and an occasional shout. Greg's back-up party had arrived and gathered Victor's men. Now they were looking for Victor.

Ally would've gladly helped them out, but she didn't dare even whimper as she rose. Evil oozed off the man. No doubt about it, Victor would put a bullet between her eyes rather than be caught. So why didn't he?

The things Greg told her in the car tightened her muscles. No. No way would Victor cart her off for that. She would make a horrid prostitute. Without conscious thought, her muscles locked up and she dug her heels into the muddy forest floor.

Fast as a striking viper, Victor swung around and backhanded her.

Through ringing ears, she heard Greg yell her name. Everything in her screamed in response. She shook with the effort it took to resist answering. Victor waved the gun again, indicating the path in front of him, leading her deeper into the trees. Away from any hope of rescue. Her cheek throbbed and her knees trembled.

She bit her lip, tasting mud and forest, and trudged through the thick trees and bushes. She made no attempt to be quiet. The storm was moving away, but thunder still rumbled in the sky and rain continued to fall. Her nightmare had become reality.

Victor prodded her through the forest.

After an eternity, they emerged from the trees into a small parking lot. Victor grabbed her arm hard enough to bruise and led her to an old sedan. In another lifetime she would have laughed. It was exactly how every movie she'd ever seen depicted a pimp-mobile. Black-tinted windows, gleaming chrome, dull-green paint and fancy rims. The alarm beeped and he opened the rear door.

He shoved her inside and followed, forcing her to the center of the big bench seat. Terror coiled inside when he grinned, exposing rotten gums and stained teeth. She fought the gag threatening to choke her.

Victor leaned forward. She leaned back. He grabbed her arm. Her stomach churned. He pulled her hand to the far corner of the seat, turning away as he did, and she sagged into the seat.

Her relief was short-lived. Cold metal clamped around her wrist. He leaned over her and grabbed her other arm. Bile rose at the stench of body odor and heavy cologne. Ally struggled, twisting her wrist, but the image of his gun kept her from fighting too hard. Seconds later, arms spread wide, she wore matching bracelets. Defenseless.

Sitting back, he grinned. She didn't know what was more frightening, his grin or the handcuff rings permanently attached to either side of his car.

Beady black eyes perused her body. She averted her face, feeling violated.

"I expec' you'll clean up good." He nodded. "You'll do."

His words were magnanimous enough, but deep inside, a horrifying certainty grew. The car, the handcuffs, his inspection...tears Ally could no longer control filled her eyes as Victor climbed out.

Despite its obvious age, the engine purred like a well-loved animal when he started it. He steered out of the parking lot, driving away from any lingering hope of salvation. Tears rolled unchecked down her dirty cheeks.

All sense of direction fled as they drove. Whether from sheer paranoid habit or necessity, Victor wove an intricate pattern through the streets. By the time he pulled over and killed the engine, they might as well have been in Peru. Ally swallowed repeatedly before she recovered the ability to speak.

"Where are we?"

"No need to worry yer head abou' that, doll face." He turned around and shot her another creepy grin. "Now, you jus' sit tight and I'll be back in a few minutes."

He climbed out, chuckling.

Really, he could take all the time he needed. Growing old right there in the seat held definite appeal. She would mummify in his pimp-mobile without the tiniest whimper of complaint. With absolute certainty, being handcuffed to his car was preferable to whatever awaited her.

Chapter Twelve

Too soon, Victor returned and unlocked the handcuffs. Ally cringed back, stomach churning, but he hauled her out of the car. He dragged her by her wrist, grinding the bones together, up the worn concrete steps of an inconspicuous building.

The simplicity ended at the door. The entryway's garish, brilliant shade of purple escalated her throbbing headache. A chandelier hung from the tall ceiling, dripping crystals and tassels. Sconces echoed the same design, lighting a path down the hallway, enticing visitors to explore the hidden depths.

Ally trembled, immensely grateful for her empty stomach. Victor didn't allow time for sightseeing and dragged her through a maze of hallways and nonsensical stairways as they descended to the seventh level of hell. They finally stopped in front of a solid, intimidating door. He opened the industrial-strength lock, light reflecting dimly off his massive key ring.

With a grotesquely out-of-place courtly gesture, he motioned her inside. Ally looked from him to the doorway. She'd rather face white-water rapids in spring than obey. An unholy glee lit his eyes and she changed her mind. On trembling legs, she crossed the threshold.

Victor followed, flicking on an overhead light.

An iron cot with a thin, uninviting mattress occupied one

corner, a metal chair another. There were no windows, which made sense, since they were buried beneath the earth's crust, well within the mantle. Buried alive. Goose bumps rose along Ally's arms and she rubbed them, turning a slow circle.

Besides the one behind her, a single door led off the room.

The only escape was out the door clanging shut. The jingle of keys and the snick of the lock nullified that idea. Ally flinched but refused to turn. She couldn't bear to watch him lock her in, especially with him on *her* side of the door.

Victor's footsteps approached and she crossed her arms to hide their shaking. He swept her hair off her neck, baring her nape. The fine hairs stood on end.

"What are you doing?" The cool, controlled sound of her voice surprised her. Gratified her.

"I thou' we could get to know one another," Victor purred, his fetid breath washing over her skin. She ruthlessly suppressed a shudder of revulsion.

"You're not my type."

His hand tightened on her hair, yanking her head back so hard a vertebrae popped. She gasped.

"You'll discover soon enough tha' you don' have a type. You'll learn to enjoy *every* type, doll-face. And if you don'…well, your enjoymen' don' really matter."

"What do you mean?"

Victor released her hair and strolled around in front of her. Ally rubbed her throbbing scalp, looked at the bed, shuddered and dropped her gaze to the concrete floor. He grabbed her chin and forced her head back up, his cold eyes drilling into her.

"It's simple. I pu' out the word tha' you're dead. In reali'y, you'll be working for me. On your back. I'll ge' paid twice over."

"Like hell."

"Tha's up to you. It can be hell, alright."

Rage obliterated her common sense. "It must be annoying not to be able to pronounce words properly. How long have those T's been dropping off your speech?"

One minute she was standing, the next he had her on the floor, sitting on her belly, hitting her. One cheek, then the other, cold concrete biting into her backside under the press of his weight.

Her ears rang and black spots swam at the edge of her vision. She'd never been hit before. She instinctively raised her hand to block the blows. He yanked her arm down hard and her shoulder popped. Ally shriveled deep inside, recognizing on a visceral level the threat Victor represented to her sanity. She retreated within herself, to a place of rain-scented pines and blossoming sun-yellow tulips.

She went numb, barely feeling the hard blows raining down on her. Eventually Victor stopped, panting, and climbed off her.

"You shouldn' have made me lose my temper." Genuine regret colored his voice. "It'll take you days to heal. I can' presen' you to clients looking like this."

Well, that explained the regret. She was cutting into his profit margin. A bottom-line kind of guy. The urge to laugh rose and nearly choked her, but she clamped down hard on the rising hysteria.

"I suppose it doesn' matter tha' much, though. You'll need training. Time to learn your new role and all the necessary tricks of the trade. We'll keep you out of sigh' in the meantime."

Ally remained silent, ears ringing.

"Excellen'." Satisfaction oozed from the single word. "Regretfully, we'll have to postpone sex. I no longer find you tha' appealing."

His footsteps moved toward the door. Ally's muscles loosened with relief.

"No need to worry, though. I sample all of the girls before they hi' the floor." He could have been talking about clothing. "There's a bathroom off this room. I sugges' you make use of it. You reek. Your clothes will have to be burned."

Victor locked the door behind him when he left, an eerie silence settling in his absence. Ally rolled to her side. Sucking in a deep, painful breath, she forced herself up onto all-fours. She swayed and clenched her muscles, forcing them into obedience to gain her feet. Weaving like a drunken sailor on shore leave, she stumbled into the little bathroom and dropped to her knees beside the toilet.

She'd been wrong about the empty stomach.

Just not enough to prevent dry heaving for an eternity of agony. Finally spent, she collapsed on the cold floor and surveyed the bathroom through eyelids swollen almost closed. A pedestal sink—no mirror. A toilet. A shower stall—no curtain.

Wow. The place could be mistaken for The Ritz.

On her hands and knees, Ally crawled back into the poor excuse of a bedroom. Agony rippling through her body in waves, she hauled herself onto the disgusting mattress. She refused to contemplate the filth. Shutting her eyes, she prayed for the sweet oblivion of sleep.

Where was Greg right now? She pictured him, brought him vividly into focus in her mind's eye. Dipping further into her imagination, she felt his hands on her, soothing, and an ache started deep inside.

She hadn't trusted a man, really trusted him, in a very long time. If ever. Her dad had taken a back-row seat to the theater of her childhood. Never stood up for her, never interfered when her cousins picked on her, never took her side against her domineering mother. Even so, she had learned to accept him and love him before he died. She still wouldn't have trusted him to take care of her. Something she'd need in the man she married.

Ally slammed on the brakes. No way was she looking at Greg as husband-material. Even if they had sex—a thought she couldn't dwell on in her current situation—it would just be sex. Mutual satisfaction. Nothing more.

In some ways, Greg's Surfer Dude persona fit him to a tee. Here today, gone tomorrow. Once something was no longer fun, he'd head for the next wave, the next best thing.

Illusions were a luxury she could no longer afford.

Shaken awake, Ally groaned. When she tried to open her eyes, only one would sort-of cooperate. Swollen and bleary, the other refused to focus on anything. She made out the hazy form of a woman bending over her.

"You wake now? Eat."

An Oriental accent. Was she in this hell-hole voluntarily?

She drifted. The hand jostled harder. Focusing came a bit more easily this time. The woman didn't look very old. Ally's age and exquisitely beautiful.

"You eat."

Right. She'd mentioned that. Ally struggled to sit up and bit back a moan of pain. She felt like she'd been run over by a car—or a train—and dragged face-first through gravel.

The woman set a tray on her lap. Ally peered at a bowl filled with a mysterious, gelatinous substance. A piece of toast shared the tray alongside a glass of milk. The toast was cold and the milk warm.

"Eat." The woman settled on the end of her bed, obviously intending to watch and make sure she obeyed.

Ally spooned up some of the runny, lumpy stuff. The food lacked any taste. She swallowed with effort, pain creeping in and rapidly escalating as more body parts awakened.

"What's your name?" she asked, desperate for distraction.

"Jia Li."

"That's pretty. What does it mean?"

"Good and beautiful. Your name?"

"Ally."

Jia Li's English was pretty rough. Learning another language couldn't be easy.

"Pretty too. What it mean?"

"I haven't the faintest idea." As best she could manage through one eye, she studied Jia Li. Her face held the timeless beauty unique to Asian women. A shining curtain of black hair fell to her waist. Her beautiful clear-blue eyes held sorrow, pain and an acceptance of her situation that broke Ally's heart. "How long have you been here?"

"Two year, three month, twenty day."

Ally swallowed. A long time. All those months of pain and degradation. She clenched the edges of the tray, fighting the urge to hurl the whole thing across the room. Jia Li would probably be punished if she did.

"I have to get out of here," she said hoarsely.

Jia Li's eyes flooded with sadness. "You eat. Need strength."

That didn't sound good, but Ally knew she was right. She had to stay alert. Had Victor already collected for her "death"? Her chest hurt. Would Greg believe it?

Shoveling in mouthfuls of slop, she thought about her family. Her mother had wanted grandbabies. Her dad too. Despite their death, she'd planned on making their dreams come true.

She had to get out of there.

Ally pushed the empty tray away and Jia Li nodded.

"Good. Feel better now."

The other woman lifted a small bag onto her lap from the floor and tentatively scooted closer. Ally squinted as Jia Li unzipped some sort of first-aid kit.

Jia Li opened a container of ointment and faced her. "I help. This make it better."

She dipped a slender finger into the jar and dabbed the cream on Ally's face. The cold stuff stung, but Ally bit her lip and endured. She wasn't vain, but neither did she want to carry physical memories of this place for the rest of her life.

Ally swallowed thickly and stared at Jia Li. "Your eyes are such a beautiful blue."

Pink darkened Jia Li's high cheekbones and her lips tightened, but her chin rose. "My father was an American." She met her gaze. "Because of him, I am a very valuable whore."

She flinched and closed her good eye against the pain in Jia Li's expression. Damn her big mouth. Jia Li finished applying the sticky substance and capped the jar.

"You be good," she said.

It took her a minute to realize she was being given advice. Ally shook her head and winced. "I have to get out of here, Jia Li."

"You be good." Jia Li's gaze drifted around the room before focusing on Ally again. Was she trying to tell her something? Her eyes flicked to the empty wall again.

Was there a hidden camera in the room? Someone watching her?

Jia Li placed the bag on the empty tray. As she grasped the edges of the tray, she pushed something into Ally's hand. Ally flinched and met Jia Li's steady gaze. She dipped her chin a fraction in a subtle nod. Ally curled her fingers around the cool, metal object and tucked her hand out of sight against the side of her leg.

A mixture of hope and fear filled Jia Li's eyes as she stood. Ally understood. If she escaped, Jia Li had hope. On the flip side, Victor might figure out where it had come from. Whatever *it* was.

Jia Li locked the door behind her. Ally relaxed her hand, stretched painfully, and glanced down. A little pair of surgical scissors rested in her hand. They seemed so small and useless, but they were better than nothing.

Shifting, she shoved the scissors into a tear in the mattress she'd discovered last night. She had ignored Victor's instructions to shower. Her muddy clothes were dried to crispy stiffness. Her skin itched and she smelled.

There was nothing for it but to shower. If there was a camera in the bedroom, odds were there was one in the bathroom. She shivered in revulsion.

Slowly, Ally climbed to her feet and stretched. Her face hurt. The lack of a mirror was probably a good thing.

Turning the water all the way to hot, she stripped as unceremoniously as possible. No need to give anyone a show. She stepped under the water and sighed over the simple pleasure. Tiny bottles of shampoo and conditioner occupied a ledge in the shower, along with a small square of soap.

The entire container of shampoo went into her hair. She rubbed the conditioner in and soaped her body. Her belly tightened. She glanced around the small, steam-filled bathroom and rushed through rinsing off, careful to keep her face out of the water. The water stung her abused skin.

Shutting off the shower, Ally snatched a miniscule, threadbare towel off the sink. She didn't remember any towels from last night. Maybe Jia Li had brought one with her. The thing was so small, she might as well have been drying off with a washcloth.

As best she could, she wrung her hair out before using the cloth. Dropping the sopping towel on the floor, she reached for her filthy clothes, only to come up empty. Disbelieving, she stared. Dried mud scattered the floor where they'd been. No clothes.

Keeping her body inside the bathroom, she peeked out the door. Not a stitch of clothing anywhere. Crap. She'd known taking a shower was a mistake.

She snagged the towel off the floor, but the cover it provided was laughable. As quickly as she could, Ally crossed the room and scooted onto the narrow bed. Dread congealed in her belly.

Thirty seconds later, the lock turned and the door creaked open.

Heart sinking, Ally crossed her legs and clutched the tattered towel to her breasts. Victor appeared in the door, grinning and congenial.

"Good morning, doll-face." He made a tutting sound, more like he was spitting than anything. "Your face is not so pretty this morning. We'll have to work on that."

As if her condition wasn't his fault.

"Not so mouthy now, I see." He nodded in obvious satisfaction.

Much as she hated pleasing him, she kept her mouth shut.

"Good, good."

He gestured through the open door and Jia Li appeared. In one hand, she carried several scraps of material. In the other, a different bag from the one she'd had earlier.

"Jade is going to help make you presentable," Victor said.

Ally's gaze darted to Jia Li. Jade? The woman gave an almost imperceptible shake of her head. Jia Li must be her real name.

Victor closed and locked the door behind Jia Li. Strolling across the room, he settled into the sole metal chair. Oh, man, he was going to watch. Her stomach rolled, threatening to divulge her unappetizing breakfast.

Jia Li laid out the material on a small folding table she had brought along. Lingerie, Ally realized. A bra, tiny excuse for panties and a garter belt, all in brilliant garnet-red. Beside these, Jia Li set black stockings.

Ally's gaze flew to Jia Li's. Sympathy shimmered there. Her mutinous stare moved on to Victor. "I don't even get clothes to wear?" she sneered. "What kind of second-rate outfit are you running here?"

His nostrils flared. "The kind that cares more about the client's pleasure than your comfort."

She longed to launch herself across the room at him, but his beady eyes watched her closely. Her fear fed his ego. She lifted her chin and held his gaze.

His eyes narrowed.

Jia Li made a soft sound of distress and Ally's attention shifted to her. She shot her a pleading look as she laid out an assortment of cosmetics on the table. A hairbrush was among them and a large jar.

Knuckles rapped against the door. Jia Li moved to answer it, but Victor waved her back and rose. Two men, massive muscles bulging, came in. They stood on either side of Victor, lust in their eyes as they stared at her.

So not good.

"If you please," Victor gestured toward her.

They started toward her and Ally scrambled back on the bed. She didn't get far. The dark one grabbed her wrists and the blonde guy snagged her ankles out of midair as she kicked out. The towel went flying. She screamed, kicking and wriggling and squirming. They held firm.

The blonde guy tucked both her ankles into one hand and reached under the bed. An old-fashioned shackle appeared, which he deftly attached to her ankle. Moving to the other side of the bed, he repeated the action. The heavy chains weighed down her legs and held her thighs wide open.

The dark one licked his thick lips. The guy with sandy-colored hair stood at the end of the bed, crossed his arms over his massive chest and stared at her crotch.

Ally's whole body flushed hot with shame.

The dark guy placed her wrists in narrow shackles on either side of her head and stepped back to survey his work. Hot rage flooded her, banishing humiliation, and she glared at the men. "Gee, I'll bet your mothers are real proud."

The blonde guy flushed and his gaze shifted away. The darker one grinned.

"Jade," Victor said.

Jia Li moved forward, mouthing a silent sorry as she set the large jar between Ally's spread thighs. Heat emanated from the jar.

Jia Li carefully applied the hot wax and methodically ripped every speck of hair from her pelvis. Staring at the ceiling, Ally pictured brilliant blue skies and fluffy white clouds drifting overhead. While Jia Li tore out hair from the most sensitive place on her body, Ally bit her lip hard enough to draw blood and refused to cry. She wouldn't give Victor the satisfaction. Without a doubt, he would derive a great deal of enjoyment from her pain.

Finally, thank you, God, Jia Li finished. Gently, she rubbed oil into the abused area before stepping back.

Victor rose. Ally's whole body tensed. He leaned down, his despicable face inches from her freshly bared pelvis, inspecting Jia Li's work with entirely too much interest.

"Very nice. Very nice, indeed. You have a very pretty pussy, doll-face."

Ally withdrew deep into the safe little space she'd created. She counted cracks in the ceiling. His breath feathered across her skin, and she pulled even tighter into herself. Without touching her, he stepped back and she wanted to weep for such small favors.

Jia Li came forward with another pot. Ally couldn't imagine anything worse than the hot wax. Jia Li unscrewed the cap and placed it on the bed. The pleasant woodsy scent of jasmine filled the room.

Victor settled in the chair as Jia Li rubbed the cool scented lotion into her skin.

"I've decided your name will be Jasmine. I like my girls to smell like their names, so this will be your new scen'. You'll wear it every day, rubbing it into your skin to keep it sof' and swee' smelling."

"All my girls are pampered and well cared for," he added, "as long as they behave."

Ally met Jia Li's eyes. Yeah, *his girls* were as happy as clams. Clams dumped in a steaming pot of boiling water.

Finished with her second task, Jia Li stood back. Curly and Moe, aka Victor's henchmen, came forward and unchained her. Moe, the blonde, ran his hand up her thigh.

"No touching," Victor barked and Moe jerked his hand away.

Curly and Moe went back to holding up the wall and Victor chuckled. "Don't worry, gentlemen. You'll get your turn. Eventually."

Ally shivered and sat up, crossing her arms over her chest. Jia Li handed her the lingerie. Something was better than nothing, right? She did her best to wriggle into the barely-there shelf of a bra without flashing more flesh than absolutely necessary. Silly after being spread out like a Thanksgiving turkey, but she didn't care.

Holding up the panties, she stared at the slit in the crotch before turning narrowed eyes toward Victor. "Real classy."

He just smiled his slimy smile.

Through a feat of sheer determination, she shimmied into the panties and garter belt without spreading her legs. The stockings came next. She rolled them up her legs and hooked them onto the garters. The smooth, silk panties felt strange against the bare skin of her pelvis.

Jia Li moved behind her and gently untangled the knots in her hair before drying and styling it. A fine mist of hairspray set the style. With gentle fingers on Ally's swollen and bruised skin, Jia Li applied makeup. Ally had never had someone else do her makeup. If she closed her eyes and pretended really, really, *really* hard, she could almost believe she was in a salon getting the full treatment.

Jia Li stepped back and folded her hands in front of her. Obviously she had done all she could. Ally didn't feel the tiniest bit curious about how she looked. Belatedly, she realized Jia Li had not uttered a single word in Victor's presence.

Victor rose again. "Stand up."

Stubbornly, she glared and remained seated.

"I'm sure these two fine men would be more than happy to help you."

She hesitated until Curly stepped forward. Trembling, she stood. Victor surveyed her from head to foot, making her feel like a side of beef on market day. She studiously avoided looking at Curly or Moe.

"The shoes."

Jia Li hurried to the collapsible table and pulled a pair of strappy heels out of the bag, handing them to Victor.

"Sit."

Ally sat.

Victor knelt in front of her. She badly wanted to kick him in the face. The fantasy played out in her head, the thin heel of one shoe buried deep in Victor's temple. Too bad his faithful dogs hovered nearby. Freed from their leashes, she had no doubt they would be all over her in a heartbeat.

Victor gently picked up her foot from the floor, rubbing his thumb along her arch. "Such pretty, delicate feet."

He lifted her foot to his mouth. Her eyes widened. He sucked her big toe into his mouth, his tongue darting between her toes. Oh, gag. Her skin crawled; her stomach churned.

Tenderly, almost reverently, Victor removed her foot from his mouth and slipped the shoe on. Damn, he was one sick puppy. He put the other shoe on, forgoing the sucking and licking routine. Then he tugged Ally to her feet and surveyed the result with obvious satisfaction. His gaze drifted back to her face and he made a comical moue of distress.

"Ah, well. You will heal and be as beautiful as ever. Come. Is time for your firs' lesson."

Achingly self-conscious of all her bare skin, she avoided looking at Jia Li and obediently followed Victor out the door. Curly and Moe fell in behind. Victor didn't look back as he walked, evidently expecting his goons to keep her in line. About halfway down the hall, he stopped in front of an unassuming door.

"You two wai' here."

Ally followed him into a narrow space, more hallway than room. Victor flipped a switch on the wall and a section moved, revealing a glass partition. And so much more.

A man stood in the center of the room, completely naked. A young woman knelt in front of him, brown hair sweeping down her back, bare breasts swaying. The man's head dropped forward as he thrust in and out of the woman's mouth.

Something seemed...off. Ally narrowed her eyes, struggling to focus through her good eye. And then wished she wasn't able to see.

A thin red rope was wrapped around and fisted in the man's hand and encircled the woman's slender neck. He pulled up and thrust hard into her mouth, burying himself to the hilt. Ally winced and closed her eyes.

"He's enjoying himself, don't you think?"

Ally tightened her lips.

"Come." He pushed her out the door.

Swaying on the stilettos, Ally trotted after him down the hall and into another narrow room. Again, Victor flipped a switch and a section of wall slid away. Ally stared at the floor, refusing to look. The reverberations of a scream trembled the glass in the wall. She flinched, shaking so hard she fought to remain standing.

"Watch," Victor hissed. He fisted her hair and yanked her head up, holding her still. Before she could even think to close her eyes, she focused through the glass.

A woman braced herself on hands and knees in the middle of a big bed, while a man knelt behind her. Thin rivulets of blood trailed from her back, down her sides, to drip onto the pristine white sheet beneath her. Ally flinched when the man brought a thick-handled, multiple-strapped, short whip down across the woman's back. He repeated the action, whipping her in time with his thrusts.

The man thrust hard and slapped his hand on her torn flesh. The woman's scream vibrated the glass again. The man threw his head back, mouth open and gasping, clearly coming through the woman's pain. Desperately, Ally tried to turn away, but Victor tightened his hold until pieces of her hair snapped free in his grasp. Bile rose, burning her throat alongside the tears scorching her eyes.

"Not all our guests have such violen' tendencies, of course," Victor whispered in her ear, his tepid breath raising gooseflesh. He released her, roughly jerking his fingers free of her hair. "Come along."

Ally followed on trembling legs. Again, they entered a narrow room and a portion of the wall slid aside. With her tender scalp still burning, she didn't dare not look.

This woman's head was drawn back, a mix of pleasure and pain written across her beautiful face. She didn't look more than sixteen. The middle-aged man beneath her gripped her hips hard, his fingers digging in, guiding her up and down. Another man knelt behind her, undoubtedly adding the pain to her expression. He held her long fall of auburn hair in his fist, driving into her bottom with no care for her tender young body. Both panting men were old enough to be her father.

Although far less violent than the last, the scene sickened her.

Sex between a man and woman was a beautiful, natural expression of love and desire. The perversion of that precious moment coupled with the gutter rat beside her was more than she could bear.

"See, the girls who are difficul' get the difficul' clients. Those who behave, like Lotus there, get to enjoy the clients with more... natural inclinations."

Alongside the pounding of her head, understanding dawned. The continuation of her mutinous behavior would result in her sharing the fate of the first two girls. Beyond bloodshed, there wasn't a whole lot of difference between the scenes. If he thought she was going to be obedient and let a bunch of sicko perverts screw her, he had another think coming.

"Do you understand, Jasmine?" The vile man glided his slimy fingers along her bare skin. "Which will you be?"

Clenching her jaw until pain shot through her head, Ally kept quiet. Sharing her thoughts didn't seem like a wise idea. Refusal to be cowed did not equate stupidity.

He sighed, ushering her out of the room. "I see obedience is still beyond you. I'm in a generous mood after the earlier show you provided, so I'll give you one more day."

Like that will make any difference. On second thought, the more time she had to plan, the better.

Chapter Thirteen

Barefoot, Ally paced the small confines of her room. The shoes were the only thing she dared remove. Lunch and dinner had come and gone, brought by a different, silent woman, who kept her gaze fastened to the floor while Ally ate.

Reaching the far wall, she turned. There had to be some way to get out of this place.

The lights clicked off. She'd learned early she had no control via the wall switch. Victor controlled everything. At least in the dark, no one could watch her.

She hurried to the bed and ran her fingers over the mattress until she found the hole. Inside the tear, the metal of the tiny scissors was cold.

Feeling her way along the wall, she found the door and knelt. Using her fingertips to guide her, she stuck the tip of the scissors into the lock. The scissors clicked and rattled inside the lock in time with her shaking. She didn't have the first clue how to pick a lock.

What if Victor splurged on night-vision video cameras? Or had someone standing guard on the other side of her door?

She fumbled, searching for the locking mechanism inside. Beads of sweat broke out on her forehead. Leaning close, Ally shut her eyes and concentrated, listening for a click, feeling with all of her senses.

She had no way of knowing how much time had passed. Hours, minutes...She collapsed against the door, tears of frustration and fear slipping down her cheeks.

How was she going to escape?

Was she truly going to end her days servicing countless men in untenable ways?

Sobbing, she crawled back to the pathetic excuse for a bed and curled up. There wasn't even a blanket. She cried and shivered, longing for Greg's heat. Eventually, she fell into a troubled sleep.

The lights blinked on. Rubbing her eyes, Ally sat up and adjusted her clothes, such as they were.

She stiffened when the door creaked open. Jia Li appeared and Ally relaxed. Jia Li shoved the door closed, quickly walked over and set the tray down on the bed. Returning to the door, she bent down.

Ally yawned, scooting up to sit against the headboard. She bent her leg to sit Indian style, but painful awareness of the slit in the crotch of her tasteless red panties stopped her. Instead, she stretched out her legs and crossed them at the ankle.

Jia Li returned to the side of her bed and roughly deposited the breakfast tray on her lap.

Ally stared at her in surprise.

Jia Li opened her palm and an object clattered onto the battered metal tray. The small scissors. She looked at them, then the floor in front of the door, before lifting her wide eyes to the other woman's expressionless face.

"Be careful," Jia Li hissed, her expression blank and her lips barely moving.

Ally took in how close she stood, her body angled toward the tray. Blocking their movements. Jia Li knew where the camera was located.

Jia Li shifted again and Ally palmed the scissors from the tray and tucked them into the mattress.

Picking up the spoon, she started eating the lumpy, bland gruel.

Jia Li moved away and sat at the end of the bed. This time when she spoke, Ally didn't see her lips move at all.

"You try to escape last night, yes?"

Ally shoved a spoonful of mush into her mouth. "Um-hmm."

"Lock very sturdy."

Ally grimaced.

"He come soon." Jia Li shot her a glance through the thick fall of her black hair. "Alone."

Ally swallowed, the tasteless gruel turning to ash in her mouth and sliding down her throat with the ease of porcupine quills.

Could she do it? Did she have enough inner fortitude to physically harm someone?

Her gaze drifted around the cold room before stopping on the foot of her bed. One of the iron shackles they'd used on her yesterday lay on the mattress. Her belly burned with the memory. The torment of the other girls flared hot inside her and determination hardened her heart.

"Thank you, Jia Li."

The woman rose and took the tray from Ally's lap, her beautiful blue eyes holding hers for a brief second. Ally almost quailed beneath the desperate faith she saw there. Instead, she dug a little deeper and stiffened her spine.

She could do this. She *would* do this.

Jia Li sidled out of the door, shooting her one last look before disappearing. Ally waited for the lock to latch into place before rising. Hurrying into the bathroom, she took care of pressing needs and splashed cold water on her face.

The swelling had gone down around her eye and her face felt pretty much normal again. Since she couldn't actually *see* herself, she could be grossly mistaken. She smoothed her hair as best she could and checked over her microscopic clothes.

Then she walked back to the bed and sat down to wait. Her fingers wriggled against the mattress, checking her location against the rip holding the precious scissors.

Closing her eyes, she pictured her mom and dad, long gone now. Greg. Too handsome for his own good, stubborn, intractable, bossy, caring, sweet, protective, Greg. Emotion pinched her heart.

Ally sighed with longing. Sure, he'd trample her poor, chubby heart to smithereens. She didn't care. Besides, she'd already surrendered to the inevitability of loving him.

The lock clicked open and her muscles cramped. Her moment of reckoning had arrived. Quickly, she pressed her back to the headboard, wrapped her arms around her chest to cover as much as possible of her breasts and crossed her legs tight at the ankle.

Alone as Jia Li promised, Victor strode into the room without stopping to lock the door behind him. Either he thought she was suitably cowed or he was confident in his ability to control her. Deliberately, she relaxed without changing position, one muscle at a time forced into submission. She would never survive the tension otherwise.

"Good morning." Victor's cold gaze moved over her. The unholy gleam in his eyes made her womb shrivel up and hide.

"Yes. Lovely morning, isn't it?" Retreat into sarcasm worked for her. "I so enjoyed the beautiful sunrise over the city."

His lips curved in a horrid smile. "I'm glad to see you still have spiri'. It will make this so much more enjoyable."

He looked over his shoulder, made a hand gesture at the wall and pointed toward the hallway. She frowned. Why? He faced her again and she stilled in momentary shock. The camera. Victor had just instructed them to turn off the camera. Or at least leave it unmanned and exit the small room on the other side of the panel. She was free to carry out her plan uninterrupted.

He moved closer and her momentary elation dissipated into a shiver of revulsion. Repulsive lust lit his eyes. She tensed, waiting for him to leap on her. Instead, he sat beside her and casually dropped his hand on her silk-encased leg. As if he had the right. Fury bubbled beneath Ally's eerie calm.

"Beau'iful lingerie never fails to arouse me."

Gross.

His hand moved to her knee, sliding over the stocking to her thigh. Thankful for the thin separation of fifteen denier between her skin and his, she narrowed her eyes and focused on keeping her breathing even. Closer, he had to be much closer before she attempted anything.

He shifted farther up the mattress, beside her hip. His hand touched the top of her bare thigh. Ally's muscles coiled in preparation.

Her palpable tension seemed to please him. Despite her concentrated efforts not to, from the corner of her eye she noticed his visible arousal. Mouth dry, throat convulsing, she remained still.

Freakishly soft fingers skimmed her pelvis before covering her belly. She trembled. He smiled. The sick pervert was having a grand time.

Maybe she should aim for his joystick. Put him out of commission and do women everywhere a huge favor.

"You have beautiful skin, doll-face."

Grinning, he yanked her down flat on the mattress. Her body covered the rip, hiding her only means of self-defense and sheer, unadulterated panic surged through her. Her brain fogged.

She lashed out, hitting him with her fists and trying to wriggle out of his grasp.

The sick freak laughed and jumped on top of her. He grabbed her wrists and anchored them over her head in one hand, his grip so hard her fingers stung. His erection pressed against her and she screamed.

"Music to my ears," Ally heard him say through the haze of terror.

His lips cruised over her neck as she strained away from him. He bit and sucked, and her skin crawled with revulsion. She lurched upward into a hard arch, trying to fling him off. He groaned and rubbed his erection against her.

Sliding down, he nudged aside the flimsy bra, licked her nipple and bit down. Pain crashed through her and she bowed off the bed, her scream echoing in the room.

Fighting her fear, she pushed through the veil of pain. Instinct demanded she withdraw to the safe place in her mind. Common sense said otherwise. She could *not* slip away or she'd be trapped in this hell forever.

Victor lifted off her slightly, glanced down her body and groaned. She followed his gaze. What few clothes she'd been wearing had shifted in their struggle, spreading her thighs and baring her pelvis completely. Degradation burned. He licked his lips, released one of her wrists and slid his fingers into her most intimate folds.

Closing her mind to what was happening to her body, she reached under her back and fumbled for the rip in the mattress. Tears ran down her temples and into her hair as she searched, fingers trembling. Victor moved to her other breast. He viciously bit the tender underside of her breast, ripping another scream from her.

Sobbing, she found the hole and curled her fingers around the small scissors. Heart thundering, she clutched them.

Ally drew a mental picture of his anatomy and calculated the best place to strike. She would have to touch him to make sure. Steeling her nerves against the revulsion racing through her, she pressed her fingertips to his chest. He didn't even seem to notice while she counted ribs.

Arriving at the location she sought, she maneuvered the sharp point of the scissors into place. She braced her palm over the handles and with a deep breath pushed, putting all her terror, pain and fear into it.

Victor screamed and rose above her on his knees. She followed and gave one more vicious shove, forcing the handles to follow the tip between his ribs. He gasped and his eyes rolled back into his head. He started to fall on top of her, but she used his momentum to propel him off the bed and onto the floor.

A dull satisfying crack echoed in the room as his head made contact with the cement floor. She flew off the bed, panting, adrenaline racing through her veins. Whether she'd killed or only temporarily incapacitated him, Ally didn't dare hang around to find out. She spun away but paused. The opportunity was too much to resist. Drawing back her bare foot, she kicked him in the balls as hard as she could.

Damn, that hurt.

Yanking the door open, she stuck her head out and looked up and down before creeping out into the long hallway.

Biting her lip, she beat back the urge to run, screaming and sobbing like an asylum escapee. Close to the wall, she moved as fast as she dared, shoving her inadequate bra cups back into place with trembling hands. Her knees were like Jell-O and her head swam.

She reached a stairway and went up, grateful she wasn't wearing the heels Victor had forced onto her feet yesterday.

Pausing on the next level, Ally searched the shadows. Nothing moved and her nerves jangled. In a building filled with unwilling sex slaves and who knew what else, the stark silence and empty hallways were eerie. She licked her lips and started down the long hall.

No matter how hard she tried, she couldn't remember how many flights of stairs they'd gone down. Panting with fear, strung out on adrenaline overload, Ally passed numerous doors and wondered how many women lived in this house of horrors.

Another staircase. The lack of consistency in the building's floor plan made it harder to focus and harder to decipher the layout.

Ally climbed up to yet another long hallway. At the head of the stairs, she paused and sidled into deep shadows to catch her breath. Her breathing was coming too fast and she struggled to calm down, to shut out the danger and her fear.

Leaning against the cool wall, she focused on deep, even breathing. She didn't dare close her eyes and refused to count the passing seconds. Her racing heart slowed along with her respiration rate, and she started moving again. A sigh of relief escaped when she reached the end of the hall. Hand on the rail, foot on the first step, she paused—if only she could remember how many stairs Victor had dragged her down.

A big hand clamped over her mouth, a muscled arm clamped around her bare belly and her feet left the stairs as she was yanked into the dark recesses beside the stairwell and held fast against a hard body. What little composure she'd regained fled like seagulls before a hurricane; her vision went black with terror and she screamed.

Chapter Fourteen

His hand muffled what should have been ear-shattering shrieks. Ally fought and squirmed in his grip, jabbing her elbows back. She made contact and a satisfying grunt of pain followed.

"Damn, you have pointy elbows, Ally." The steel band around her body tightened. "Calm down, sweetheart. Shhhh."

Warm breath ruffled the damp hair alongside her face as he whispered in her ear and rubbed her arm. Greg's low voice and familiar touch popped her bubbling panic and she sagged against him.

He soothed her, his touch and scent so reassuring tears stung her eyes. "That's right. Just breathe. You're okay. You're safe."

No. She wouldn't be safe until she was far, far away from this place.

A door slammed somewhere in the building, followed by a shout. Fear sprang back to life with fangs and Ally whimpered.

"It's okay, baby."

By increments, he eased his hold on her, as if afraid she'd collapse. When she stood on her own, he took her hand.

"All right. Follow me and stick close to the walls."

Staring at his back, she did exactly that. He'd found her. Braved the lion's den to rescue her. Her heart swelled.

Shouts and thuds followed them as they raced through the

maze of hallways and stairs. Down a long hallway, Ally spotted light ahead. Brilliant, beautiful, natural sunlight.

Her eyes widened. Men slinked past in the opposite direction wearing black vests buckled over their chests with big black guns cradled in their arms. Greg had brought the troops to rescue her. Thick emotion tightened her throat.

The men stalked like silent predators down each side of the dim corridor. One of them turned, gave her a quick salute and grinned.

She and Greg burst out the door. Ally closed her eyes against the blinding sunshine, tripped and slammed into Greg. He swore beneath his breath and swept her up into his arms.

She hid her face against his neck. Buried alive came the closest to describing the feeling. Surely months had passed in the interim.

Squinting, she raised her head to stare at the building looming over them. Greg's long stride carried them across the street and out of its menacing shadow. He sat her on the crisp sheet of a stretcher and someone draped a warm blanket over her bare shoulders.

His eyes narrowed, clouding with concern. The hot sting of shame swept over her and she turned away, closing her eyes against his scrutiny.

Greg gently tugged the blanket closed. "You had me worried."

Sighing, she looked at him. "Sorry." Unsure what else to say, she stared at her lap.

"How are you feeling?"

"Okay." Outside the open rear doors of the ambulance, people hurried past. Ally's head throbbed. Had everyone gotten out of the building? "What's going on?"

"We're taking apart Victor's little business. If I had my way, it would be brick by brick." His mouth tightened to a grim line. "And limb by limb."

She appreciated—and shared—the sentiment.

"What's going to happen to the women?" She fiddled with the edge of the blanket.

"That depends. It will take time to sort everyone out and find out who belongs where. I imagine some will be in desperate need of medical attention."

Ally nodded, fighting back visions of the violence she'd witnessed. "There was a beautiful Oriental woman. She helped me. Her name is Jia Li. I wouldn't have…" She paused, swallowing hard. "I don't think I would have survived without her."

Greg's fists clenched. "I'll ask around." He hesitated. "Ally, I…" He ran a hand through his blonde hair. "Damn, I was so worried I wouldn't be able to find you in time. Tracking down Victor's holdings, finding the right one and getting a warrant took so long. Too long." His chest expanded and he squeezed his eyes shut. "Can you tell me what happened in there, sweetheart? Did anyone… Were you…Ah, hell."

Nausea swirled through her with the realization of what he was asking. She'd lived with the horrid possibility for three days, but her worst fears had gone unrealized. Fragmented light spilled through her badly tarnished thoughts. "I wasn't raped."

His head snapped up and he stared hard at her, took a step forward, stopped and shoved his hands in his pants pockets. More light spilled into her, dispelling the gloom. Hope.

"Greg, would you hold me? Please?"

He closed the space between them in a blink and eased her into his arms like she was made of spun glass. She closed her eyes and snuggled into his embrace. He felt so good. Smelled so good. The horror of her captivity receded. The memories weren't gone by any stretch, and likely wouldn't be for a long time, but they were less stark.

She'd missed him so much. Her belly tightened. *So not panic-worthy. Get a grip.* If he stomped all over her heart, she'd survive and be stronger for it. Just like she had survived the last few days.

Ally opened her eyes and looked at his shirt fisted in her hands. Hands covered in Victor's blood. She gasped and jerked back, but the damage had been done. He had bloody prints on his shirt.

Greg stared at her, as if he could see right through her, into her. He glanced at his shirt. She flinched. After everything she'd witnessed inside that hell-hole, she didn't want him seeing the evidence of what she'd been reduced to. Turning her face away, she squeezed her eyes shut against the hot sting of tears. A few escaped anyway.

"Baby." His thumb followed the damp trail down her cheek. "It's okay. The paramedic will clean you up while I try to find Jia Li for you." He turned her back to face him, but she kept her gaze focused on her lap. Sighing, he released her. "I'll be back in a few minutes."

He jumped down with the ease of a natural athlete and disappeared around the side. A rush of emotion slammed into her like a tsunami and her shoulders drooped. The interior of the ambulance was all sparkling and sanitary. Her wavy reflection in the cabinet caught her eye; a motley of blue, green and yellow, with a few ragged cuts thrown in for interest. She grimaced.

A package of wet wipes sat on the narrow bench beside the gurney. She roughly scrubbed her hands, front and back and in between her fingers. The large wipes turned pink, then dirty brown. There was even blood under a few of her fingernails. She scrubbed those clean too. If only the memories could be scrubbed away so easily.

Snapshots of the past few days swarmed. Her throat closed and her vision swam.

Greg reappeared as Ally debated the merits of a full blown melt-down, so handsome it hurt to look at him. He grinned and stepped aside.

"Jia Li!"

"You did it." Jia Li clasped her hands in front of her, looking two seconds away from bowing. "We all free now. You did it."

"You did it too." Ally reached out her hand, and Jia Li clambered into the ambulance and sat beside her. Jia Li didn't take her hand, keeping her own tightly clasped in her lap.

Greg leaned a shoulder against the doorframe and crossed his arms.

Jia Li shook her head. "I do nothing."

"That's not true." Ally leaned forward, intent on making Jia Li see the part she had played in freeing herself. "You had the courage to give me those scissors. I would never have gotten past Victor without your help."

Jia Li shivered. Ally badly wanted to hug the woman, to share her pain and offer comfort. She refrained. From her own short experience in the hell-hole, she knew Jia Li wouldn't be comfortable with casual physical contact. Instead, she poured her heart into her words.

"You are a remarkably brave woman, you know."

Jia Li's demure posture remained unchanged.

Ally fought a frustrated sigh as she met Greg's eyes.

"You must be one strong lady," Greg said.

Jia Li glanced at his face before focusing on a spot over his shoulder.

"There's a reward on Victor's head. Sounds to me like you were instrumental in his capture and deserve the money."

Ally's eyes widened and Greg winked at her. Light pink suffused Jia Li's cheeks, a sparkle lit her blue eyes and her slender shoulders straightened. The dawning of hope.

Greg had given Jia Li the means to start a new life. Except, there wasn't a reward. Or there hadn't been. With absolute certainty, Ally knew the reward money would be coming from Greg's personal account. Beaten and bruised, sitting in the back of an ambulance in slutty underwear and a scratchy wool blanket, Ally lost the last piece of her heart.

A commotion across the street drew Ally's gaze, but Greg blocked her view before she could see what was going on. She frowned and met his gaze just as a vulgar curse spoken with a familiar lisp colored the air. Light-headed with dismay, she squeezed her eyes shut.

"Victor is still alive." Her voice sounded flat, even to her.

Greg sighed and touched two fingertips to her cheek. "You don't want his death on your conscious, sweetheart. No matter what he did, it's a heavy weight to carry."

After seeing Jia Li safely off, Greg whisked Ally to a downtown boutique hotel and took her painfully given statement before disappearing. Taking care of police business. The flash of big hulking male hovering outside her door when he left reassured her she'd be safe in his absence.

After wandering aimlessly through the ridiculously large suite, Ally sank into the whirlpool tub in the bathroom and scrubbed away the memories and humiliation until her skin was rosy. Steam rose. The citrus oil she'd poured into the water scented the air. The hot water numbed her skin and soothed her muscles, melting away her assorted aches and pains.

She rested her head against the tub pillow and closed her eyes. The past several days seemed more nightmare than reality. Unwilling to dwell on them, she shoved the unpleasant memories aside.

Pounding on the bathroom door woke her.

"Ally? You okay? Ally!"

"I'm fine." She couldn't have slept long, the water was still hot. "I'll be out in a sec."

"No problem. Take your time."

A few minutes later, she emerged, a billow of lemon-scented steam following her out of the bathroom. The fluffy white hotel robe covered her to the tips of her toes, and an equally fluffy towel was twisted around her head.

She had resisted looking in the mirror. As if the depravity she'd witnessed, the horror and hours spent locked in the subterranean levels of a building would be stamped across her features. Rationally, she knew it wasn't possible, but her emotional side wasn't so sure. Plus, part of her was vain enough to be worried about permanent damage.

Greg was seated at the table in front of the balcony, sipping from a coffee cup. Wonderful aromas wafted from the large white bag sitting on the round table.

Bypassing all of the lovely temptations of Greg and food, she stood in front of the glass-paned French doors and stared out over the city. The brilliant colors streaking the sky as the sun set soothed her soul. Sunshine and the freedom to look out the window with the world at her feet.

Ally opened the French doors and walked to the edge of the balcony, closing her eyes and tilting her face. A light breeze kissed her skin.

Greg came up behind her and grasped the railing on either side of her body, surrounding her. Leaning back against him, she watched the sun sink beneath the horizon. The feel of him, the warmth, the solid strength, his spicy scent wrapping around her, was so right she bit back a moan of appreciation. He wrapped his arms tight around her and she tipped her head back to rest on his shoulder. Heaven.

Two seconds later, she needed more. She turned in his arms, needing …him.

Wrapping her arms around his neck, wallowing in the fathomless green of his eyes, she toyed with the curls at the back of his neck and drank him in. He must have read her feelings, her intentions, in her expression.

"Ally, are you sure? After all you've been through…"

"I'm sure. Please," she whispered. "I need this. I need you."

His eyes shuttered and her heart clutched.

She couldn't stand it if he denied her now.

"I don't know if this is such a good idea."

"Please, Greg. Wipe away the ugly memories. Give me new ones. Good ones." She should have been embarrassed to plead with a man to make love to her.

He cupped her cheeks in his big hands. "A woman like you doesn't need to beg. You were made for loving."

With his words echoing sweetly in the air, his mouth took hers.

No hesitation, no room for second thoughts. His tongue swept inside her mouth, and she matched him stroke for stroke. He pulled back and snagged her hand. As soon as they cleared the threshold, he pressed her up against the wall and untied her robe.

His callused fingers smoothing over the tender underside of her bare breasts sent shivers across her skin. She allowed her head to fall back and Greg took advantage by dropping soft kisses along the column of her throat. He licked and sucked at the crook of her neck. Desire coiled, tightening her belly.

She throbbed and ached, moaning. He shattered her inhibitions. Desperate for the feel of his skin on hers, she tugged at his clothes. He grabbed the back of his shirt and pulled it over his head.

Ally rubbed against him, brushing her hard nipples back and forth across the rough hair on his chest. They both groaned. Sweeping her up in his arms, he laid her on the bed.

His mouth and hands drove her to the brink and soothed her down, time and again, until she thought she'd go mad. Squirming and writhing in his arms, arching against him, Ally tried to pull him up so she could reach more of him. He evaded her attempts deftly, frustrating her.

"Greg. Please."

"Please what, sweetheart?"

"Let me touch you." She barely recognized her husky voice.

"Not this time, baby."

His mouth slid down her soft belly. A distant, old part of her urged her to squirm away in self-conscious agony, but she ignored it. Greg demolished every prior, lackluster memory of sex, until all she knew was him. His scent, his mouth and the glide of his hands and clever fingers. His low whispers of praise should have tinted her cheeks pink with embarrassment.

Greg twirled his tongue around her, pushed two fingers inside and she burst through the invisible barrier. Wave after wave of pleasure washed over her.

Sated, limbs weighted down, Ally opened her eyes to stare at him. He leaned over her, his big body blocking out everything but him, his deep gaze trapping her. Greg slid his arms under and around her, holding her tight as he pushed into her body. He took her soaring with him, every stroke and every touch of his body taking her higher.

Gaze locked on his, she wrapped herself around him. Her legs around his hips opened her more fully and he thrust deep inside her. Another orgasm crashed through her and she cried out, her inner muscles milking him until he stiffened, groaning his pleasure into her neck.

The words tumbled from her lips before she could snatch them back. "I love you."

Greg kissed a sensitive spot on her neck. Dread coiled in Ally's belly, replacing the lingering warmth. Slowly, his head came up. Still buried inside her, he wore his cop face, unreadable to the world. Even so, turmoil roiled in his eyes.

Without a word, he kissed her, deep and long. He moved, thrust and she gasped. He was still hard. Part of her savored his desire for her, while another, deeper, part wept. Greg didn't love her and likely never would.

Helpless to resist her body's response, Ally arched into him. She wrapped her arms and legs around him, trying not to hold too tight, as he took her to paradise again.

Chapter Fifteen

Opening her eyes to the sun streaming through the windows, a smile grew. The memory of every perversion of intimacy she'd witnessed had been banished to distant lands, thanks to Greg's mind-blowing lovemaking. While the city outside their windows slept, Greg had learned every inch of her, until her body responded to his touch like a well-honed instrument.

Rolling onto her belly, Ally searched the room. She wanted to thank him properly. Thoroughly. In a way she'd never thanked a man before.

The stillness of the room finally penetrated the lingering fog of sleep and passion-induced languor. She sat up, the sheet sliding to her waist. Ignoring it, she scrambled off the bed and stood naked in the middle of the room. While she wasn't surprised Greg had taken off, she couldn't quite suppress the stinging pain of reality.

Running a hand through her tangled hair, she sighed, wincing. Greg's last impression of her must have been lovely. Mouth wide open, drool pooling beneath her cheek, bird's nest of hair.

In the bathroom mirror, an alternative vision greeted her. Instead of something the cat dragged in, she gaped at a well and truly pleasured woman, unmarred by the yellowed bruises and healing cuts. Snapshots of last night rolled through her mind. Sensory memories pebbled her nipples and reawakened desire pooled low in her belly.

A-cat-got-the-canary smile spread.

Her gaze traveled over all the naked flesh reflected back at her. Days ago she would have flinched away. A newfound sense of self, of her value, unfurled and stretched. Assorted marks, reminders of Greg's incredible lovemaking, were scattered across her creamy skin, much more memorable than the ones from Victor.

A hot bath was in order, with fizzing bath salt from the jar the hotel provided. As she sank into the steaming water, she realized what a difference a few hours could make. Just yesterday she had laid her head in the same spot, pushing aside her horrifying experiences at Victor's hands.

Today, she relished the little aches reminding her of Greg's hands. And mouth. And…other body parts.

Reluctant to wash Greg's scent off, she nonetheless set to work scrubbing her skin pink and shampooing her hair. Laying back in the water, eyes closed and ears submerged beneath the water, she drifted.

"You're so beautiful." Greg's mouth had brushed back and forth across hers, teasing her. In the moonlight, his eyes were dark and mysterious, gleaming down at her. She wrapped her arms around him.

"No, I'm not."

"And argumentative. You remind me of a Greek goddess; gorgeous curves draped in fabric, lounging on a couch while some poor besotted fool dangles grapes against those gorgeous lips."

The image he painted in husky whispers enraptured her. Then he kissed each and every one of the curves he adored, until she was a mindless puddle of female satisfaction. Every square inch of skin thoroughly worshipped and praised.

Ally blinked the memory away and wiped a few bittersweet tears from her cheeks. Skin tingling, she dried off slowly, rubbing lemon-scented oil all over her body. Savoring her memories of the previous night.

As she put the finishing touches to her hair, she arrived at several important decisions.

The best way to deal with a snake was to cut its head off. So she needed to find out who was after her, one way or another. This had gone on long enough. Too many people had been hurt.

More importantly, she would no longer hide in her job and her home, avoiding life and love. Even if it hurt, even if it broke her heart, the time to embrace life was now. Last night she'd gained more than a night of incredible lovemaking.

Ally had found herself.

In the bedroom, she made the big bed, smoothing a hand fondly over the sheets. She picked up a few scattered pillows and tossed them onto the comforter. Straightening the room made her feel better. A stranger coming in, mercilessly stripping the bed bare and carting the sheets away without a thought seemed…wrong.

She was reaching for the door when it burst open.

Greg stopped shy of dumping two steaming cardboard cups down her front. Which would have been a real shame, since she wore the gorgeous sundress she'd found draped over a chair.

"Hi," they said in unison, grinning at one another like a couple of teenagers.

Greg cleared his throat and stepped around her. "I brought breakfast." He headed for the little table beside the balcony. "I figured you'd be starving."

"I am." She was unable to wipe away her smile.

"Yeah, me too." He grinned, so handsome and endearing, she stumbled.

He grabbed her arm, bringing her flush against him. "Whoa."

Faces inches apart, his eyes focused on her mouth, and her body leapt to life. Ally wet her lips. Greg dropped her arm and stepped back, shoving a hand through his hair.

"This okay?" He gestured to the table behind him, "Or would you prefer to sit outside?"

"Whichever." She wanted to stomp her foot. How could she feel awkward with him after last night?

"So…" they said at the same time.

"You first." Ally took a sip of her nonfat chai tea latte and ducked her head, smiling. He remembered what she liked from Starbucks.

"I spoke with my captain this morning. I snuck you away from the scene yesterday, no one the wiser, for a reason." He pushed a slice of pumpkin bread across the table. She broke off a piece and savored the moist explosion of flavor on her tongue.

"My captain agreed with me. We've already discovered several leaks in the department, and I've come up with a way to use them. The world at large is going to go on thinking you're dead—for a few more days, at least. Other people will soon hear otherwise." He held up his hand when she opened her mouth to object. "Let's discuss it with the captain before you say yes or no, okay?"

She tightened her lips, frustration humming and tingling in her fingertips.

Greg's eyes narrowed. "Ally…"

"You know best. I just hate all this." She reached for the comfort of his hand.

Greg sat back, out of reach, his expression closing down as thoroughly as a bank vault at five on Friday. "This is the best plan we can come up with for flushing this guy out. I know it won't be pleasant for you. If there were any other solution, I'd be all for it. So, unless you have any ideas…" He stared at her with a raised brow.

Misery and rejection tightened her stomach. She pushed away the half-eaten pumpkin bread. Her appetite had fled as surely as a flock of geese before a group of noisy hunters. Which was about how she felt. Hunted. "No, I don't have any ideas."

Silence descended. Ally sipped her latte.

Greg seemed lost in a world of his own.

"This sucks."

"Yeah." He rose and held out a hand to help her from her chair. For a second, she debated refusing and remaining where she was, which served no purpose except to annoy him, and no matter how satisfying that sounded, it was also childish.

So she accepted with more grace than she felt and stood without touching him. "What now?"

"Now we bait the trap."

Dread and resignation reigning supreme, she followed him to the door and paused, turning to glance around the suite one last time.

Her gaze swung back to Greg, but his eyes were inscrutable. Just her luck to fall for a man petrified of his emotions. Or maybe he was afraid of hers. Regardless, the result was the same. She was a child with her nose pressed against the glass of her favorite candy store and no money in her pocket. So close and yet so far.

She pulled the door closed. "What trap? Do I even want to know what the bait is?"

"I won't sugarcoat it. Our plan involves the most risk for you. If I could change places with you, I would in a heartbeat."

Little tension lines popped up around his eyes. Eyes that wouldn't meet hers. The new expression wasn't any better than his blank mask. "Why should you take on more danger than you already have?"

"Because it's my job!" he shouted.

His words echoed in the stark silence. Another peek at him revealed a reddish tint to his cheeks. Shocking. And amazing. All the different personality traits one conversation could reveal.

"Okay. Still, your friend and your sister have already been hurt by this." She sucked in a breath and straightened her shoulders. "Which is one of the reasons I'm willing to do whatever it takes to finish this. Plus..." She forced a smile, trying to lighten the mood. "You can't be on twenty-four/seven guard duty forever. What will happen when you have to, oh, I don't know, work?"

"I've *been* working. What do you think all this has been about?" He gestured down the hall toward the room. The beefy guard from last night stood five feet away, studying the tips of his shoes.

She barely registered his presence around the roaring in her ears.

Blood rushed to her cheeks then away again, leaving her chilled and shaken. Believing he refused to get emotionally involved because of his history was one thing. Knowing he viewed her merely as another case was entirely another. Just a citizen to serve and protect. Or service. All her old insecurities rushed in to choke off her new growth.

"Ally, I didn't mean..."

She held up a hand. Took a deep breath. Another. She pushed aside a lifetime's worth of self-doubt and poor self-esteem. Tossed out her mother's incessant nagging and her classmates' cruel digs about her weight.

Greg swore and reached out a hand, which she neatly sidestepped.

She knew, with steely-eyed certainty, if he touched her now, she'd lose it. So she fought back her emotions and waited until she was certain she could speak without pain strangling her voice.

"Please don't. It's fine. Really." She even managed a smile. "Let's just get this over with, okay?"

"I didn't mean being with you was work, Ally. I had a great time last night."

A great time. Well, good to know. The way her stomach was cramping, she wouldn't be able to eat for a week. Since he seemed to be awaiting a response, she forced a smile. "That's ... great."

"You're a great girl."

Ally flinched and Greg muttered another curse, running his hand through his hair.

"I'm doing this all wrong, aren't I?"

She had no response and glanced down the hall at the guard, her cheeks burning. He was giving the tried-and-true break-up speech in a hotel hallway with a stranger to witness her humiliation. This week just kept getting better and better.

"I just...I don't do the whole relationship thing, Ally." Greg held his hands out, looking confused and frustrated and breaking her heart with every word.

"I know. You told me before." Her dry eyes were hot with emotion. She blinked a few times and forced another smile. "It's fine, Greg. Let's just go."

She waited out of sight while he checked out of the hotel, feeling mildly slutty as he paid for the room and she remembered how they passed the night. Guess she'd learned more from Victor than she thought. Silent as a tomb, she followed him out the rear entrance and graciously let him hustle her into his rental without complaint.

He settled into his seat and sat with his broad hands, hands intimately familiar with every inch of her body, clenching the steering wheel.

Staring straight ahead at the uninspiring alleyway scenery, she broke the thick silence. "Tell me what you need from me."

It was a loaded question, but she fully expected him to dodge any personal interpretation. He didn't disappoint, even if he appeared to be gritting his teeth, judging from the muscles working in his jaw. In another lifetime, after she'd swept up the shattered pieces of her heart and painstakingly glued them back together, she might even manage to feel sorry for him.

Right now, such a generous emotion was simply beyond her. Sitting near him and listening to the rumble of his deep voice took every ounce of strength, every bit of nerve she'd so recently learned she possessed. To smell him and breathe through the certainty she would never be able to call him hers, her boyfriend, her lover, her husband, her anything.

He outlined his plan in meticulous detail. What he was asking of her made her heart throb heavy and hard. Nerves she hadn't known she had a week ago jangled in alarm.

At the police station, he bundled her in a back door. Since there was no back entrance into the captain's office, he threw a long trench coat over her dress and tugged a ball cap low over her face. He swept her down hallways and past curious stares without a word.

Hand on her arm, he steered her, unrelenting as a jungle python gripping its evening meal. Frustration and anger built with each step, until the top of her head felt ready to blow.

She dug in her heels, yanked her arm free and swung around, glaring at him.

"I'm not your prize Doberman out for a brisk evening stroll, Detective." Despite her mounting irritation, Ally managed to hiss the words instead of shouting.

His lips twitched.

Twitched!

Oh, that's it. Spinning on her heel, she marched down the hall. The first bathroom she came to, she darted inside and slammed the door shut with a less-than-satisfying thud. She yanked off the stupid coat and threw it on the floor. Her single lap around the small room came to an abrupt halt when Greg pushed through the door.

Ally narrowed her eyes, blood at full boil. "You can't come in here."

He leaned against the closed door, crossing his arms, watching her with his irritating unfathomable expression. The big jerk.

"Actually, I can. This is the men's room."

She focused on the urinal-lined wall. If wishes counted, Greg would be a frog about now. A big warty one. "I don't care. Get out."

"Make me."

His low voiced taunt froze her in place. "What?"

"Make. Me."

He didn't look unruffled now. His eyes gleamed, watching her like a big cat staring at cornered prey.

She glanced below his belt buckle and her eyes widened. Good night, he had a hard-on. Heat raced over her skin, her traitorous body revving up in response to his arousal. Readying for him.

Oh, hell no.

Greg uncrossed his arms, grabbed the garbage can and heaved it in front of the door before taking a step toward her. She retreated, only recognizing her mistake when his eyes sparked with triumph. He stalked forward, closing the distance. She retreated again.

Just short of a bathroom sink, she stopped and snapped her spine straight. "This is ridiculous. If you think we're going to fool around after all the crap you've thrown at me, you're beyond thick-skulled."

Pulling the tattered mantle of her dignity around her, Ally tried to sidle around him.

"We're gonna more than fool around, babe." He grabbed her around the waist and unceremoniously deposited her on the cold ceramic sink. The chill permeated the sundress so quickly she might as well have been naked. She started to slide backward into the sink. With a small shriek, she lunged forward and latched onto Greg's hard biceps.

His gaze dropped to her lips and his mouth followed, thrusting his tongue inside to tangle with hers, demanding complete surrender.

Not gonna happen.

If they were going to do this – her body gave a resounding cheer of approval – it would be on her terms. She pulled him closer, sank her fingernails into his shoulders and rubbed her breasts against him. His attack paused and his hips twitched. She slid her hands up, grabbed handfuls of his thick hair and angled his head for easier plundering.

He bridged the remaining distance and tugged her bottom closer until she teetered on the edge of the sink, melding her softness against his steel. Ally moaned into his mouth. His palms slid down her thighs and under the hem of her dress, pulling the material up as his hands journeyed toward her hips.

Never breaking from the battleground of their kiss, she impatiently tugged open his blue jeans. Greg's erection sprang into her waiting hands, and she wrapped her fingers around him. His hands reached the junction of her thighs, her thong panties and bare skin offered no barrier when he parted her swollen folds. Thick fingers spread her slick arousal over her and she almost came.

He brushed aside her hand and positioned himself at her entrance.

Breaking their kiss, he held her gaze. A rakishly angled broad hat on his blond head and the image of a victorious pirate would be complete. Something in the depths of his eyes, though...

Greg sank to the hilt and her head dropped back, the exquisite pleasure trembling across her lips on a husky moan. Not giving an inch, she wrapped her legs around his waist. One hand on her bottom, he tugged her head back up and kissed her as he began to move.

Deep and hard, each thrust pushed her closer to the edge. His lips were gentle, the exact opposite of the demanding press of his hips. Greg explored her mouth with delicate thoroughness while his body took unhesitating command of hers.

Ally clung to him, a rock in the storm.

"Ally," he whispered against her lips.

She swore the same emotion she'd seen in his eyes twisted through his passion-roughened voice.

His lips skated along her jaw and down her throat to the sensitive curve at her shoulder. She shivered. He kissed her skin and she trembled. He sucked gently and her muscles clenched. He nibbled and she tumbled into a swirl of exploding stars.

His hips jackknifed against her and he groaned low against her neck as he came.

Gradually, the hard press of the sink against her bottom demanded her attention. The reality of her situation popped the delicate bloom of post-coital glow.

Greg lifted his head, eyes once again shuttered and unreadable. Just as well. She didn't need any more confusion where he was concerned.

She refused to look at him as he helped her off the sink. Frowning over the dampness between her thighs, she adjusted her clothes.

He'd been the poster boy for safe sex the night before.

"I didn't use protection," Greg said, as if reading her thoughts.

He sounded so matter of fact, no hint of regret or apology. Strange. A man like him wouldn't want any unsanctioned rug rats running around. A vision of a baby with blonde curls and eyes the color of the Aegean Sea temporarily blotted out the bathroom.

She managed a careless shrug. "I'm sure it won't be an issue."

Snagging the trench coat off the floor, she brushed past him, pulling the coat on and raising the collar to shield her face. She tugged the cap back into place, painfully aware of Greg's presence right behind her. Respecting the invisible wall she'd erected between them, he didn't lift a finger to help her.

Ally tried to shove the metal garbage can away from the door, and about wrenched her shoulder from its socket. "What is this thing made out of?"

He reached around her and slid the can aside.

Right. Gritting her teeth, hand on the doorknob, she glanced at him. "Shall we?"

With effort, she ignored the wet slide of her thighs as she followed Greg down another hallway. He stopped in front of a closed door, glanced up and down the empty hall, opened the door and basically shoved her inside. Relief etched across his face, he followed her in and shut the door.

"About time you got here, Marsing," a rusty voice barked, startling her.

Hunched over the array of papers scattered across the scarred surface of a massive desk, glaring at them from beneath a shock of bushy white eyebrows, sat the man she'd already met several times. He still in no way resembled her image of a police captain. The extravagance of his eyebrows made up for the lack of hair on top of his head, not counting a few lonely strays, topped off with an overabundance of attitude.

Attitude directed toward Greg. Her sympathy was almost piqued. Almost.

"Sorry, sir."

She hung up the trench coat that smelled miserably of Greg and tossed the cap in a chair, which Greg promptly sat on. He glared at her and yanked the smashed baseball hat out from under his rear end.

Gracefully sitting as far from him as possible, she gave him her most angelic smile.

"This is my favorite hat." Greg slapped the misshapen cap against his thigh.

"Oh?" She batted her lashes, shaping her lips in a round moue of distress. Petty of her, but a woman took her revenge where she could. "What a pity. I do hope it'll be alright."

Ignoring the way his eyes focused on her lips and darkened, ignoring her answering surge of desire, she turned to the captain—who was avidly following their byplay. Which annoyed her to no end. So she hopped up, leaned over the desk and offered her hand.

"Pleased to meet you." Sheer willpower kept her expression bland.

"Oh, right." Greg spoke up behind her. "Captain, meet Ally Thompson. Ally, this is Captain Morgan."

Was the name Greg's idea of a joke? She glanced over her shoulder, but his gaze was fastened on her rear end as she bent over the desk. Guess he wasn't joking. He was too busy being a guy. Captain Morgan grasped her offered hand, and she turned back to him.

His grave expression betrayed nothing, but his gray eyes twinkled. He gave her hand a brisk squeeze. She half expected him to pat her on the head, too, and quickly found her seat again.

"Well, young lady, has Detective Marsing told you all about our little plan?"

"Yes, he has."

The twinkle departed like yesterday's news. "What do you think?"

She bit her lip, unsure how to respond. "Umm…" She glanced

at Greg.

He sprawled in his chair, glowering at nothing in particular.

"Well… frankly it scares the hell out of me."

Greg's eyebrows shot up.

"But I'll do it."

"Good." The Captain's alert gaze shifted to Greg. "How 'bout it, Marsing? We all set to move on this?"

Greg straightened from his slouch. "Yes."

"Run me through the plan again. Let's make sure there aren't any holes for Miss Thompson to fall through."

"As we discussed, I've run my mouth all morning about how some woman I'm protecting is insisting on going back to the scene of her abduction today to show me where Victor abducted her and walk me through the process. Locker-room talk, the works. I've got a few ex-military buddies providing back-up at the park, where I hope to pick up the head honcho. He's got to be frustrated at this point, hearing about this latest failure on top of the other ones."

"You trust these friends of yours?" the Captain asked.

"With my life. They'll keep the area tight as a tick's ass, sir." Greg gave a respectful nod.

Ally rolled her eyes. "What's happening with the Victor situation?"

They exchanged a look she couldn't interpret.

"Well…" Captain Morgan folded his hands on top of the desk. "Victor is under armed guard at the local hospital. As soon as he's released, he'll be transported to jail. That'll be a bit yet, since his injuries include a collapsed lung and other internal damage." He grinned. "Nice job, by the way."

Tension crept up her spine. She didn't want to think about what had happened within those walls, not even her escape. Jia Li, though… "What about the women?"

His expression turned serious. "That's a bit trickier. Some of them were there so long they hardly know anything else. Identifying the women and tracking down families will take time. In some cases, we're dealing with young girls who've been missing so long they no longer resemble any photos, on top of which they're so traumatized or ashamed they refuse to speak to anyone—male or female. Composite sketches have to be created and run through missing persons. Meanwhile, we're fielding thousands of calls from parents of abducted children, attorneys, press and every Tom, Dick, and Harry—otherwise known as concerned citizens, within four hundred square miles." He spread his hands. "We're doing all we can, and they're as comfortable as possible in the meantime."

"Where are they?"

"You can't see them, Ally," Greg said. "You don't want that kind of attention. The media is camped outside the place."

She refused to spare him a glance.

"We've moved them all to a local women's shelter. The place has tight security because of previous run-ins with abusive husbands, not to mention on-staff counselors to help any of the women who want it. Unfortunately, we have to keep them in lockdown. The women who've accepted our help or are underage, anyway. There's some concern about the men they've…uh…associated with could try to get to them. Victor had some pretty high-powered people as clients. Once we've sorted everyone out, I imagine some of the women will enter the protection program."

Ally crossed her arms, not pleased. Those poor women had gone from one cage to another. Still, she could see the rationale of it. Even if she didn't like it.

"We're doing everything in our power to help them. I believe we've covered everything, Detective. I'm counting on you to make sure nothing happens to Miss Thompson. She's taking a huge leap of faith here. Let's not reward her confidence by failing to keep her safe. Again."

Greg's hand tightened under Ally's elbow as he lifted her from the chair. She hid a shiver of awareness. Greg was so good at maintaining his careless façade, she had no way of knowing if he was aware of her reaction. At the door, Ally shoved her arms into the smothering trench coat and slapped the ball cap over her head.

Tipping the brim up with a finger, she caught Captain Morgan's roguish wink and smiled.

"It was lovely meeting you again, Captain Morgan."

"You too. Hopefully next time will be under more pleasant circumstances. Take care out there. I hate putting you in this situation after all you've been through. If we had any other option…" He shook his head and waved her out the door.

Ally highly doubted there would be a "next time," but she held onto her smile and nodded. They didn't exactly move in the same circles. Neither did Greg, who steered her out the door.

This time, thank you very much, she left the building under her own steam. She even opened her door, got herself into Greg's car and shut the door. All alone. See what a grown-up girl she was?

Ally barely restrained from snorting. Yeah, right.

Refusing to look at Greg, she glowered out her window. They were parked in a corner between two buildings, most of the car hidden from view. The sounds of him settling into his seat and the musky, spicy scent of his cologne magnified. Ally shook her head in disgust. Somewhere in the past twenty-four hours, her body had clearly gone into overdrive, determined to make up for the sad state of her love life the last few years.

Oh, who was she kidding? Her love life had been a pathetic, scrawny, substance-deprived, weed of a thing ever since she'd developed an interest in *having* one. Throw in the insidious little voice whispering in her ear, telling her to enjoy every aspect of Greg while he was still available, and she had a regular World War III. Her heart versus her head. Either way, something was going to wind up bloodied.

Everything revolved around one question, really. Did she want to spend the fraction of time she had left with Greg pouting?

Ally became aware of the painful degree of silence within the confines of the car. Wary, she met Greg's gaze. "What?"

"Just wondering how long your little snit is going to last. We have a lot to accomplish and I don't want it interfering."

So much for romance. More the fool for even thinking such a thing. Sweet as apple pie à la mode on a hot summer day, she smiled. "My mood is dandy. I'm just contemplating the previously unknown joys of bathroom sex. Don't worry yourself about coming up a little…" She glanced down at his lap and widened her smile. "Short."

He continued to stare at her. Waiting for a second head to sprout?

"What?"

Greg shrugged, finally starting the car, but he made no move to shift into drive. Probably missing the rumbling power of his Camaro. The sedate, uninspiring mid-size sedan, hardly compared.

Maybe she'd trade in her Prius for something else. Something a bit more fun, a bit more sporty. *Not* a Camaro.

Licking her lips, she tasted Greg. The memory of his body against her, inside her, sped up her pulse. She shifted in her seat. Her panties rubbed against her clit and Ally bit her lip against a moan. She dropped her head back against the headrest and closed her eyes. *Focus on something else. Anything else.*

When had she turned into a raging nympho? She met Greg's gaze. "So, uh…you've put the word out? All systems are go?"

"Oh, yeah." His voice dropped an octave, the husky tone setting her squirming in the seat again.

She didn't know who moved first. Greg hauled her across the narrow space to straddle his lap while she voraciously ate at his mouth, sucking on his tongue and nipping his lips. She coasted her hands under his shirt and moaned into his mouth at the feel of his skin.

Ally yanked off his shirt and curled her fingers in his coarse chest hair, reveling in the sensation. His hands massaged her bare bottom, and she sent out a silent thank you for the indecent panties she was wearing. She'd been too mad and too far gone to appreciate the lack of coverage in the bathroom, but no more.

One of his hands disappeared. A click sounded and his seat dropped back, offering her so much more to touch and more room to maneuver. He fumbled his pants open, lifted her up and onto him. They both groaned as he slid into her slick heat.

Watching the passion etched across his face, she began to move. Greg pushed the straps of her dress down, baring her breasts and cupped them. He rolled her nipples between his fingers. She sucked in air and slammed down on him a little harder than she'd intended.

His eyes narrowed to slits and the muscles in his neck corded, but his hands remained gentle, teasing and tormenting her. Ally found a rhythm she liked, hitting the perfect spot inside and out. Each stroke of her body over his drew her muscles tighter.

She fought for control, her movements jerky. He gripped her hips, helping her slide along his rigid length. Watching her ride him. Seeing too much.

Love swelled and pressed like a trapped bird against her ribcage. Emotion had to be written all over her face. She didn't care; she was determined to selfishly take everything he offered.

She sobbed with the effort to hold back.

"Shhh, baby." Greg pulled her head down to him, spreading gentle kisses across her flushed face. Big hands smoothed up and down her back as he held her, cradled her close like she mattered to him. As if all of his words to the contrary meant nothing.

She ached in a way she couldn't describe. Sometimes, actions really did speak louder than words. He fought so hard to keep her safe, to rescue her when she needed. What lay between them couldn't be all about his job. The way he made love to her didn't feel like a temporary fling, even if she didn't have a ton of experience to draw from.

Ally tightened her muscles around his throbbing erection and his hands returned to her hips, guiding her up and down. The musky scent of their lovemaking filled the steamy interior of the car. She kissed him and his hands tightened, squeezing her bottom.

Greg gave her everything she needed, and his tenderness was her undoing. She cried out, sinking down onto him. Felt his answering groan against her lips and the throb where their bodies were joined.

She rested her cheek on his bare chest, his thundering heart beneath her ear and pressed a kiss to his skin. Aware of the unrelenting passage of time, the sound of cars coming and going around them and thankful for the tinted windows and overcast sky. The steady rhythm of his heart soothed her.

"We need to go, sweetheart."

"I know."

Reluctance made her limbs heavy as she sat up. Greg's expression was tense, his green eyes guilty. Why? For making love to her? Because she loved him? Or for using her as bait? She ran a finger along his square jaw.

"None of this is your fault, you know."

"It's not exactly yours, either."

"No. I just think you try to take on the world, and this isn't something I want you to bear the burden for. You carry enough on your shoulders."

His eyes turned bleak. "I care about you, but I can't stop who I am, Ally. It's my job to take risks. I'm damn good at my job. At least, I used to be. You shouldn't have to put yourself in danger to catch a bad guy."

"It's my decision to make, Surfer Dude."

Greg smiled, but it didn't reach his eyes.

Her heart squeezed.

"Did you join the police because of what happened to your parents?"

"I don't know. Maybe." His gaze dropped and he fiddled with her dress. "Experiencing something like that firsthand probably influenced my choices. Guess I wanted to be someone's hero, after failing my family."

"How can you think that?" Holding his face in her hands, she waited until he met her eyes. "What happened to your parents was completely out of your control. You became a father figure to your sister. You took care of her and provided a home for her. You stood beside her, even with your own life destroyed. You are the definition of a hero, with or without your job."

He didn't say a word.

"You don't want any real relationships with a woman because of what happened to your family."

His expression shut down so fast she blinked. "What?"

Ally glanced down where her fingers lay tangled in his chest hair and shrugged. "I saw a picture of you with a girl at some formal dance. You were doing a pretty good imitation of a couple and you looked young, high-school age, so I just thought..." What could she say? That she wanted to believe she was more than a convenient lay?

"Look, I care about you. I've already told you that. I don't know what more you want from me."

She flinched. Stretching past him, she snagged his discarded shirt off the backseat. She ran the fabric through her fingers, fighting tears. Blinking rapidly, she pressed the shirt against his chest and slid off his lap into her own seat.

He *cared* about her. Rubbing her hand over her heart, Ally turned away.

Greg drove out of the parking lot. Anything could happen, but ten to one, tonight would be the last time she saw Detective Greg Marsing. A tear slipped free and she impatiently brushed it away.

Chapter Sixteen

Greg pulled into the park—the same park Victor had abducted her from only days ago.

Ally fought the urge to vomit. *Crap. I can't do this.*

"You okay?"

Deep breath. This was totally doable. Piece of cake. "Dandy."

He threw the car into park and took her cold hand in his. "Ally, you don't have to do this."

She pulled her hand free. If only she believed him, she would walk away without a qualm. "You said you were bringing in a couple of friends and the area is secure." See? She could be reasonable. "Who are these friends, anyway?"

"I grew up with them. Frank is a commercial airline pilot who did time in the Air Force. We're lucky he happened to be in town. Ted is a chef at Les Poulets Rouge. He's scary with knives. Probably goes back to preparing meals for Special Ops guys. Then there's Georgie. She's fierce, but three tours of duty and she retired to decorate people's houses." He shrugged. "Go figure."

"You trust them?"

He rubbed a hand over his face and tightened his other one on the steering wheel until his knuckles shone white. "With my life."

Ally tried on a smile, for his sake as much as hers. "If you trust your friends to keep us safe, so do I."

She made a grab for the door handle, but Greg was faster. He pulled her back for a quick, fierce kiss. His expression was unreadable when he released her, but one side of his mouth kicked up.

"Let's do this, Sugar Lips."

"Right, and I'll just pretend my legs aren't rubber after that kiss." She shoved her door open. He was standing at her side before she'd even closed the door. "What exactly did you 'accidentally' leak?"

"The usual crap. How lame it was to be forced to follow some chick on a self-help trip."

"Gee, thanks."

"No problem, doll-face." He grinned.

An image of Victor leering at her flashed before her eyes and she swayed.

"Don't ever call me that. Ever. Victor…he liked…that's what he called me."

Greg took a step back. "Never again. I promise."

His voice sounded harsh, choked, and she glanced at him. Set in granite would be a good way to describe his expression, except for the ticking muscle in his jaw.

"So…" Ally cleared her throat. "How do I know your buddies from the bad guy?"

"You won't see Ted or Frank. Georgie will be around. She said something about a disguise. One thing we do know is our man is exactly that. A man. So unless Georgie comes gussied up like a guy, we're good."

A woman ran past pushing a baby jogger. Long and lithe, toned to a painful degree of perfection. Ally turned and stared until her ponytailed form disappeared around a bend in the trail.

"Speak of the devil."

"What?" They closed in on the curve leading them to the little lake. *We're going fishing and I'm the bait.* Her stomach rolled. Then she got it. "*That* was Georgie?" At his nod, Ally rolled her eyes. "Good night. Why do all the women you know look like supermodels?"

He attempted an innocent expression. Not a good look for him.

The woods opened up and the sun slipped out of the clouds. The glare off the water hit Ally in the face. Squinting, she lifted a hand to shield her eyes.

Something popped. Greg hit her with a football tackle and they slammed into the dirt. Dazed, she lay on the packed-dirt path. Fluffy white clouds floated by overhead. Pain unfurled with slow breath-stealing agony.

Over the buzzing in her ears, someone shouted and Greg rolled off her. Footsteps thumped past.

"This way," a male voice hissed.

Greg jumped to his feet. "You take the right flank, I'll take the left. Set Georgie on the front and Frank on the rear. Do *not* let this guy get away. Ally, stay put."

No problem.

A cloud came into view shaped like a teddy bear. Footsteps thudded away. More pops and the sound of branches breaking. Answering gunshots came from multiple directions. Ally tentatively ran her fingers along her collarbone to the source of the intense pain beneath her right shoulder. Her fingers came away sticky and glistened red in the afternoon sunshine. Black spots flickered on the edge of her vision and she sucked in a painful breath. Getting shot officially sucked.

More gunfire, sounding farther away this time. Shouts, then ominous silence. At least it felt ominous, considering she was lying on the ground bleeding and helpless, and didn't know what was happening.

Someone rushed toward her and she instinctively tried to flinch away, only to be rewarded with searing pain. She gasped.

"We got him, Ally."

Wanting to share his pleasure, she tried to smile but couldn't quite manage it. "Good."

"Yeah."

Greg's handsome face came into view, marred by a dirt smear, a concerned frown pulling his eyebrows together as his gaze took her in. The color drained from his sun-bronzed face and he dropped to his knees beside her. Something warm ran down her side and pooled underneath her. She shivered.

Greg yanked off his T-shirt and pressed the warm fabric to her chest below her right shoulder. Fresh pain roared through her and she closed her eyes.

"Come on. Stay with me, sweetheart."

Ally licked her lips and whispered. "You are *so* bossy."

His laugh sounded strained and shaky.

She struggled to focus on anything other than the exquisitely sharp pain digging deeper into her with each breath. Footsteps thudded to a stop beside her.

"We got him, man. You guys ok…ay? Damn." The new arrival's voice softened. "Bad?"

With more effort than she liked, Ally pried open her eyes and stared at the man looming over them. Big and tanned, with spiky black hair and laugh lines fanning out from sharp, bright- blue eyes. The good ol' boy charm emanating from him was slightly off tune with the bump in his nose and assorted scars on his face.

He also wore a two-thousand-dollar suit, complete with a pink and soft-blue paisley tie and matching pocket triangle. This guy took down a nasty criminal two minutes ago?

"Nah. She'll be up and giving me hell in no time. Ally, this is Ted."

Greg didn't look so good. A little green around the gills and eyes dark with concern.

Ted knelt down on her other side, replacing Greg's hand over the T-shirt. He smiled, remarkably gentle and easy-going for such a big man. "How're you doing, beautiful?"

"Wonderful." She managed to only wheeze a little. "Just give me a sec and I'll be on my feet."

"No rush." His gaze shifted to Greg, who still knelt in the dirt.

Greg's expression shook her more than anything. All the world-weary cynicism was gone, leaving behind wide-open vulnerability—like a lost little boy.

"Marsing."

Greg jerked upright at Ted's bark.

"You need to call this in. Get the medics here ASAP."

"Right. Yeah. Of course." Greg took a few steps away and pulled out his phone.

"So you've been hanging out with ol' Marsing, huh?" Ted's words pulled her attention away from Greg. "He's a real pain in the ass. Don't know how you've stood being around him so long. Pretty sure I would've shoved him off a building by now."

"I resisted. Barely."

Ally never expected to feel this way. Then again, she never thought she'd get shot, but she wouldn't mind seeing a doctor about now. An EMT, a nurse. Heck, she'd settle for a candy striper. Ground vibrations heralded the arrival of more people. Good to know she'd become one with nature.

A tall, good-looking man leaned against a nearby tree, his face inscrutable. The jogger, Georgie, dumped her stroller and spared Ally a brief glance before striding to Greg's side. Georgie and Greg stood shoulder to shoulder, their backs to her. They looked good together. A different kind of pain twisted through Ally and she turned her head away.

Her gaze met Ted's and he winked. "I know what you're thinking, but you're wrong. Trust me. They'd kill each other."

None of her business. Greg had made that clear. "That's Frank? He doesn't look like a Frank."

Ted snorted out a laugh, glancing at Frank before leaning closer to her. "I'll tell you a secret, but he'll kill me if he finds out."

An elephant had taken a seat on her ribs. All the response she could offer was a raised brow.

"His real name is Frankfurt."

"I've always said your big mouth will get you killed one of these days, Ted." Frank didn't move from the tree he was holding up or even change expression. "That day could be today."

Ted winked again. The warmth of his expression and cheerful demeanor didn't quite conceal his concern. Sirens wailed in the distance.

Greg knelt beside her, glanced at Ted and bent so close she could make out the specks of green in his eyes. "Hanging in there, sweetheart?"

Her eyelids were growing unbearably heavy, but Ally managed a wan smile. Sleep was very appealing.

The sirens were louder now. Surely a little nap wouldn't hurt? Just close her eyes for a few minutes?

Greg glanced back at Frank. "Where is he?"

"We made him real cozy a few yards back. He's not going anywhere, but he's not talking either." Frank's voice sounded very different, low and hard. Dangerous.

Greg met her eyes. "I'll be right back."

Ally was losing her battle against the pull of sleep.

"The pros will be here real soon, beautiful," Ted murmured, "and they'll take good care of you."

With effort, she cracked her lids open. Georgie hovered a few feet away, staring at her. Probably trying to figure out the appeal to Greg. Well, what did she know?

"Do you need anything?" the nurse asked, a floral arrangement in her arms.

"I'm fine, thank you." Ally scooted higher in the bed. Nerves tightened her belly as she stared at the flowers.

"These are beautiful." The smiling nurse placed the vase on the window sill, pulled the card out and presented it to Ally. "You're one popular young lady. You've gotten so many flowers in the three days you've been here this place looks like a florist shop."

"It does seem to get people's attention when you return from the dead." A wry smile twisted Ally's lips.

The nurse smiled, checked the water level in a couple of the vases and fiddled with the I.V. bags. She set a tray of bandages on the bed beside Ally's legs, unsnapped her hospital gown, and gently peeled back the bandages from her wound. The nurse set the dirty cotton aside.

"You're healing nicely. There's a very small amount of blood and some clear seepage, which is positive. The stitches from the surgery to repair the damage to your tendons look good." She stepped back and smiled. "I'll get some warm water and bath the edges so you don't feel sticky, then we'll put some clean cotton and tape on you."

She turned away to fill a small bowl at the room's sink, giving Ally a modicum of privacy. She opened the card and hope wilted. Another one of her coworkers wishing a speedy recovery and welcoming her back to the land of the living.

A few minutes later, the nurse left and the silent room settled around Ally. A hollow feeling made itself at home in her stomach. Greg wouldn't be putting in an appearance. He'd told her more than once he didn't do relationships. Sadly, forewarned didn't always equal forearmed.

The door creaked open again and Ted glided in on silent feet. Probably a handy attribute in a busy kitchen for a man his size. She'd never been to Le Poulet Rouge. Five-star restaurants were a bit out of her modest price bracket.

"Hey, beautiful." He dropped a kiss on her cheek. "You're looking perkier by the day."

"Thanks."

He set an elegant take-out container on her bedside tray and glanced at the door. "Contraband," he whispered.

"More?" She reached for it.

He put his hand on top of the box. "No peeking until I've gone. You might injure my fragile ego."

Nodding, she did her best to look earnest. Fragile ego her butt. He dropped into the chair pulled alongside her bed and stretched out his long legs. Despite his expensive suit, he was incongruous with the flowers crowding every nook and cranny. Ted turned his astute gaze on her and addressed the white elephant in the room. "Heard from Marsing?"

Becoming absorbed in a loose thread on the blanket, Ally shrugged. "I've been so busy with coworkers and hospital staff coming and going, I haven't had time to think about it, but now that you mention it, no."

Liar, liar, pants on fire. She'd looked for him upon waking from anesthesia, heart jumping every time the door opened. The second day, she was more hopeful than expectant. By this morning, she'd slipped into a resigned state of depression she refused to dwell on.

"Not even a bouquet of flowers, I see."

Startled, she glanced up. He hadn't even looked at the cards.

"I know Marsing's style. Pretty low, not sending so much as a card."

That stung. "What do you mean? Have you spoken to him?"

He shot her a look full of pity. "It was pretty obvious you two were involved in a lot more than an investigation."

Past tense was more appropriate, apparently. She focused on an especially lovely spray of tiger lilies and forced a smile. "I don't need more cards or flowers. So, how've you been?" Not the smoothest subject change.

"Oh, fine. Took a few days off. I've been keeping Marsing company on and off. Got my head bit off this morning for my trouble, so I thought I'd bestow my presence upon you again. Figured a lovely lady such as yourself would be too gracious to snap at me like a grumpy old bear."

"This grumpy bear is going to throw your ass out in the hall," a familiar masculine voice growled from the doorway.

Ally's heart skipped a beat before setting a pace fast enough to make a racehorse proud. Fingernails biting into her palms, she drank him in as he crossed the room. His lazy saunter and laid-back attitude were nowhere in sight.

"Hey, baby. How are you feeling?"

"Good."

Greg gently untangled her fingers from the loose blanket threads, his touch sending her already racing pulse into the stratosphere. "Your fingertips were turning blue."

"Oh." Ally stared at him.

"Well." Ted's voice startled her. "Guess I'll head out. Take care of yourself, beautiful."

Ted leaned over to kiss her cheek, like he had every day, but at the last second, he tilted her chin up and kissed her lips. She froze, staring into his sparkling blue eyes as he lingered over her mouth. A rumble of what sounded suspiciously like displeasure came from Greg as Teddy's lips curved against hers. When Ted straightened, no sign of amusement remained.

"Problem, Marsing?"

"What do you think?"

Tension thickened and Ally divided her gaze between the two men on either side of her hospital bed. Should she be worried about one lunging across her and slugging the other?

Ted rocked back on his heels, stuffed his hands in his pockets and shrugged. "You've laid no claim. Far as I can see, the turf's wide open."

"So you decided to make a play."

"Why not? It's a gorgeous day and I'm with a beautiful woman. Besides, I'm lonely."

Not an ounce of humor brightened Ted's dark expression. Greg's face was inscrutable, his hands tightly fisted at his sides. She ran her gaze over him. His whole body vibrated with aggressive energy. Perked up considerably, she glanced back at Ted.

"Nothing to say?" Ted shook his head. "Pathetic, man. Just pathetic. You've got an incredible woman you should be holding onto with both hands, but you're too blind and pig-headed to see it."

"The only reason you aren't picking yourself up off the floor right now is out of respect for how long we've been friends." Greg's voice was low and dangerous. "But you're treading on thin ice, man."

Ted planted his fists on the side of the bed and leaned in, inches from Greg. "You really think I haven't noticed your little issue? The thing with your parents...I feel for you, man, I really do. But it's time to move on. Live life and quit hiding." Ted straightened. "Trust me, you'll be a better man for it."

Ally released the breath she'd been holding, afraid to look at Greg. She'd had the exact same thoughts.

"If you're finished doing your armchair shrink bit, I'd like a word alone with Ally."

Ted's shoulders sagged. He nodded and winked at her, but his usual sparkle was MIA.

As soon as the door closed behind him, Greg turned. "How are you really, Ally?"

The gentle tone of voice took her by surprise, as if the last few minutes of thick tension hadn't occurred. He tucked a strand of hair behind her ear. She longed to tug him down into bed with her. Guess she was feeling better. He trailed a fingertip down her cheek and rubbed his thumb over her bottom lip. Her fingers curled into the bedding.

"I've missed you, sweetheart."

Ally's eyes widened. Quite an admission from Playboy of the Year.

"Have you missed me?"

Had she missed him? Anger flared in her belly. He'd known where she was for the last three days. If he missed her so much...it didn't matter. Greg didn't *do* relationships. They weren't his *thing*. What difference did her missing him make?

Ally's gaze dropped to his mouth. All the deliciously naughty things he'd done to her flashed through her mind.

Greg leaned down and teased her lips apart, kissing her until her thoughts fizzed and popped, dissipating into the air. She lifted her arms to wrap around his neck and flinched, gasping as pain ripped through her.

Frowning, concern darkening his eyes, he pulled away. "Do you need more pain meds?"

"I'll be okay. Just give me a sec." Ally took a breath and willed the pain to subside.

The concern didn't leave his expression. He ran a hand through his hair and settled into a chair. "The guy from the lake confessed. Looks like he's our man."

She perked up. "Really? Good of him. Very selfless."

"Yeah." Greg chuckled.

"Did he say why he wanted me dead, by any chance?"

"No."

Her heart sank. A reason for all the torment she'd endured would have been nice.

"He lawyered-up and quit talking. When do they spring you from this joint?"

"When the doctor was here, he mentioned tomorrow. I'm going stir crazy."

"Any plans for getting home?"

"A woman from work offered, but I turned her down. I made other arrangements." Just an hour ago. She kept hoping Greg would show up and play errant knight in shining or even slightly tarnished armor. Now he was here…well, a girl had her pride.

"You sure? I'd be happy to be your escort."

Despite her anger and hurt, hope made a surprising recovery.

"It's the least I can do after…" He waved an expansive hand. "Everything."

After…she got shot? After sleeping with her and dumping her? After abandoning her in the hospital for three days? Warm and fuzzy flat-lined. Alongside their absence came a sharp realization.

She needed to do this. A bullet from a would-be killer had done serious damage just below her shoulder, shredding muscles and nicking her lung. What had come before with Greg didn't bear thinking about. Getting home from the hospital seemed like an excellent start to reclaiming her life.

"You're sweet,"—*Not*— "but I called a car service to drive me home. I'm splurging."

"You shouldn't call me sweet. I'll develop a complex and there won't be any living with me." He grinned. "On second thought, go ahead. I live alone."

She forced a laugh but gasped as pain washed the room in shades of gray and she bit her lip. The equipment she was hooked to started beeping. "Guess I'm not as recovered as I'd like."

The nurse bustled into the room, tutting and rearranging Ally's pillows and checking her bandage. She pushed a syringe full of clear fluid into her IV, shot Greg a dirty look and left.

"Damn. She's a real bulldog. You okay?"

"Nurse Betty is very nice. She doesn't like me getting so many visitors."

"Was that a hint?"

"I am a bit tired." Ally straightened her blankets one-handed and avoided his gaze.

Greg stood and leaned down, invading her personal space. "I'll go, but I'll be back to discuss your ride home."

Her heart cracked, but she put on a smile. "I'll be fine, Greg."

Impassive, he nodded and left.

Ally sagged into the bed, staring at the muted show playing on the television. A soap opera of some kind. Fascinating. Not. She gingerly shifted onto her side and watched clouds drift by outside, waiting for the painkiller to kick in. If only they had one for heartbreak.

Chapter Seventeen

The helicopter tilted to the side in a wide arc around the bay. Ally's lunch shifted dangerously in her stomach. Swallowing, she focused on the scenery spread out below like a beautiful buffet, courtesy of Mother Nature. She'd gone from bland hospital walls to wild adventure in just a matter of days. Amazing how getting shot could change a girl's perspective.

"Gorgeous," she breathed. And breathtaking. She laughed.

The pilot grinned and headed inland. Coastal landscape gave way to rugged mountains.

A wild river slashed through a canyon below. Along the edge, a herd of elk leapt up and disappeared into the tree line.

The pilot spoke through the earphones. "The noise of the chopper startled them."

Brawny and good-looking, in his mid to late thirties, there'd been no mistaking the gleam in his blue eyes when he greeted her at the small landing pad. Or the way his gaze lingered with notable appreciation on the fit of her new clothes over her curves.

A few weeks ago she might have followed up on the invitation in those eyes. Then again, a few weeks ago she never would have been on a fun weekend get-away. Especially alone. She was thankful to be alive, she reminded herself yet again as tears blurred the striking vista below. Her last conversation with Greg ran through her mind with startling clarity.

"I missed you at the hospital. Guess you made it home okay?"

Greg's achingly familiar voice wrapped around her throat like barbed wire. Resolute, she clung to her poise. "Yes, thank you."

"I wanted to let you know we've gotten the word out about Big, Bad and Ugly being in custody and there won't be any more commissioned jobs." He'd stolen her nicknaming habit? "We're still working out all the angles, since he clammed up after confessing to ordering the hit. I hope to have an answer on why he went after you soon. The important thing is, you're safe now." He paused. "So, uh...how are you doing?"

"Good, thanks." She forced a smile into her voice. "I take it this means I can get on with my life?"

"Yeah. I don't see why not."

"Great."

Silence hummed on the line, and Ally bit her lip to resist filling it.

"Okay, well, I'd better run. Talk to you later, Sugar Lips."

The pilot glanced at her as the helicopter touched down. Ally saw instead Greg's blue-green gaze. Remembered the feel of his blond strands in her hands as she stared at the pilot's ruffled brown curls when he helped her onto terra firma.

Ally smiled against the heartache and waved good-bye. Probably wrong to enjoy the regret on his handsome face as she grabbed her small suitcase from the storage area and climbed into a cab to the airport.

She went through the motions of checking in and boarding the homeward-bound flight, but her mind was elsewhere. Even the pat-down at security didn't faze her. Preoccupation with redesigning her life and wondering if Greg would carve out a space for himself had its benefits.

The drone of the idling airplane filled her ears as Ally dug through her handbag. "Drat. I know I put my earbuds in here."

"Lose something?"

She jerked upright and gaped. "Greg? What are you doing here?"

"I thought a quick trip would be fun. Too bad I missed out on the chopper ride."

"The chopper..." She narrowed her eyes. "How do you know about that?"

Greg shrugged, sat down and opened a magazine.

Two could play his game. Ally sat back and crossed her arms. If he thought he was getting off so easy, he was mistaken. "So, you just *happen* to know about my weekend trip and you just *happen* to be on the same flight home?"

"Yep. Small world."

Irritated beyond belief with his recalcitrant attitude, she glared. "I could get a restraining order, you know."

He snorted. "Good luck with that."

Ally gritted her teeth and bored a hole in the side of his head.

Finally, he met her gaze and sighed. "Fine. I was worried about you, okay? The past few weeks were pretty stressful for someone who..."

Ally raised her brows, daring him to complete his sentence.

He cleared his throat. "Who isn't used to it. I wanted to make sure you weren't going off the deep end. Sky diving without a parachute or some other crazy stunt, but I couldn't get off until late last night. I missed you at the helicopter pad earlier. Then you boogied out of there so fast, I figured I'd just meet up with you here."

Great. He'd bought a round-trip ticket to babysit her, just in case she needed a reservation for her very own padded cell.

"How adorable." Toxically sweet, she smiled, glancing to her left. A big guy sat there, looking uncomfortable in the ever-shrinking airplane seat.

"Hi," she said.

The dark-haired man glanced up and Ally experimented with what she hoped was a flirtatious smile. To her gratification, his eyes widened and he shifted to face her more fully.

"Hi. You coming or going?"

"Going. How about you?"

On Ally's other side, Greg noisily flipped magazine pages. She ignored him.

"I'm headed to my parents' for a few days. It's their fortieth anniversary tomorrow, and my sister is throwing a big party." His gaze skimmed over her body. It did nothing for her, unlike when Greg gave her an appreciative once-over.

"Really?" She upped the wattage of her smile.

Greg slapped his magazine down.

"That's great. You don't hear about too many couples staying together very long anymore." Ally shifted so her back was to the annoying passenger to her right. "Do you live here in Seattle, then?"

"Yeah. I play for the Seahawks. Name's Mark Gresham." A hundred-watt smile with perfect white teeth about blinded her.

"That's nice. I don't watch much baseball."

Greg snorted.

The power of Mark's smile died down to a more manageable glow.

"My name's Ally."

"Pleased to meet you, Ally." Mark held out his big hand, but instead of shaking, he brought her hand to his lips while holding her gaze. No doubt the practiced move paved serious in-roads with women.

She could have sworn Greg growled.

Mark's dark-brown eyes twinkled. "The Seahawks are a football team, honey. Just so you know."

"Oh." *Don't I feel like a moron?*

Behind her, Greg snorted again, so she upped the wattage of her smile. "Football is a very demanding sport. You must be in incredible shape."

Mark grinned. A very cute grin. "Yeah, it can be pretty rough. I can't complain, though. The pay is great and the activity keeps me in shape."

"I can tell." Heat climbed into her cheeks at her boldness. Well,

Rome wasn't built in a day. She plowed ahead. "I'm impressed your parents have been together for so long. So many people are like small, frightened children about commitment these days."

Ally literally felt the weight of Greg's glare on the back of her head.

"Uhm ... yeah. Thanks. They've set a great example for my sister and I."

She forced herself to relax and grin. "That's great."

"What do you do back home?"

"I work for an insurance company at the moment, but I've been thinking about changing careers."

"Oh, yeah? Bold move."

Ally basked in the appreciation heating his eyes for all of two seconds before something smacked her shoulder and she jerked around. Greg smiled with more teeth than was necessarily polite.

"Sorry, miss."

Smiling with sugary sweetness, Ally cooed, "Not at all. I'm sure controlling muscle spasms is difficult at your age."

Mark's cologne and handsome face invaded her peripheral vision as he leaned around her. "Try to be a little more careful, buddy."

Greg went from poker-face innocence to dangerous cop in a blink.

Ally stiffened and parted her lips to intervene, but the stewardess began preflight instructions. Both men subsided into their respective seats. Ally buckled her seat belt, fiddled with the emergency-exit pamphlet, fluffed her hair, straightened her blouse and avoided Greg's hot glare.

An hour of studiously avoiding looking directly at Greg while maintaining a stream of flirtatious conversation with Mark frayed her composure to the breaking point. A few minutes of solitary in the miniscule airplane bathroom sounded like heaven.

Ally climbed over Greg's long, muscular legs to reach the aisle, forcing her into direct contact with the hunky body she knew intimately. Halfway over, turbulence knocked her off her feet and onto his lap.

His hands latched onto her waist, her butt inches from the heat of his crotch.

She glanced over her shoulder. "Sorry."

Heaven help her, his mouth was an enticing two inches away. She licked her lips and his gaze dropped to watch. A moan caught partway up her throat. Pathetic. A little direct contact, a few heated looks and her panties were damp.

She scrambled off his lap. Five steps down the aisle, feminine instinct made her glance back.

Greg's gaze was glued to her butt.

Shutting the bathroom door, Ally collapsed against it. Not two seconds later, someone knocked. Hadn't they seen her walk in? "I'll just be a sec."

"Ally, let me in."

Greg? What did he want? She opened the door an inch. He crowded his way into the room with her. They stood chest-to-chest in the tiny space as he locked the door. She noted the familiar gleam in his eyes and took a step back, but her heel hit the sink cabinet and the tiny counter bit into her butt.

"Greg, what are you doing? What if someone saw you?"

"No one did."

"This isn't…."

His mouth over hers shut her up and chased away every thought in her head. With a low moan, she twined her arms around his neck and sank into the kiss like a starving woman with a buffet of homemade, just-out-of-the-oven cookies. Big hands cupped her bottom and brought her flush with his arousal. The contact tipped her over the edge of sanity.

Hands shaking with desire, Ally yanked his T-shirt over his head then moaned again at the feel of his taut skin under her hands. Greg did one better, tugging her shirt over her head and her pants and panties down to her ankles then pulling her bra cups down until her breasts spilled over the edges.

While their tongues mimicked what she so desperately wanted their bodies to be doing, he cupped her bare bottom in his hands. The friction of his chest hair against her nipples started a dull roar in her ears. He planted his foot between hers and lifted her free of her pants, setting her on the bathroom counter. Ally fumbled with the button on his jeans. She wanted him inside her now.

Greg pushed her hands aside, shoved his pants down, took hold of himself with one hand, used the other to grab her butt and thrust home. Fully seated inside her, he threaded his fingers into her hair and kissed her. Two hard thrusts and she came, moaning into his mouth. The threads of his restraint seemed to snap. He lifted her off the counter and pounded into her.

The feel of him around her, moving inside her, their combined scent, his passion, all wove a tight web. Emotion swelled and her body tightened around him again. Tearing her mouth free, she buried her face against his neck. Another orgasm, more powerful than the first, swept through her and she bit his shoulder.

Beneath her hands, Greg tensed. One more hard thrust and he gave a low guttural moan. Arms and legs wrapped tight, she held him as he found his own release.

Ally licked and kissed the spot she'd bitten. She kissed a line up his neck, along his jaw. At his mouth, she paused and pulled back to meet his glittering, unreadable gaze. Difficult man. If she didn't love him, she'd have to club him over the head. She might anyway.

She leaned forward and brushed her lips back and forth across his. His arms tightened. Firming her lips over his, she poured all of her heart into the kiss. He twitched inside her and lengthened.

Instead of following up on that unspoken promise, he stepped back. The drag of him withdrawing from her sensitive flesh left her twitchy and flushed. He pulled up his pants, not bothering with the zipper or button before he leaned back and crossed his arms, staring at her.

Naked as the day she was born, his hooded gaze made her feel far too vulnerable. She grabbed her shirt off the counter. Greg snatched it from her.

She narrowed her eyes. "Greg, I need to get dressed."

He tucked her blouse out of reach between his back and the wall. His feral smile slammed Ally's defenses into place. "Not just yet. I like you this way. My cum seeping out of your sweet pussy; flushed and satisfied from a thorough fuck."

She flinched and bit her lip.

"What's the matter, sweetheart? Don't care for my terminology? Well, neither do I." Leaning forward, his face an inch away from hers, he growled, "You deserve better than an easy fuck with some big-time player. Don't do something you'll regret just to get even with me."

So this had all been his way of showing her he didn't appreciate her flirting with some guy? Tears stung her eyes, but she refused to give in to them. Not here. Not in front of him.

"Who said I intended to fuck him, Greg?"

He scowled and some of the tightness in her chest eased. Ah, revenge. Good to the last drop.

"I engage in a little harmless flirting and you barge in here to teach me a lesson with some lame bathroom sex? Well, fuck you, Marsing."

"You just did."

She slapped him. In the stark silence, Ally's heart pounded in her throat and her palm tingled.

Greg squeezed his eyes shut. "I deserved that. I'm being an asshole. I'm sorry, baby. Jealousy is eating me alive, and I'm not used to feeling emotional crap over a woman. I lost it. Fact is, you make me feel things I've never felt before."

Ally crossed her arms and looked away. Tried to close her legs, but he moved between them.

"Forgive me?" He nudged her entrance and she glanced down, jaw dropping in disbelief. Fully erect and veins bulging as if they hadn't just had sex, he pushed inside her. Biting her lip to withhold a moan, she met his eyes.

"Please?" Balls deep inside of her, Greg didn't move, didn't touch her anywhere else.

She swallowed hard, upset swirling in her belly. His apology went a long way toward soothing the wounds his words created, but she hated how much he could hurt her. How vulnerable being in love with him left her. She could totally understand his difficulty in dealing with foreign emotions; she was right there with him.

"Don't do it again." There was steel in her tone. She was no man's doormat.

"I won't." Greg withdrew to just the tip.

"Watch, sweetheart." His voice roughened and he grasped her thighs and spread them further apart. "Watch how good we are together."

If he thought they were so good together, why was he afraid of an actual relationship? He thrust and her thought process fractured. Slow and thorough, his hips pumped back and forth.

Ally's vision hazed and she fought to focus. Missing a single moment wasn't an option. She'd never seen or experienced anything so erotic. So thick, he spread her lips apart as he pushed into her, reappearing slick with her arousal and his cum, combined with the drag and pull across her nerve endings until she tumbled over into an orgasm. The heat of his climax poured into her.

"That's what we're like together," he rasped into her hair.

From somewhere, she summoned the energy to lift her head from his shoulder to whisper in his ear, "You remember too, Surfer Dude."

Greg stiffened but didn't pull away until both their breathing returned to normal and her grip on him loosened. In silence, he helped her wriggle back into her clothes in the cramped quarters.

The rest of the flight passed in tense awareness of the man to her right and obliviousness to the one on her left. The scent of their lovemaking clung to her nostrils. Everything he'd said swirled round and round her head until her temples throbbed.

Ultimately, he hadn't clarified anything between them, and there was no way she was having a deeply personal conversation on a crowded airplane.

She gathered her things once the plane landed and joined the de-planing throng. The joy of her adventurous weekend had dissipated in the haze of uncertainty clouding their relationship.

Walking through the airport, bittersweet longing tugged at her as couples and families greeted one another. Greg came alongside her, wove his fingers through hers and nudged her into a deserted lounge area. Her stomach clenched with anxiety.

"So..." she laced her fingers behind her back and stared at his chin. "I'm a little confused about where we stand."

"I don't know what you want from me. You're the kind of woman a man comes home to every night, makes a family with... that's not me."

Acid churned in her stomach. He was dumping her? After the way he'd driven every muscle in her body into plaintive lassitude? Either Greg had a real cruel streak or he was having trouble deciding what he wanted. Regardless, the constant push and pull was killing her.

Ally lifted her chin and met his gaze. "You need to make up your mind. One minute you care about me and we have something special, the next you're saying you have nothing to offer. Except sex." Cynicism twisted her smile. "If you figure it out, let me know."

Dignity wrapped around her like a long winter coat, she turned and walked away. At the door, she paused, took a deep breath and looked back over her shoulder.

Greg stood with his hands fisted and lips tight, color riding high in his cheeks. Maybe he did want her for more than sex, but she hadn't come this far to shove herself down a man's throat. Either he wanted her, all of her, or he didn't.

"Just don't take too long," she said. "I won't wait around forever."

With a heavy heart, Ally walked away. In the parking lot, she stared at her little Prius. A boring car for a boring woman.

A car lot drew her gaze on the way home. Why did she have to be boring? Maybe her image just needed a little…fluffing. And some high-dollar therapeutic shopping to ease what ailed her. Trading her Prius in a year before she paid off the loan wasn't the wisest financial decision, but she pulled in anyway.

She coasted to a stop beside a bright-red VW convertible. Entranced by the color, Ally climbed out and walked over to admire the interior and read the sticker. Black-leather interior, black-convertible top; very nice. Even the color's name spoke to her. Salsa Red.

Before she quite knew what had happened—possibly temporary insanity—she was wheeling away from the dealership in a shiny new VW Beetle convertible. Soft leather upholstery, a nice sound system and the scent of new car improved her mood considerably. No doubt a fleeting high brought on by the toxic new-car smell, but she enjoyed it nonetheless.

Smooth as silk, the little car accelerated up her drive and into the garage. She walked inside with a jaunty step and checked her answering machine. Joel, her real estate agent slash cousin, had left several irate messages. Excitement bubbled in her chest. Her town house already had a buyer. Wonderful. Now she just had to find a new place to live.

"It'll be fun." She wheeled her suitcase into her bedroom.

The stillness of the house grated on her nerves. Silence had never bothered her before. The tan walls irritated her. Unless it was the color of her skin after a relaxing weekend in Saint Lucia, her fixation with tan was definitely over.

"Now that would be a great get-away."

Great. Now I'm talking to myself. Throw in a cat—or ten, and I can be the neighborhood's crazy lady. A thud from downstairs made her jump and she threw her purse on the bed. Who had burst in without invitation this time?

"This is getting ridiculous." Ally stomped down the stairs. "Do I have an OPEN sign on my front window or something?"

She walked into the kitchen and her muttering came to an abrupt halt. Her heart, stomach and several other vital organs plummeted to her feet.

"Hello, doll-face."

Chapter Eighteen

Mother of God, this is not happening.

Victor peeled himself off the wall and strolled toward her, smiling. The friendly expression was ill at ease on his face.

Panic beat against Ally's ribcage.

He leaned against the island. "You look good, doll-face. I migh' have to reconsider the rule about my girls wearing clothes." His expression turned ugly. "But then, your de'ec'ive friend made sure I no longer have any girls, didn' he?"

She took a step back. Victor was under armed guard, on his way to forever-after in a jail cell. Greg had said so. Why was he standing in her kitchen? Oh, God, she couldn't breathe.

Fleeing front and center in her mind, Ally spun on her heel and smacked into something. Someone. Curly wrapped his beefy arms around her and squeezed her butt. If only looks *could* kill. He'd be howling on the floor, the sleaze.

She smiled sweetly and stomped as hard as she could on his instep. He howled but didn't let go. Instead, he spun her around to face Victor and held her arms in a bruising grip.

"Now…" The telephone rang, cutting Victor off. He held up a hand. "Don' move, doll-face."

Like she had a choice. Her answering machine clicked on.

"Ally, we have a problem." Greg's voice filled the room. "Victor escaped during transport. I don't know if he'll try to find you, but don't open the door for anyone except me. I'm on my way."

The machine clicked off and Victor grinned. "Hero to the rescue, huh? Tha' makes this so much more fun."

Her belly tightened. He was way too calm and collected for her peace of mind.

"Come on, boys." Victor waved Curly and Moe, his favorite pet guard dogs, toward the door. "Let's get ou' of here. We don't wan' to make this too easy for Detective Marsing."

Curly twisted her arm high behind her back, lifting Ally up on her toes. She cried out in pain. His crotch pressed into her bottom. Ally's stomach turned. Now she'd have to burn a brand-new pair of pants. Pants she really liked.

Ticked off and grossed out by Curly's onion-scented breath, she forced herself to think. Inspired by his heavy breathing, she brought her head forward and flung it back as hard as she could. She saw stars. Curly cursed and released her.

Blood gushed all over the front of his pristine bowling shirt. Ally made a mad dash for the back door. Something hit her hard in the back and slammed her to the tile floor.

She'd hoped Moe wouldn't be so fast on his feet.

Ally glared daggers at Moe pacing in front of her. Per Victor's instructions, he'd tied her hands behind her and her legs to the oh-so-comfy metal chair she currently inhabited. The good thing about her position was no one would be taking off her clothes or molesting her. No matter how creative a guy got, sex just wasn't possible with her tied to a chair like this.

And if anybody stuck anything in her face, well, she was only too happy to bite his appendage off. She'd be doing mankind a favor. Or womankind, at least.

"Are you going to pace all day?" she asked sweetly.

"Shut up."

"Charming. You must be a real hit with the ladies."

Moe stirred up the dirt on the floor as he approached and she sneezed. This place hadn't been occupied for a very long time—by any two-legged creatures, anyway. Dust and grime covered every surface.

The filth didn't seem to affect Moe, who didn't stop until he was right in her face. "If you don't shut up, I'll shut you up."

"You should consider a tic-tac. I'd offer you one, but I'm a little tied up at the moment." She smiled, biting back the rising bile of fear and nerves swirling inside her belly.

Moe spun away with a grunt.

She could have sworn his lips twitched, but it had to be a trick of the light. No way Big, Bad and Ugly had a sense of humor. Okay, he wasn't ugly, but personality beat out looks every time.

"So, where's Curly?"

"Who?"

"The other guy."

"He's icing his nose. I think you broke it."

"Gee, that's too bad."

With an enigmatic shrug, Moe resumed pacing. Back and forth, back and forth in the small room until she wanted to scream. She tapped her toes on the floor and admired the charming Dust Bowl era décor instead.

Not Victor's old establishment, and he hadn't had time to set up a new one. He'd only just escaped. Which dirty cop helped him out this time? Dirty cop. Good night. Like she was in some corny TV show. *Cops Gone Bad* or something equally stupid.

"So…"

Moe spun, tension in every line of his body. "Just shut the hell up! Please."

"Since you said please." She muttered, dropping her gaze to her lap.

"Oh, man. I am gonna freakin' lose it."

Ally frowned. What kind of bad guy said freaking? Tension and frown lines marred his forehead. Like he was thinking hard, concentrating, plotting and planning. Wasn't plotting Victor's job? She hoped Moe didn't hurt himself. Much.

Muted voices and footsteps approached.

Moe spun on her so fast, she flinched. "Look, I'm begging you. Keep your mouth shut and let me handle this if you want any chance of getting out of here alive."

Wow, that was the most words he'd ever strung together at a time. Remarkable. Then what he'd said penetrated. Ally's eyes widened.

Moe shot her a warning look.

Victor strolled in, his heavy cologne filling the room and reminding her of the concrete chamber in his old basement. Her stomach twisted and panic tried to gain a toehold. She lifted her chin, praying it wasn't trembling.

"Hello, doll-face. Glad you're awake. You've go' a nasty bump on your forehead. Shame abou' the cabine' and all."

"Isn't it, though." Ally smiled tightly. "Shame about your lisp too."

Victor's face darkened, but his slimy smile remained in place. Creepy. "I see you go' your smar' mouth back. We'll have to take care of tha'." He took a threatening step in her direction.

"How's Joe?" Moe asked.

Victor paused and shot Ally a look. "His nose is broken. He go' wha' he deserved, letting a woman get the better of him. He'll be in shortly."

"Oh, goodie," she muttered.

Moe's exasperation became a tangible thing and she bit her lip. When had she become so mouthy? Probably all those years of repressing her feelings coming to bite her in the butt.

A calmer Victor pushed past Moe. Hopefully, he was also less inclined to slap her around. She didn't especially enjoy being slapped around.

"I hear the rich SOB who ordered your hit go' caught." He chuckled. "Good thing I got paid firs'."

Ally bit her tongue hard.

"Finally learning your place. Perfec'."

The door creaked open, admitting Curly. Gratification swelled. Both of his eyes were black and his nose had swollen to enormous proportions. His glare held a lot less power, thanks to the broken nose.

Ally winked at him.

He lunged. Moe snatched him back just in time. A rush of wind followed his fist past her face, missing her by a hair. She gulped.

"If you can' control yourself, you can leave." Victor glared at Curly. "I don' wan' her messed up. No' ye' anyway."

Moe slammed Curly against the far wall, thick arm pressed against his windpipe, holding him in place. Impressive. Curly was a big guy.

Curly made a strangled sound and Moe released him. Moe stepped back but kept an eye on him, a fact Ally appreciated. Curly was one loose bolt away from falling apart at the seams.

Victor watched the two men, head cocked to the side.

Striving for nonchalance, as much as a woman tied to a chair could achieve, she quirked her brow. "Where are we anyway?"

"A little place I know from my younger days." He turned back to her. "It'll take a while for your detective to figure out where we're hiding. Plenty of time for the boys to have a little fun."

The panic she'd been holding at bay sailed in and dropped anchor. Curly surged forward, but Victor narrowed his reptilian eyes and Curly subsided into sullen silence, lounging against the wall.

"I believe he deserves the privilege." Victor pointed at Moe, then turned his cold gaze on Curly. "You allowed a woman to ge' the bes' of you."

Relief surged, until Moe leered at her. Ally's heart began to pound. Had she mistaken his intention to help her? He stalked forward and she shrank back in the chair. The hard metal back pressed into her skin.

"Take her in the room next door," Victor said. "You'll have to untie her legs, but keep her hands tied." He pressed a hand to his ribcage. Right where she'd stabbed him. Grim satisfaction filled her.

Moe grunted in response and knelt to deal with the ropes. As soon as the rope fell, she tried to kick him and stand. He grabbed both her ankles and jerked hard. Ally toppled over his beefy shoulder as he rose, her face in his butt and her heart in her throat.

Victor chuckled. "I see you two will ge' along jus' fine."

She spat at him. Hanging upside down didn't make for good aim. She missed by a mile. Distaste crossed Victor's face then he smiled. An icy shiver snaked along her spine.

Moe opened the door, crossed a narrow hallway decorated in early roach mixed with rat infestation, opened another door and carried her across the threshold. Not a romantic, back from our honeymoon, threshold. Especially when he dropped her unceremoniously on a creaky old bed. A thick cloud of dust rose and Ally sneezed. One sneeze followed another, then another.

The dust and her sneezing fit finally subsided. She opened watery eyes. Moe stood over her, big arms crossed over his burly chest. Her heart skipped a beat. If he followed through on Victor's offer, she didn't have a prayer of stopping him. He was built like a Hummer—the military ones.

"You are a load of trouble, woman."

Biting her lip, Ally eyed him.

He didn't fall on her, ripping her clothes off. "I feel sorry for the man who takes you on."

She bristled. "Hey."

Moe checked his watch. "Time to scream."

"Uhm...what?"

"I'm supposed to be..." He waved a hand toward her pelvis and Ally reflexively crossed her legs. "You know, having my way with you. My reward for being a good boy."

"Seriously? 'Having your way with me'? Nobody says that." Ally rolled her eyes and struggled into a sitting position, no easy feat with her arms tied behind her back.

"Just scream already."

She pictured a big, fat rat crawling up her leg and screamed at the top of her lungs.

Moe winced and fell back a step.

She kept screaming. Moe leaned against the far wall with his arms crossed, the skin tight across his cheekbones and his eyes narrowed. He'd probably love to cover his ears but didn't want to hurt the whole tough-guy, macho thing he had going. He could give Greg lessons in inscrutability, and Greg wasn't any slouch.

Moe's lack of interest in raping her went a long way toward convincing her something else was going on. Despite the general absence of expression, switched up with a look of bored menace, which must come in handy in his line of work. DEA? FBI? CIA?

"Shut up," he bellowed.

Ally started and shut her mouth with an audible snap.

He walked to the side of the bed on silent feet. An impressive achievement, considering the age of house and its creaky floorboards. "Sorry." His voice was pitched low. "I figured it fit the situation. Besides, one of my eardrums blew two minutes ago."

His lips twitched and she grinned. If she weren't in love with Greg, Moe could throw her for a loop, now that he was on her side. He was very handsome, in a thickly muscled, too much testosterone, "me strong man, you little woman," sort of way.

"Would you mind scooting over?" he asked.

Ally scooted. He sat beside her and flipped open a deadly looking little switchblade. Her saliva dried to dust as he leaned close. Guess she wasn't quite convinced of his stellar intentions, after all. Moe grabbed her bound hands. The cool metal of his blade pressed into her wrist and she was free.

Massaging her abraded skin, she eyed him. He winked, reached behind her and began banging the headboard against the wall. Repeatedly.

Heat flooded Ally's cheeks. "Good grief."

"If possible, I'll hold off until Detective Marsing arrives," Moe said between thuds. "Arresting Victor, rescuing you and holding Joe at bay at the same time could be tricky otherwise."

"So you *are* some sort of undercover agent."

Gray eyes void of expression, he merely continued the rhythmic thumping. The pretend sex rattled her.

"You have a rather high estimation of your...err, capabilities, don't you?"

Something crossed his face, enough to remind her he'd seen her naked and spread-eagled.

"Not really."

She swallowed. A woman would have to be dead to be immune to Moe's virile appeal. Especially once he stopped snarling at her.

He stopped hitting the headboard against the wall and groaned, loud and long, still holding her gaze. Ally couldn't look away; her flush deepened until her face was on fire.

He winked again and stood, breaking the spell. "Lay down."

Refusing to look at him, she obeyed. Moe stood and yanked open her blouse, scattering buttons everywhere. Then he flipped open the buttons on her jeans. She gasped, slapped his hands away and yanked the ends of her shirt together then shifted her hips to the side. "What are you—"

He smacked her. The sting spread through her mouth. Numbness followed. Ally froze, eyes wide. Blood trickled down her chin. She put the tip of her tongue to her lower lip and tentatively felt where the skin had split.

"I'm sorry," he whispered, "but if you don't look like you put up a fight and I did some damage, they'll never believe..."

The door creaked. His hands went to the fly of his pants. For an endless minute, he stared down at her then dropped his hands and turned.

Moe blocked her view of the door, intentional or not she didn't know and didn't care. The metallic taste of blood filled her mouth and her face throbbed.

"If you're through, bring her back into the other room," Victor instructed from the doorway.

Ally imagined Victor's smug smirk and shrank back on the bed. Moe didn't say a word, just nodded.

"She must've been a damn fine lay, to have struck you speechless."

Victor closed the door, but his chuckle penetrated the thin wood. Moe turned back around and she lurched back, smacking into the wall. He didn't move, simply watched her. "You okay?"

"Do you care?" She flinched.

"I wouldn't ask if I didn't."

Biting her tongue, Ally faced the wall. Then she glanced back, too afraid of his lightning- fast moves not to.

"I'm sorry, Ally." He'd never used her name before. "I did what I had to do to keep you safe and me under the radar. For now. It would've been worse if I warned you ahead of time."

He didn't look sorry. As a matter of fact, his complete lack of expression was downright creepy. The few times he hadn't been without expression passed through her mind—when she'd taunted him, amused him or when he'd winked at her—but she shoved them away. Moe was clearly not trustworthy. The throbbing of her cheek was reminder enough, thank you very much.

He sighed. "Let's go."

Ally scooted away from his outstretched hand and slid off the end of the bed.

Moe opened the door, grabbed her elbow, despite her attempted evasion, and ushered her into the room next door. He none too gently pushed her into the metal chair and knelt to retie her legs.

Curly still held up the same portion of wall, eyeing her with vivid dislike. His nose seemed to have swollen more in her absence and his lips were parted to allow him to breath. She'd earned his enmity and couldn't care less.

Victor, on the other hand, bothered her big time.

He eyed her critically. "You need to learn to cooperate, doll-face.

You wouldn' ge' slapped around so much." He strolled over and pressed a finger against the tender skin on the side of her face where Moe had slapped her. She winced.

His sleazy smile emerged, not big enough to reveal his tobacco-stained teeth, but evidence enough to warn smart people away—the ones with a choice. "You might even find you enjoy it. 'Sides, I can' keep having my property getting messed up."

Oh, hell no. Ally glared up into his slimy face. "I'm no one's property, especially not yours. And enjoy it? Seriously? You are one sick freak."

Moe's soft sigh penetrated her irritation and she glanced down at him. His eyes held a warning when they met hers. He yanked the ropes tight around her ankles. She returned her attention to Victor, uncertain of Moe's motives and fighting off fear like the hard throb of a bad toothache.

Victor's smile vanished and he roughly patted her sore cheek. Her pain rose from a dull throb to rich, vibrant agony.

"One fella mus' no' be enough. Tha's okay. I have a lo' of clients who would enjoy breaking you, doll-face, so I'll le' tha' one slide."

Discovering an intensely fascinating niche in the wall, Ally stared straight ahead and ignored Slimeball. Curly snarled and straightened from the wall. Finished rendering her helpless, Moe stood and Curly subsided.

Whatever. She didn't need Moe to be her hero. Regardless of how Greg felt about her, she knew he'd arrive sooner or later.

She really hoped the sooner part applied.

Ally raised her chin as Victor left the room and met Moe's gaze. He watched her with his usual inscrutability. She barely resisted snorting. A CIA agent? What had she been thinking? Why would any government agency be interested in Victor?

Forced prostitution was illegal, but the government wouldn't be interested in a small-time criminal. She assumed he was small-time. Otherwise, why would he be hanging in a rundown, decrepit old house using her as bait to force a confrontation with a lowly detective?

The thought of being bait reminded her of last time. Which reminded her of her freshly healing injury. A throb of exquisite anguish shot through her, originating below her shoulder and radiating outward until her fingertips vibrated with pain. She struggled to bite back a sob.

Her vision hazed.

"Seems only fair I should get time alone with the little bitch." Curly's whining voice grated, but she focused on it anyway. Anything to shut out the hurt. The tank top beneath her shirt was damp and warm liquid seeped down her front. Fantastic. Her freshly sutured and bandaged wound had started bleeding again. The doctor would be so pleased.

Moe stirred. "Shut up, Joe."

"Who left you in charge?" Curly snarled.

"I did." Moe's tone alone would have made her give way, but Curly was too thick-skulled.

"She broke my fucking nose, man. The least she can do is provide a little fun while we wait." Curly curled his fists, knuckles white.

Moe leaned against the wall, not even looking at the other man, watching her. "No."

Face red, fists rising, Curly took two steps toward Moe. Moe whirled and pinned him to the wall. Again. How much humiliation could one man take? Curly flailed uselessly.

Moe leaned in close. "You heard what the detective on the phone said. You wanna be caught with your pants around your ankles and your dick flapping in the breeze when the SWAT team arrives?"

"My dick doesn't flap," Curly snarled.

Despite his belligerence, his fists relaxed and the color receded from his face. Moe let him go. Curly's feet thumped to the floor.

Ally's eyes widened. Sure, Moe's muscles bulged and stretched the sleeves of his simple T-shirt, but Curly was no lightweight. The guy was huge. Massive. WWF material.

Victor slammed into the room, his typical *savoir-faire* gone with the wind. His pale cheeks were flushed, his scraggly hair sticking up and his pockmarked face covered in a thin sheen of sweat. The clip-on tie of his business suit—Did he fancy himself the CEO of a successful sex-trade company or something?—sat at an odd angle.

A burst of unholy amusement caught Ally by surprise. Counseling, and lots of it, clearly lay in her future.

"He's here." Victor's voice was high-pitched and almost feminine. "Move, you morons. Guard the doors."

The dude had lost it. His bellowing could probably be heard a block over. Real clever way to surprise the enemy. Or the good guys, in this particular case.

Victor latched onto a handful of her hair. Her amusement fled. Pain shot through her skull and she winced. He pressed the muzzle of a gun she couldn't see against her temple.

Moe hadn't moved since Victor's dramatic entrance. "What are you doing?"

"Wha' the hell difference does it make? Ge' in position." Victor ground the gun against her temple and Ally fought back a cry of pain. She wouldn't give him the satisfaction.

"Too late, Victor."

Greg. Ally's gaze flew to the doorway, where his broad shoulders filled the frame. Victor pressed his gun even harder. She ground her teeth and fixed her gaze on Greg, on the grim determination in his eyes and the ridged line of his jaw.

"Wha' are you gonna do, Detective? One wrong move and doll-face here is splattered all over the walls and tha' fancy sui' you're wearing."

Greg was wearing an awfully nice suit. Ally frowned. Had he rushed to her rescue from a hot date? A very formal hot date? The no-good, two-timing jerk. Her stomach rolled and her narrowed gaze shot back up to his.

"Give it up, Victor. This dump is surrounded. You're not going anywhere."

"Oh, no? No' even…" Victor yanked on her hair.

She gasped.

"If I take *her* along for a little walk?"

"I'm not letting you leave this room with her, let alone for a stroll outside."

Greg widened his stance and Ally flashed to a movie scene. An old spaghetti western, the bad guy and the sheriff facing off at high noon on a dusty street. Granted, the bad guy didn't have a gun to the head of a hostage in that movie. And the sheriff/hero wasn't wearing a designer tuxedo. She frowned.

A metallic click made her jump.

She closed her eyes and swallowed. Hard. She didn't know a whole lot about guns, but she was very fond of movies. The click had sounded an awful lot like a firing mechanism snapping into place.

Eyes squeezed tightly shut, it took a second to identify the scrabble of feet across the hardwood floor, followed by a grunt. Her world tilted. The pressure at her temple disappeared and she crashed sideways onto the floor, still tied up.

Ally snapped her eyes open.

Greg rushed forward and relief flooded her. He blew by—*Rude!*—leaving her lying on the nasty floor. More grunts followed. Squirming, she managed to turn the chair around. The three men rolled in a heap, the smack of flesh hitting flesh filling the room.

Victor went limp. Greg and Moe sat back on their heels, eyeing one another. Greg broke first. "You must be Agent Daniel St. James."

Chapter Nineteen

A muscle twitched in Moe's jaw. "I don't know what you're talking about."

Greg stood and offered him a hand up, which he took with every appearance of wariness. "Really? DEA agent working undercover for over a year, gathering evidence of drug-dealing to put Victor away and take apart his operation? Ring any bells?"

"I don't know what you're talking about."

Amazing. Moe *sounded* totally pissed off, but his expression remained bland.

"I have a few connections, Agent St. James."

"Pretty high connections, Detective Marsing."

Greg inclined his head and dusted off his suit. Ally knew from her up-close perusal the grime was an unholy combination of animal droppings, paint shards and dirt. The suit was a total loss. Pity.

Ally cleared her throat and both men turned. "Hi. If you two aren't too busy…"

"Right."

"Sorry."

Moe, err…Daniel, uhm…Agent St. James reached her first. He sliced through the rope around her ankles with his trusty pocketknife. She rolled into a sitting position and he reached behind her to free her hands. Again.

Greg's gaze landed on her cheek and his expression hardened. "What happened to her?"

Moe glanced at her cheek and winced.

Fists clenched, Greg took a step forward. "So help me, if you did that, you won't be walking out of here."

Ally let Moe help her up. Nibbling on her lower lip, she looked between the two men and raised a placating hand. "He didn't mean to, exactly."

Greg turned glittering eyes on her. "*Exactly?*"

She took a step back.

Agent St. James spoke up. "You weren't here, Detective Marsing. Things happen."

"Not to Ally. You were supposed to protect her."

"No, my job was exposing Victor for the drug-dealing slime he is and getting him and his drug pushers off the streets. Not protecting some woman foolish enough to get caught by Victor. Twice."

Ally straightened and glared at St. James. "Hey—"

Who just kept talking over her. "Even if she is your girlfriend."

"She's not my girlfriend," Greg growled.

Ally sucked in a breath. Way harsh. Apparently, convenient fuck-bunny defined her better.

"Then there's no reason for you to be concerned." Agent St. James stepped closer, placing her in the shadow of his well-muscled frame. Ally didn't move, her muscles solidified by betrayal and heartache. She turned her face toward St. James, closed her eyes and breathed in his spicy cologne. Anything to distract her from Greg.

The heavy thud of feet heralded the arrival of several police officers. Under Greg's direction, they hauled Victor to his feet. He came to and the words pouring out of his surly mouth didn't bear repeating.

Greg followed the officers carting Victor to the door. He paused, his gaze darting from St. James to her. Eyes narrowed, Greg opened and closed his mouth several times. His lips thinned and he turned on his heel. Ally sucked in a quiet breath and blinked away a flash of pointless tears.

In his absence, the totally embarrassing and extremely intimate things Agent St. James had witnessed flooded Ally's memory. Cheeks warm, she looked down.

"You okay?" he asked.

"Lovely. You?"

"Well, I could use a vacation." He grinned. For a man so out of practice with smiling, it was lethal when unleashed. Warmth unfurled in her belly, pushing aside the pain of Greg's denial. She returned his smile.

"Yeah, I know the feeling."

St. James nodded to the blood soaking through her shirt. "Your Detective Marsing seems like the thorough type, so I imagine there's an ambulance out front. Better get that looked at."

Ally stiffened. "You heard him. He's not my anything."

He arched his brow and walked away. She followed St. James out and let an EMT do her thing. Having assorted boo-boos patched up after being mauled and abused by some criminally inclined psycho was getting to be old hat. The EMT finished up with a few dire warnings about reopening injuries, and she hopped out of the back of the ambulance.

St. James offered his arm. "Shall we go?"

She grinned at the chivalrous gesture and accepted, even if she didn't entirely trust him, ignoring the speculative looks cast their way by the police officers. Awareness of him as a man, an attractive man, further confused the emotions swirling through her.

"Miss Thompson?"

Hard muscles tightened beneath her light touch. Ally turned and smiled at Captain Morgan.

"Miss Thompson, I am so sorry about all of this. On top of everything else you've been through." He shook his head. "If there's anything I or my department can do for you, just say the word."

"Did you catch the guy who helped Victor escape?"

The captain's expression turned grim as he nodded. "A man with fifteen years on the force. I can only hope that's the last of it, but I intend to make certain." Captain Morgan's gaze shifted to St. James and her hand tucked securely in the crook of his arm.

"Captain Morgan, I'd like to introduce you to A…" St. James' arm turned to granite. With barely a pause, she continued. "… Mr. St. James. He came to my aid before the police arrived. I don't know what would have happened without him. Mr. St. James, Captain Morgan."

Polite greetings were exchanged. Captain Morgan turned to her.

"We'll need you to stop by the station as soon as possible and give a statement." He glanced at St. James. "You too, Mr. St. James."

St. James inclined his head.

Ally doubted Captain Morgan would lay eyes on Agent Daniel St. James again.

Captain Morgan walked away, a tall, white-haired figure amongst the sea of navy-blue uniforms. Greg leaned against a nearby squad car, arms crossed, watching them. Her heart hoped for a sign, a gesture, anything to indicate his interest. Her mind wanted to slap some sense into her heart.

St. James pulled her around. Burning awareness of Greg's gaze stayed with Ally until she and St. James turned a corner. Willingness to suffer for love and a longing to tell Greg to stuff it where the sun didn't shine twisted her into knots. She kept her back straight and shoulders back. Some degree of dignity had to be maintained.

"Thinking of Detective Marsing?"

She glanced at St. James. "For a man who reveals so little, you have an uncanny ability to read other people. Not that you're right."

"Of course not. And reading people comes in handy. It's kept me alive a time or two."

The slight inflection in his voice revealed a lot more than his words. His could not be a pleasant job. He must really believe in what he was doing to be willing to deal with such perversion of human nature on a regular basis.

"Where can I drop you?" He opened the passenger door of a black sports coupe parked at the curb.

Ally eyed the dark interior of the car. Sticking her hands in the front pockets of her jeans, she rocked back on her heels. "Uhm, ya know, I'll just call a cab."

He crossed his arms. "Don't trust me?"

She shrugged.

"You're welcome to call a cab. Though I know for a fact..." St. James paused and his gray eyes darkened a shade, just enough to make her feel itchy. "...You're not carrying a cell phone. Nor do you have any money to pay a cab driver."

Her cheeks warmed. Again. There should be a law on how many times a woman blushed in one day. Like she needed to be reminded that a really, *really* attractive man had searched her? Thoroughly?

She glared at him and lied through her pearly white teeth. "There's always a pay phone tucked away every few blocks, somewhere. And how can you be so sure I don't have any money? I always carry a bill discreetly tucked away. So unless you strip-searched me..."

His brow went up and the bottom fell out of her stomach. Bad enough knowing he'd seen her naked, but if he'd really had his hands all over her, intimately...*holy cow*.

"You don't have any money and there aren't any pay phones. You know my name; you even know what I do for a living and for whom I work. You're as safe as a newborn baby with me."

"I don't expect I'll need to have my nappy changed any time soon." His attitude grated. "Besides, how do I know all that stuff isn't dangerous? In an 'I can tell you, but I'd have to kill you' sort of way. Then there are the numerous so-called," she made air quotes with her fingers, "*respectable* police officers who've tried to kill me."

Gray eyes sparkling with amusement, he grinned and placed his hand over his heart. Wow, when the guy let his mask drop, he let it drop. "Allessandra Thompson, I promise, I have no intention of killing you. Now or ever. Well, if you start dealing drugs I may have to rescind the last part."

She rolled her eyes.

"Now, would you get in the damn car?"

Captain Morgan and Greg knew his name and that she was with him. Besides, if he wanted to kill her, he could have done so earlier and blamed her death on Victor.

So she climbed into his car. And suffered a flash of panic when he drove away from the curb.

"Home?"

Ally swallowed. "Yes. Do I need to even bother to give you the address? You must have a mile-thick file, since you know everything there is to know about me."

"Not quite. For example, I don't know the name of the first boy you ever had a crush on, although I do know the name of the first one you ever slept with."

She stared. "Are you serious?"

"No." He chuckled. "I only know a few facts of your life. Victor's arrest is the only reason I even know that much. We assumed he was safely out of circulation, so I did a little research during my few days off. And," he flashed a Cheshire-cat grin, "the file isn't a mile thick.

"I can't believe I even have a file." Ally cleared her throat. "So I'll take that as a 'no, I don't need to give you my address.'"

"No, you don't."

"What should I call you? Agent St. James? Mr. St. James? Daniel? Danny-boy? Moe?"

"Moe?"

"Long story."

"I can't wait."

"Well, it's not a long story." She tucked a strand of hair behind her ear and smoothed her shirt. "See, I have a habit of, ya know, naming people when I'm in a stressful situation. So you became Moe and the other guy Curly."

"Ah."

Thirty seconds passed while she gnawed on her lip and counted her heartbeats thudding beneath her jaw.

"You can call me Daniel. Or Moe, if you prefer." He grinned.

Ally couldn't deny a little niggle of relief. Some people found her habit annoying. Daniel pulled into her drive and she climbed out, heading for the remote pad beside the garage door. Greg's muscular frame unfolded from a petite wicker chair on her porch and she nearly tripped over an invisible crack in the concrete driveway.

"Greg?" She detoured down her walk. "What are you doing here?"

His gaze went past her. "Look what followed you home."

She glanced back. Daniel hovered behind her, expressionless mask in place, less than a foot between them. "He gave me a ride."

Greg's eyebrows rose. "Not a wise choice, Ally."

Wow. She folded her arms across her chest. "I don't recall asking your opinion. How did you get here before us?"

"I didn't have a headstrong female to convince into my car." He glanced behind her again. "Nice ride, St. James."

"It's a rental, Marsing. Don't get your panties in a knot."

Animosity and testosterone practically vibrated in the air. She sighed. *Men.* "Feel free to tear each other apart in my absence. I'm going inside, where I plan on sitting down with a very large glass of wine and possibly not getting up again until sometime tomorrow. Try not to make too much noise and don't break anything."

She left them staring after her and let herself into her condo. Cool air wafted over her, the scent of cinnamon and apple from the plug-in air freshener welcoming her home. It would have to be enough. Weary beyond description, she kicked her shoes off in the hall closet. Who knew if Greg would ever pull his head out of his butt.

The front door opened and closed. Her entry promptly shrank, but she didn't bother to turn around.

"Would either of you like a glass of wine?" She walked into

the kitchen without waiting for a response, selected a bottle and rummaged through a drawer for the opener.

"Here, let me do that." Greg pulled the bottle from her hands and took the opener she'd unearthed.

"I'll get the glasses." Daniel opened and closed cupboards in search of them.

Huh. Well, if two handsome, strapping men wanted to wait on her, who was she to object?

"Cupboard to the right of the sink." She indicated the appropriate one and collapsed onto her couch. A thump and grunt came from the kitchen, then silence. She sat up. "Everything okay?"

Another thump, a deeper grunt, and a tinkling crash. Ally jumped to her feet and screeched to a halt in the kitchen, eyes wide. Chests rising and falling rapidly, shards of crystal glasses at their feet, St. James and Greg squared off between her crystal and fine china. She crossed her arms and noisily cleared her throat. They spun to face her, quickly straightening their shirts and smoothing their hair. Ally didn't know whether to be amused or annoyed. She glanced at the glass shards and pursed her lips to hide a smile.

"Oh, sorry," they said simultaneously, elbowing one another and jostling to get to the broom closet. Daniel reached the handle first and shoved a strategic elbow into Greg's ribcage. Greg "ooomphed" and slammed into the wall. A large framed poster of Paris shimmied, then crashed to the floor.

Ally sighed and crossed her arms, casting her gaze heavenward. "Seriously?"

"Sorry." Greg grabbed the picture and rehung it.

Daniel snorted on his way into the kitchen with the broom and dustpan. Exasperated with them both, she lay down on the couch and crossed her ankles on top of the armrest. She didn't even care about the dented corner of the picture frame. After all that had happened, she could barely tolerate her home. She sat up straight with a start.

Joel had called earlier with an offer.

While the two men puttered in her kitchen, peacefully this time, she picked up the cordless and had a quick conversation with her cousin. By the end of which she'd sold her condo and made an appointment to start searching for a new...something. Apartment, house, another condo, she didn't know at this point.

She didn't especially care, as long as it wasn't this place.

Greg and Daniel walked in. She eyed the two of them. Something about the way they moved linked them in a way nothing else could. They shared the instincts of a predator. And they were in her home, serving her wine. Freaky.

She took a sip. The sweet red wine went down with a polite bite. Greg sat in an overstuffed chair beside the couch she was hogging. Daniel chose a chair by the front windows.

They both stared at her.

"What?"

The men exchanged a glance and her back stiffened.

Greg leaned forward. "I'm worried about you, Ally."

"Why?"

"For starters, your life has been threatened repeatedly over the last few weeks."

"*C'est la vie.*" Not very nice of him to rub salt in her wounds. Settling deeper into the couch, Ally glanced at Daniel. "Did you have something to contribute?"

He grinned. "I think I'll just seduce you. Nothing like great sex to relax a person."

"Funny."

"Who was being funny?"

"I almost liked you for a few minutes," Greg growled.

Ally took another sip of wine, watching them.

"If she were under you," Daniel said, "I wouldn't be here."

"If you think I'm just going to sit here while you sweep her off her feet—"

"Greg," Ally interrupted, "Daniel is talking about sex, not marriage."

Daniel laughed. "I like a girl who isn't afraid to call it like it is."

"I appreciate the offer, but I'm not interested. Kinda like someone else I know." She slanted a narrow look at Greg.

"She's got you there, mate." Daniel leaned back and took a drink of his wine.

Greg grinned tightly. "Now, sweetheart, you know that's not true. I'm more than happy to take you to bed."

Ally snorted. "Yeah, like that's gonna happen."

"Please." Daniel raised a hand in the air. "You'll traumatize my young ears."

She laughed, relaxing into the cushions, a pleasant buzz dulling less-agreeable emotions. Like a fractured heart and irritation over Greg's attitude.

"So, what are your plans now, Ally?" Daniel asked.

"For what?"

His eyebrows went up. "Oh, come on. You aren't just going back to your boring life, are you?"

"Boring?" She bolted upright, indignant. "What do you know about my life, anyway?"

"I read your file, remember? Twenty-nine-year-old insurance claims processor, owns a modest condo in the suburbs, never travels, stays home a lot. Alone. No boyfriend, no mysterious lover, no significant other."

"Well, when you put it like that." Ally slid down in her seat. "You said the file was thin."

"You shouldn't believe everything you're told." Greg glared at Daniel.

A speculative look lit Daniel's eyes. "Have you ever considered working for—"

Greg snorted. "Don't bother."

Daniel shrugged and went back to sipping his wine. He'd swirled the wine, stuck his nose in the glass and inhaled deeply, then sipped. A real connoisseur. Daniel St. James had unplumbed depths, but she'd leave the plumbing to another woman.

She yawned. The sun had set and she was crashing fast.

Daniel rose and scooped the empty glass from her limp fingers on his way out of the room. A few seconds later the water in the kitchen came on. A man who did dishes. Didn't know they made those anymore.

Ally yawned again, curling up on the couch as her eyes drifted closed.

"Oh no, you don't." Greg scooped her up into his arms.

Wrapped in his strong arms, the steady beat of his heart beneath her ear, hand fisted in his shirt, her heart cracked a little more.

"About what I said earlier," he murmured against her hair. "I didn't mean it the way it sounded."

"I am your girlfriend?" Hope stirred, but the silence stretched a little too long.

"I'm not..." He sighed. "It's not that easy, sweetheart."

She released his shirt and settled her hand limply in her lap. "Okay. Well, I appreciate all of your help over the last few weeks." A huge yawn escaped, slurring the last part. "You've been great."

Greg sighed and headed for the stairs. "Up to bed."

Daniel snorted. He stood in the archway to the kitchen, a broad shoulder against the wall and his arms crossed. "At least I was upfront about seducing her."

"I'm not seducing her. I'm putting her to bed."

"Poor Ally," Daniel murmured, a wicked gleam in his eye. "Are you sure you don't want any company, darlin'? Someone to help warm your bed?"

Relaxed against Greg's familiar warmth, Ally belatedly remembered the pain pills the EMT had forced down her. No wonder a single glass of wine had hit her so hard. She'd be down for the count soon.

Her sluggish brain caught up with the conversation and she frowned. "Not unless it's Greg. And he won't, 'cause he doesn't like me anymore."

Greg's arms tightened before he gently sat her on her bed.

She fell back against the soft mattress with a sigh.

"Are you going to let her sleep in her clothes?" Daniel asked.

"Go 'way," Ally mumbled.

"You heard her." Smugness lightened Greg's voice. "Go away before I throw you out."

"Don't worry about me." Daniel sounded closer. "I've seen her naked before."

"What?" The anger in Greg's voice roused her from her stupor. Sort of.

"Victor," she mumbled, rolling over and snuggling deeper into her bed. "Whore-house."

"You were there? You did nothing to help her?" Disgust lined Greg's words. "And people wonder why I refuse to work for the government."

Her shoes were pulled off and landed on the floor with a thud. A masculine hand settled on her hip. Greg was undressing her? Her body tingled and warmed. Trapped between sleep and wakefulness, Ally wasn't terribly motivated to stop him. She did have one worry niggling at her conscience.

"Daniel?"

The wonderful hands paused in their work for a few beats.

"He left. Went downstairs, left for good, I don't know or care. You'll be more comfortable without these."

He tugged her jeans off. Just her luck, to develop a fondness for thong panties at this point in her life, about the same time a handsome police detective decided to make her comfort a priority. Cool air washed over her bare butt, Greg lifted her the rest of the way onto the bed and the soft weight of a blanket settled over her.

"Sleep, sweetheart. Things will seem better in the morning."

His voice sounded deeper, huskier.

"Stay," she whispered, drifting. "Please."

Weighted silence followed her request. The sweet darkness of sleep beckoned, but she held off—just a few more seconds.

The rough pad of his finger traced her jawline and his sigh

ruffled her hair. "Good night, Sugar Lips."

A dart of pain hit home. Her door clicked closed behind Greg and quiet solitude descended. She pictured him sitting beside her, back before life had gotten so complicated, lazy amusement sparkling in his green eyes. It really was time to move on. A tear slipped free.

Chapter Twenty

Three weeks later....

"I don't know about this one, Joel. It's a bit...industrial." Ally turned, surveying the open configuration of the space. "Although, I do like the exposed brick and the character. What do you think, Celia?"

"I love the brick." Celia spun slowly on her crocodile stilettos. "I don't mind the exposed duct work. Once it's furnished and decorated, I don't think you'd notice it. And the kitchen... Ally, it's gorgeous. How many places have we looked at with a gourmet kitchen?"

"None. You're right. What about the empty space below? I know you said there are a few more condos on this floor, but they aren't sold yet. I'd be living here alone."

"That's true, but the building has excellent security. The first floor is set up to be a commercial lease. Or split up into several commercial leases. This is a great opportunity, Ally. Getting in on the ground floor of an up-and-coming real-estate location. Once the rest of the community gets wind of this, the prices are going to go through the roof. Imagine the equity you'll have."

"How did you find out about this, anyway?" She eyed him suspiciously. Joel was a great realtor, but she never would have suspected he had the kind of connections that allowed him this type of access.

"Another realtor turned me onto it." He shrugged, turned and scanned the room. "I love the floors in here."

Well aware he was trying to distract her, Ally dutifully admired the original wide-plank wood flooring. Carefully refurbished to retain years of wear, they'd been finished with a beautiful clear stain. In a word, gorgeous. They ran through all fourteen hundred square feet of the condo.

"I still can't get over the price," she said. "Only two hundred forty-nine thousand for this place? For this area, that's insane."

"Don't look a gift horse in the mouth," Celia quipped.

Ally glanced at her sharply, but Celia was busy admiring the large windows with the original glass, dating back to 1889 when the factory was built. The glass surviving looters and juvenile delinquents was a miracle.

"Yeah." Joel drew the word out and she turned toward him. He was staring at Celia like a lovesick puppy. Even knowing she was practically living with Detective Lucas Jones didn't stop him from mooning over Celia when she wasn't looking. Ally rolled her eyes.

Joel cleared his throat. "The low price is one of the perks of being the first to buy."

Walking around, Ally took in the brick, the floors, and the fabulous kitchen. "I think you guys are right."

"Of course I am." Celia smiled. "That's why you brought me. For my exquisite taste and expert opinion."

Ally returned her smile. Celia had blossomed in the last few weeks. Being in love and loved by Lucas had helped her accept herself. A new contentment and happiness radiated from within, increasing her stunning beauty. No wonder Joel was smitten.

Decision made, Ally grinned. "Write up the offer, Joel."

"Thank you, Lord."

"Are you saying I've been difficult?"

"Yes, I am. We've spent weeks searching every corner of this city and the outlying suburbs. At least I get paid for this torture.

I'm not sure how Celia managed."

The over-the-top, admiring gaze he turned on Celia made Ally wince, but Celia just smiled. Celia's poise left her in awe. Ally was doing her best to mimic her, but she didn't know how well she succeeded.

"Ally, could we grab a coffee?" Celia turned to Joel, all lovely tact and sweet smile. "I hate to exclude you, Joel, but it's girl-talk. You understand?"

"Of course, of course. No problem. You girls run along and have fun."

Ally rolled her eyes again.

"No problem at all. I understand completely." Joel grinned, rolling his shoulders back and propping a fist on his hip. He stopped short of bowing them out, thank heaven.

Celia slipped her arm through hers as they left, a conspiratorial grin on her face. Ten minutes later they settled at a little table in a bistro around the corner.

"Another reason to love the condo," Celia said with a smile. "You're steps from great restaurants and shops."

"Good thing I'm making an offer."

Ally sipped her nonfat chai tea latte. The last weeks had been a whirlwind of activity. Packing and moving out of her old condo had been a huge relief. Celia had offered her the temporary use of her apartment. She was pretty much living at Lucas' house, while her apartment sat empty.

Ally had gratefully accepted. On top of that, Celia's help in her house-hunt had proved invaluable.

A healthy savings account enabled her to quit her painfully boring job and future employment was very much up in the air. Talk about a life in upheaval. At least she'd always been smart with her finances. Her last place had been paid for, which allowed her to buy the new one without worrying about little details. Like a job.

A man's low voice rumbled behind her. She thought of Greg and closed her eyes against the flare of pain. She hadn't seen or heard from him since he'd left her sleeping in her bed the night of Victor's second arrest. His absence left an aching hole in her life.

"Hello?" Celia waved a slim, manicured hand in front of her face.

"Sorry." Ally opened her eyes and made a face. "Guess my mind wandered."

"Uh-huh." Celia eyed her speculatively.

"Anyway…" Blowing out a breath, Ally quelled the nerves fluttering in her stomach. "I had an idea I wanted to talk to you about. Something we've touched on a few times, which has been on my mind a lot lately."

Celia cocked her head to the side. "Sure."

"I got the idea while we were walking around looking at the main level of the building beneath the condo. What would you think about opening a women's shelter? But go all out. We wouldn't be giving them just a place to stay. We would also offer education, prepare them to enter the workplace, the ability to manage a budget and balance a checkbook. We could especially look for women who are leaving an abusive situation and prostitution, whether voluntary or forced."

Ally sat back, chewing on her bottom lip and staring at Celia. The idea meant so much to her. The beginning of a dream, stepping up and taking full control of her life. Still, she couldn't take on such a big project alone. Celia had the kind of financial backing necessary to make her dream a success. If she was interested.

Celia grinned. "I love it."

Ally clapped her hands, almost bouncing in her seat, relief and excitement rushing through her and going to her head like a cold glass of bubbly.

Celia fixed her with a determined gaze. "Just one thing. Let me handle the details of the space, okay? It'll be a joint endeavor, one hundred percent, but I'd like to take care of the real estate."

"As long as you agree to let me pay my share. It won't be much of a partnership if we start out with you biting off such a huge chunk alone."

"Ally, please. I'm a trust-fund baby." Celia voice was quietly self-mocking. "I could buy a dozen of those buildings and still have enough to last a lifetime."

Ally gaped. She'd known Celia was rich, but *that* rich? She shut her mouth and shook her head. "I don't care. I still want to pay half."

"You don't understand. All my life I've just been this flibbertigibbet-do-nothing. I shopped, I went out with friends, but I was nothing. I had nothing. I want this for more than just a way to help other women. It'll help me too." Celia leaned forward, every line of her slim body tense. "For once, my money will go to something with a purpose. Something beneficial. Let me do this."

She sighed. "Sure. Take away all my cards. That's playing dirty, Celia."

"I know. I'd apologize, but I wouldn't mean it. Just say you'll let me pay for it, and you won't regret it."

"Okay, fine," Ally smiled. "Go for it."

It took a month to get everything set up. Celia purchased the entire main floor of the building housing Ally's condo. Within a week of receiving the necessary permits, workmen were everywhere. Thanks to Celia's family connections, their permits flew through the usual channels.

Meanwhile, Ally moved into her new home. A shortage of furniture—her old space had been much smaller—sent her and Celia on a weekend shopping trip out of town. They returned with enough furniture to fill her condo, as well as some great pieces for their office downstairs. Lucas lounged against the old brick exterior when they pulled up to the curb Sunday evening.

Ally busied herself parking the moving truck, opened the back and pulled out some of the smaller pieces while Celia and Lucas reunited. Watching them kiss like lovers parted for months instead of a few days sent her unruly memories flying back in time to Greg. Misery settled around her heart. Straightening her shoulders and lifting her chin, she loaded the freight elevator with everything she could carry and headed upstairs.

Greg leaned against the wall beside her door, bringing her up short.

"Hey, Sugar Lips." He grinned and took the small hall table from her hands.

"Uhm...hi." How could he show up with zero notice, acting like they'd just seen each other a few hours ago? "What are you doing here?"

"I haven't seen the new place, so I thought I'd drop by."

"Just like that?" Ally cleared her throat and muzzled her inner bitch. "Celia and I just got back."

"Yeah, Lucas told me about your weekend expedition to the far reaches of our fair state. Knowing he was waiting down there for Celia, I figured retreat to be the better part of valor."

Wishing she could laugh, she unlocked her door. "I know what you mean."

She held open the door as he carried in the table.

"Not exactly G-rated, huh?"

"No."

She stuck a towel underneath the door as an impromptu doorstop and went back for a couple of lamps from the elevator. When she got back, Greg stood in her kitchen.

"Want the grand tour?"

"Uh..." He shifted from one foot to the other, looking uncomfortable—until his alter ego slid into place and he grinned. "Sure."

Ally gritted her teeth. When would he stop hiding?

By the time they were done, Celia and Lucas had managed to pry themselves apart to join them. The men moved the heavy pieces and Ally directed positioning upstairs while Celia handed out instructions downstairs. Two hours later, they all collapsed in Ally's living room.

"Man, moving is exhausting," Greg said.

"Tell me about it," Ally said. "I won't be doing it again for a long time."

"What if—" Lucas broke off with a grunt. Ally raised her head from the back of the couch. He and Celia shared a couch and Lucas arched his eyebrow at Celia.

Ally dropped her head back, her belly twisting over their display.

Communicating without words, loving touches... sometimes it killed her to be around those two.

"Love the new place," Greg filled the silence.

"I do too," she said. "And I can't wait until we open our shelter operation in a few weeks."

"That reminds me," Lucas said. "I talked to the security company on Friday. They'll be by tomorrow morning to look at your setup. Then they'll let us know what you need."

"I still don't think—" Celia started.

Lucas firmly interrupted her. "We agreed it wasn't up for debate, Celia."

"It's a good idea." Ally glanced between the two. "Some of the women will be coming from difficult, even dangerous, situations that could follow them to us. We don't want any of the women hurt or threatened. *I* don't want to be hurt or threatened."

"I know." Celia sighed. "I just worry the women will find the system invasive."

Lucas hugged her to his side. "They'll set up cameras around the perimeter, alarms on the doors and windows and guards on a few of the more vulnerable entrances. It may take some getting used to, but before long you won't even notice. Besides, just think how much safer the women will feel."

"That's true," Celia said.

They stared into one another's eyes.

Ally shifted, crossed her arms, glanced at Greg and quickly looked away.

Lucas and Celia clearly needed some private one-on-one time.

Lucas stood and pulled Celia up with him, confirming her thoughts. They made an attractive, if unlikely, couple. The tough, hardened detective and the delicate-looking socialite.

"We're gonna head out," Lucas said.

Celia came over and hugged her. "You'll be okay?"

"Of course."

"I had so much fun this weekend." Celia stepped back.

"Me too."

"See you later." Greg waved from his reclined position on her couch.

Celia went over and dropped a kiss on his cheek, whispering something to him before she rejoined Lucas on the way out the door.

The door slammed and awkward silence descended. What did she do now? Offer to feed Greg? Jump him? Throw him out?

"See much of St. James these days?" Greg asked a little too casually.

Jealous? In a less-than-forthcoming mood, she crossed her arms. "Not really."

"Huh. Guess I'll head home too." He stood and stretched. "It's getting late."

She wasn't about to get clingy and hate being alone at this point in her life. Ally lifted her chin.

"You'll be okay?"

She must look like some wilting hothouse flower to make everyone ask if she'd be okay. "I've lived on my own for years. I'll be fine."

"I know." He shrugged. "It's a new place. Hard to settle in sometimes."

"This isn't my first night. I moved in two weeks ago." She was suddenly very tired.

"Alright." He rose and headed down the hallway, toward the front door. "Just trying to look out for a friend."

That didn't sting. She followed him.

"Thanks for your help," she ground out through clenched teeth.

"No problem. G'night."

Ally locked the door behind him and rested against it. The

quiet closed in around her.

"Music. I need music."

In her room, she switched on the alarm radio by her bed. The loud music thumped, lightening her mood while she changed into a little nightgown. Then she sank into the plush armchair she'd positioned at an angle in one corner of her sanctuary.

She'd painted the walls a deep sea-green color. Silky bedding draped her new king-sized bed in shades of blue, green, and purple. Soft, floaty fabric accented the windows.

With a heavy sigh, Ally flipped off the lights and crawled into bed. Lying there watching the headlights of passing cars play over her ceiling, her mind hummed at a steady clip and her muscles twitched.

Grumbling under her breath, she crawled out of bed and headed for the kitchen, not bothering with any lights. She grabbed an open bottle of wine from the fridge and poured a small amount into an antique crystal glass. One of a set she'd picked up over the weekend.

Staring out her windows, she sipped her wine. Gradually, her muscles relaxed and her breathing deepened. Exhaustion and wine swept aside her body's resistance to sleep. She headed for her bedroom.

Just shy of her room, the click of a locking mechanism tumbling open froze Ally in her tracks. The doorknob on her front door rotated. All her lovely relaxation fled, replaced with the sting of adrenaline in her veins.

What the flip? Did she have the worst luck or what? Had she broken a mirror unawares and gotten seven years back luck?

Thankful she'd chosen a black silk nightie to sleep in, she crept into deeper shadows. She was tempted to sneak into her bedroom to hide, locking the door behind her. But, if one doorway hadn't stopped him, another one wouldn't either. Then again, if he only wanted to rob her blind, maybe he wouldn't bother with the bedroom.

Ally stood in the shadows, watching a very large, dark shape slip inside and close her front door. She could be lying sound asleep in her bed about now, blissfully unaware. Somehow, oblivion didn't seem like an appealing option.

The most likely scenario was definitely robbery, although why he hadn't waited until she left for the day was a mystery. Oh, right. There were workmen around all day. Still, she could hope.

He crept closer to her hiding spot and she focused on being invisible. Fingers tensing, the cut-crystal stem of the antique goblet bit into her fingers, reminding her of its presence. Wait a second. What the hell was she doing? Get the phone, dumbass!

Or—she glanced at the big shape approaching and then the remarkably flimsy little glass in her hand—a weapon at least. Well, she sorta had a weapon. Something was better than nothing.

Maybe if she kicked him in the crotch and *then* broke the glass over his head. Yeah, that sounded like a plan. Of course, she would have to let him get really close first, which sucked sour grapes.

Pressed against the wall, she held her breath. Almost there. Almost…

Ally lashed out with her bare foot and connected with solid, warm flesh. He grunted and she quickly brought down the goblet. The man caught her wrist mid-swing and flattened her against the wall. She wanted to howl in frustration.

"Damn woman, castrate a man why don't you?"

"Daniel?" She sagged in relief, swiftly replaced by fury. "Daniel!"

"Yeah, I think we cleared that up already."

He sounded a little off. Oh right, she'd kicked him in the testicles. She jerked her wrist free. Served him right.

Spinning on her heel, she marched back into the kitchen, flipping on lights en route. She rinsed the goblet and put it away, needing time to calm down. At least she hadn't broken the irreplaceable glass over his worthless head.

"I'm glad you didn't break it over my worthless head too."

She'd spoken aloud? "It would've served you right. What are

you doing breaking in anyway? And in the middle of the night. Normal people knock, ya know."

Turning to face him, she planted her hands on her hips and glared. He just grinned and leaned against her counter, unrepentant. An appreciative gleam lit his gray eyes as he surveyed her black nightie.

Clearly she hadn't kicked him hard enough. She refused to be embarrassed. Even when she glanced down and realized the cool air had pebbled her nipples.

Daniel glanced around her condo. "What fun is there in that?"

Considering this was the third time he'd broken in, she doubted there was that much "fun" involved. Ally crossed her arms and tapped her foot. Focusing on her again, his eyes darkened. She dropped her arms. Nature had given her enough cleavage.

"Might I enquire as to the reason behind this midnight visit?"

"I was in the neighborhood."

"Lucky me. You were also in the neighborhood a week ago, and the week before that, and…oh, hey! The week before that."

He grinned.

She rolled her eyes. "I'm going to have to upgrade my security staff, I see."

"That's cute. About the time a Rent-A-Cop can catch me, it's well past time I hang up my hat, darlin'." His gaze slid down over her legs, his perusal far more leisurely this time.

Swallowing and tugging on her hemline, Ally edged toward the hall. "I'll just run on down to my bedroom and slip into something more comfortable."

She honestly didn't mind his visits. He was fun to chat with, incredibly smart, witty as hell, and knew something about just about everything. Even so, it'd be nice if he just knocked once in a while. She'd just set foot in her bedroom when someone started banging on her front door. In a heartbeat Daniel was at her side, shadowing her to the door.

"This time of night," he said in a low voice, "people at the door are never a good thing."

"Funny, I've been thinking the same thing." She glared at him, still irked over how badly he'd scared her.

She reached for the knob, but Daniel brushed her aside and yanked the door open. Peering around him, her eyes rounded. Greg stood on the other side, disheveled and furious and so incredibly handsome her heart lodged in her throat.

"Detective Marsing." Daniel leaned a forearm against the door-frame above his head, filling the frame and effectively blocking the entrance. "What a fascinating coincidence, running into you here. And at this time of night. What brings you to *our* neck of the woods?"

Her heart abandoned her throat and plunged to her feet. Daniel had implied so much, she didn't even know where to start. What would Greg think? Then again, he had eloquently displayed how thoroughly he didn't care. Why should she?

Regardless, she slipped under Daniel's arm, coming to her full height in front of him. With Daniel behind her and Greg in front, neither giving an inch, she became the filling of a very intoxicating sandwich. Their heat surrounded her. A dangerous brew of testosterone and hard muscle went straight to her head.

Ally straightened her spine. Greg's gaze dropped to her breasts. She cleared her throat. His eyes met hers, his expression going all Detective Marsing—about as readable as the brick wall behind him.

"Detective. What can I do for you?"

"I thought you hadn't seen St. James."

"Like it's any of your business?" Ally scowled.

Greg's eyes narrowed and his lips thinned.

She rolled her eyes. "Whatever. Your intimidation tactics aren't going to work on me."

"Do you always answer your door dressed in lingerie?"

"I didn't..." Ally bit off the explanation and bared her teeth, uhm...smiled. "Why are you here, Greg?"

"I was driving by and saw your light on, so I thought I'd check and make sure everything was okay." He glanced at his wristwatch. "It is after 2:00 am."

Detective Marsing, ever on the job. "Well, thank you for checking. As you can see, I'm fine."

His gaze skated over her, from the tips of her fire-engine-red toenails to the top of her bed-mussed hair, leaving her burned in its wake. Then he looked over her shoulder. Daniel and all he had so helpfully implied still loomed close enough to feather her hair with each breath. Determined to end this before Greg did, she spoke.

"Thank you again, Detective. Now, if you'll excuse me, it's late."

Ally tried to back inside, but Daniel didn't move. She debated elbowing him, hard, but Greg was far too close. His spicy cologne was doing things to her hormones and clouding her ability to reason.

Fighting her body, she locked gazes with him. She would *not* do something foolish like fling herself into his arms. Desperation was unappealing. To her. She was a pretty, desirable woman. No need to reduce her self-image to sludge because of this man.

Pep talk finished, Ally managed to dredge up a smile. "Was there something else?"

"Could I have a word? Alone?"

Hope flared in her chest, but she ruthlessly squashed it. The absence of heat at her back told her Daniel had finally given ground and retreated inside, leaving her facing the man who'd broken her heart. Swallowing, she waited.

"I realize I've given up my right to ask, but are you okay?"

She barely swallowed a snort. "I'm fine."

"Why is Agent St. James here?"

"I don't see how that's any of your business, Detective. As you said, you've given up any claim to me or my time."

Greg stiffened and his eyes flickered.

She raised her eyebrows.

"I just…" He paused. Cleared his throat. "I don't want to see you get hurt, Ally."

Hearing him say her name hurt. Seeing him, smelling him hurt. She just plain ol' *hurt*. "You won't be around to see it if I do get hurt, will you?" Time to go lick her wounds in private. "Now, if you'll excuse me."

She turned, but he caught her arm. Ally contemplated his hand caging her wrist before meeting his stormy sea gaze. "You don't seem to understand, Detective." She enunciated her words carefully. "I live alone. I work alone. I shop alone. I drive alone. That's my life. I don't see it changing anytime soon. I'm not your responsibility. I haven't been for some time. So, what I do with my time, or who I spend it with, is none of your business. I can manage my life just fine."

Expression unreadable, Greg stared at her.

She didn't see the relief she would have expected. After all, she wasn't going to cling or cry or demand anything. With crystal clarity, she knew he'd never offer anything more than sex.

When he didn't move, she tried again. "I'm well aware our little…" She waved a hand, searching for the right word. "…affair is no longer convenient. *I'm* no longer convenient."

"Ally, I didn't sleep with you because you were convenient."

"You don't understand." She smiled, the crack in her heart deepening with each word. She didn't have a choice. She had to let him go. "I'm no longer available. A long-term affair doesn't interest me. Casual sex isn't my thing."

"It wasn't casual sex, sweetheart." He shoved a hand into his hair and stared at the floor. "I want to…I want more. With you. I've never felt this way about a woman before, and I don't have the first clue what to do about it." Greg flung his arms out. "I'm not *capable* of *more*, Ally."

If she lived to be a hundred, she'd never understand men. Why wouldn't he just go away already? He was killing her, one word at a time.

"Whatever. I get it. I just wanted *you* to know I get it." Dredging courage from her toes, she took a deep breath and met his eyes. "The truth is…" She closed her eyes and gritted her teeth. Sometimes, the truth really did hurt. She met his gaze, determined to see the moment through to the end. "The truth is, I love you, but I want more than you're willing to offer. I *need* more, and I deserve it."

Greg gave a jerky nod, at odds with his natural grace. His eyes were brilliant, cutting her heart into a million shards. "You do deserve more, Ally. You deserve a man who'll put you on a pedestal and worship at your feet. You deserve a man who'll give you his whole heart and hold nothing back. You deserve the world, sweetheart."

Then he walked away.

She couldn't believe he'd say all those lovely things and then just walk away.

He turned the corner, disappearing from her sight, her life, and still she stood frozen in place.

A warm arm stole around her waist and pulled her inside. "Come on, darlin'."

Daniel led her inside and into her bedroom, pushing her down to sit on the bed. He left, returning minutes later with her crystal goblet and wrapped her cold fingers around it. "Drink this. You'll feel better."

She drained the glass in one gulp. Her throat went up in flames, her stomach imploded and she started coughing. "What was that?" she gasped between wheezing breaths.

Daniel rubbed the back of his neck and grinned sheepishly. "Vodka."

"What?" The inferno in her belly reduced to hot coals. "I don't have any vodka."

"It's mine."

"You carry a bottle of vodka?"

He pulled a silver flask from his jacket pocket. "I thought we could celebrate the new place."

"You broke into my home in the middle of the night to toast my new condo? That's...oddly sweet. Creepy, but sweet." Ally smiled and pressed a hand to her gradually cooling throat. Heat and warmth stole outward from her belly. She admired Daniel, pushing aside the fresh pain of broken dreams. He was a remarkably handsome man.

A handsome man who had seen her in really humiliating positions but didn't seem to care. He was standing in her home, wanting to celebrate with her. He'd dropped by to chat every single week, despite what must surely be a hectic schedule. Most importantly, he was still there. Unlike Greg. She tilted her head to the side, gaze skimming the length of his body, lingering on the growing bulge in his pants. Maybe it was time to move on with *every* area of her life and create a new future. One where she wasn't alone.

Ignoring the twist of pain in her chest and uncertainty burning a hole in her stomach, she met his eyes. They had darkened to gunmetal gray. He knew what she was thinking. In another lifetime she would have been embarrassed. But that girl was gone, and she wasn't quite sure who had taken the place of that shy, withdrawn woman. Neither did she particularly care.

She stood and moved toward Daniel, a seductive little sway to her hips. At least, she hoped the sway was seductive. Unsure of her welcome, she rested her hand on his chest. This man had saved her from being raped, badly hurt or killed. And he was gorgeous.

Shoring up her courage, Ally walked her fingertips up his chest, over his shoulder and around his neck. She pulled his head down and pressed her lips to his. For a terrifying moment, he didn't move. Then his arms came around her, pressing her soft curves into his hard muscles, and he took control of the kiss. He devoured her mouth. His hand moved down her black silk nightie and under the short hem to cup her bare bottom.

Desire warmed her and she sucked his tongue into her mouth. His fingers bit into the tender skin of her bottom and she jumped, startled. His other hand moved to her breast, squeezing and plumping. So, he was a little rough. She could deal. Tilting her pelvis, she rubbed against his erection. Groaning, he pinched her nipple. Ally yelped.

Without missing a beat, Daniel tumbled her onto the bed and followed her down. His mouth moved to her neck, sucking and nipping. The desire that had fled returned, flaring hotter. The delicate fabric of her nightie shredded beneath his hands and he tossed the torn material over the side of the bed. Pulling back, he zeroed-in on her still-smooth pelvis.

"I'm glad you kept it this way." His voice was husky with arousal. "You have such a pretty pussy."

Ice solidified the blood in her veins. He kissed a trail down her body, oblivious. His words were a harsh slap in the face; a glaring reminder of her time trapped in Victor's basement.

Daniel licked the sensitive skin at the junction of her thighs and forced two thick fingers inside her. Her back arched, her head pressing into the bed. She gulped air and tried to relax. The pain of his invasion rippled through her body.

"You're a little dry, darlin'. We'll have to see what we can do about that."

With little regard to the extremely delicate way nature crafted the female body, he sucked her sensitive bud into his mouth. Ally fisted the comforter and whimpered.

"You like that, baby?"

Daniel shoved a third finger inside her and her control snapped. She scurried backward, biting her lower lip to keep in the cry of pain as his fingers came free, doing an excellent imitation of a crab in her desperation.

"I'm sorry." She curled naked against the headboard, panting, reaching blindly for the robe hanging beside her bed. She didn't dare take her gaze off him. "I'm so sorry, Daniel. I can't. I'm sorry. I can't. Please."

Daniel knelt at the edge of her bed, dark eyes gleaming in the light shining into her bedroom. She had no idea what he was thinking. There was no doubt he'd been aroused and no way of knowing how he'd react to her abrupt withdrawal.

Seconds ticked by. He remained still and silent. Watching her.

Panic unfurled. She didn't know this man. Fingers closing at last on her robe, she yanked it down and draped it over herself. His silence eroded the last of her self-control. Tears she'd held at bay for what felt like days spilled down her cheeks.

"I'm sorry," she wailed, trying to become one with the headboard.

In agonizing increments, he moved to sit on the end of the bed. "It's fine, Ally."

"I didn't mean to lead you on. I swear. I just thought…It's just…" She stumbled to a stop. Nothing she could say would be very flattering to him.

"Ally, breathe." Wry humor crept into his voice. "It's fine. I'll be uncomfortable for a while, but I understand."

"I'm sorry. It's just…" *Good night, Ally. Shut up already.*

"It's just I'm not Greg, and you can't have sex with a man when your heart isn't involved."

The breath she hadn't realized she'd been holding released. Daniel wasn't going to lash out or force her. She shuddered to put words to her biggest fear and realized anew that she didn't know this man.

"At first, I thought I wouldn't mind being your consolation prize, but in the end, I guess I do." On silent feet, he circled the bed to where she huddled against the headboard. "You're a remarkable woman, Ally. Everything Greg said to you was true." Ally stared up at him, outlined in the gray light of her room. He'd heard her conversation with Greg? "You deserve everything your heart desires."

Daniel leaned down and pressed a soft, gentle kiss to her trembling lips. So unlike the others he'd given her. His hand exerted gentle, tender pressure to tilt her face to his. A hairsbreadth from her lips, he spoke. "When he comes back to you…and he will… make him work for it."

Ally nodded, dazed. Daniel dropped one last lingering, achingly sweet kiss on her lips before releasing her. Then he turned on his heel and strode out of her room. Confused and shivering, she heard the quiet click of her front door closing and the locks engaging.

Automatically, she placed her robe on the hook and wriggled beneath the comforter.

Had Daniel been rough with her on purpose, knowing she was using him? Had he intentionally pushed her out of lust and into reality with his harsh words? Studying people was part of his job. He would know exactly what to say and do to get a certain reaction out of people. From the little he'd told her, his life often depended on that ability.

She pressed her fingers to her lips, remembering the gentleness of his last kiss. A different person than the man who'd been so rough had kissed her good-bye. And she'd felt...cared for. Treasured.

At least the disaster with Daniel had kept her from thinking about the sight of Greg's broad back walking away from her. Until now.

Chapter Twenty-One

Ally slammed the front door behind her, hurried down the hall, tossed her purse on the island, spun, and tripped over her sandals. Grumbling, she snatched them from the kitchen floor. Her mind had been going a mile-a-minute all day. Unpleasant exchanges with two different men, plus a serious shortage of sleep, followed by a painfully long day at work equaled an irritable Ally. The sound of someone clearing their throat stopped her in her tracks.

Her belly tightened painfully and she spun, eyes widening. The owner of the company she used to work for sat in her favorite wingback chair. What the freak? Beams of sunshine spilled through her big windows and across his perfectly styled salt-and-pepper hair, accentuating his distinguished appearance. During her five years with the company, Ally had only met him twice. He'd been perfectly polite, even charming.

Breaking into her condo wasn't especially polite, however.

"Uhm…Mr. Chesterfield." She glanced around for a clue to his presence. "What's up?"

He smiled and smoothed his pant leg. It wasn't a particularly charming smile. Which did nothing to soothe the panic growing like a mushroom cloud. "I thought I'd drop by for a visit."

"How…kind." She sidled behind the kitchen island and grabbed the tea kettle. "I'll put on some tea, shall I?"

"Aren't you a polite little hostess?"

Somehow, that didn't sound like a compliment. Had she left her door unlocked? Even if she had, how had he gotten past security? She filled the kettle with water and set it on the stove to boil. Carl was on tonight, and he was very thorough.

"Why don't you stop fidgeting and come sit down, dear?"

Dear? Eww. She started toward the couch, only to pause halfway there. Now that she thought about it, she didn't recall seeing Carl downstairs. A nasty suspicion bloomed. If her boss was behind everything that happened—timing, events, too-convenient coincidences clicked into place. Her gaze flicked to Mr, Chesterfield, the contents of her stomach congealing.

His elegant pin-stripe suit was totally out of place in her industrial-style condo. A brilliant-red tie stood out in stark contrast to the dark-blue shirt he wore under the black suit. He crossed one slim leg over the other, the high shine of designer shoes catching the light and breaking her trance.

"Your coworkers have been very concerned about you, Miss Thompson. I heard you quit after a serious injury. How are you feeling?"

He was sitting in her condo, uninvited, because he was worried about her health? Right, and she was the Easter Bunny. The long hair hid her floppy ears. Ally edged toward the island. *Where did I put my cell phone? Or a really sharp knife?* "Good."

"Excellent. I've been waiting for you to return home for some time, you know."

He was admonishing her, like a fond grandparent disappointed in his favorite grandchild. Revulsion crawled along her spine. Pretty sure her granddad had never behaved this way. "Umm...sorry?"

"Indeed. I had to occupy myself by rifling through your drawers and closet. You have excellent taste in undergarments."

The twisted old fart pawed her panties? Gross. Now she'd have to throw them all out. Tucked into a far corner clear on the other side of the kitchen, the knives weren't an option. Her gaze slid around the room. The lamp might work.

Ally dove across the room. A bullet smacked into the wall. She missed the lamp and crashed into the wall half a heartbeat after the bullet. Plaster rained over her and heat bloomed in her cheek.

She slowly turned, heart pounding in her throat, warily eyeing her boss and the little gun in his hand. Former boss.

"Sorry about that, dear, but at least I didn't hit you. You really should avoid sudden movements."

Wetness headed south along her cheek and she glanced down. Little droplets of blood landed on her shirt. Mr. Chesterfield might not have shot her, but the plaster had obviously cut her cheek.

"Now, I'm sure the last few weeks have been very difficult for you. Were you terribly frightened?" He sounded more curious than concerned.

Her pulse pounded in her ears. Fury blasted through her so hard and fast black spots danced at the edge of her vision. Careful, deep breaths restored her equilibrium and she focused on the old fart holding a slender gun and his question. "Sometimes."

"Only sometimes?" He frowned.

She imagined him trying to decide whether to be proud of her fortitude or disapproving at her lack of the proper delicate female constitution. Ally shook her head. This was surreal.

"What are you doing here?"

His sharp, brown eyes narrowed. "You really haven't figured it out, have you?"

She'd figured out that he was a very nasty man who wished her ill. Mostly, she was trying to buy time until she figured out how to reach her phone. Or a baseball bat. A Taser would be nice. "Figured what out, Mr. Chesterfield?"

"Why, that I'm the one who put out the contract on you, of course."

The condescension layering his tone rubbed her the wrong way, but she maintained her bimbo act. "Why?"

"A few weeks before you quit, a paper crossed your desk quite by accident. The same day Michael helped you with your overload of cases."

"What paper..." Belated realization dawned, stealing her breath. "You had Michael killed."

Chesterfield smiled.

Her stomach bottomed out and thick tension made her cheek throb with each beat of her heart.

"But...how did you know we'd both be at the amusement park that day, let alone that ride?"

"Don't be silly. I didn't know. He had instructions to follow Michael and take him out at an opportune moment. Afterward, he was to go to your little town house." He tilted his head. "Perhaps you should sit down, my dear. You look a little pale."

Delay, Ally. Think! "Why did you have Michael killed, though?"

He shrugged. "I couldn't be sure which one of you had seen the paper. So I had no choice, you see."

"What paper?"

"A paper addressed to an...acquaintance of mine, in regard to getting rid of my annoying wife."

Oh, freak. She leaned against the wall.

"You really should sit down, before you fall."

"It's just a little nick. As you well know, I've had much worse. So, you were going to have your wife killed. Ever heard of divorce?"

"Sarcasm is so unattractive in a female. Divorce isn't an option. The pesky creature holds all the purse strings, you see. I can't afford it and I'm not willing to give up all her lovely money. I simply don't care to live with her any longer."

Oh, God above. He was definitely going to kill her. No way would he tell her all this and walk away. After evading numerous hit men, a sicko pimp and a skilled marksman, she was going to meet her maker in her new home.

Her knees trembled and Ally locked them. Shifting the sandals still in her hand, she tapped her thumb against the wood sole. She tucked her hand behind her and hefted them, testing their weight, eyeing the distance between her and her boss. It was risky. Then again, standing around chatting didn't seem to be accomplishing much.

"You didn't even see it, did you?"

Ally blinked. Oh, right. The paper. "I look at hundreds of claims, tons of reports. So no, I don't have any idea what paper you're talking about. It must have gotten stuck inside a file or something."

She frantically tried to remember any out-of-place paper crossing her desk.

A noise reached her, out of place in her home. A soft click. She eyed the dignified lunatic sitting in her chair, but he didn't seem to notice. Not knowing what the sound meant added to the already palpable tension. *Please, please, don't be Celia. Or if it is, let her go for help.*

"I don't get it, Mr. Chesterfield. A man confessed. No one has come after me for a while now."

"Yes." He smiled. "Brilliant, wasn't it? I paid very well for that distraction while I figured out what to do. I assured him he would be released. Maybe he will. Maybe he won't. Not my problem. I withdrew the whole hit-for-hire thing." He waved a casual hand. "It wasn't working. I decided to wait a bit, until you relaxed your guard and that obnoxious detective went his way. Then I waited some more, but my patience has run out. My wife is driving me up a wall. So, here I am." He sighed. "Well, I suppose we'd best get on with it, Miss Thompson. No use putting off the inevitable, I always say." He rose, tall and fit, the picture of refinement.

Ally's heart rate increased to the approximation of a hummingbird in flight. "Is this necessary, Mr. Chesterfield? Couldn't we just forget this conversation happened?"

He chuckled. His behavior scared her more than his gun. Who pointed a gun at someone intending to kill them and *laughed*? The man clearly needed help, the in-depth psychiatric kind, with a straight-jacket and padded room thrown in for good measure. Ally edged toward the kitchen counter and the muzzle of his gun followed her. Another sound reached her, like the scuff of a shoe.

Surely one of Mr. Chesterfield's guys would just walk in. Could it be Ted? Maybe he'd come by to check on her, like he had during her hospital stay. Or Daniel, though he seemed an unlikely candidate after last night's disaster.

Greg thought he had his man, so it couldn't be him. Except, surely the man they had under arrest would have told them by now. Weeks had gone by. So, maybe it *was* Greg.

"Where would you prefer we do this, Miss Thompson? You've always been a good employee, diligent and hard-working. I don't mind allowing you a choice. Perhaps you'd be more comfortable in your bedroom, lying in your bed?"

She swallowed hard past her dry throat, tracking the gun in his hand, and took a few more little steps to the side. "I just bought the bedding. I'd hate to ruin it with all the blood."

"The kitchen then? It seems to be your destination at the moment."

"Uh, sure." Bile rushed up her throat. He sounded so calm.

Ally crossed from the rug onto the hardwood. She didn't dare look down the hallway to see if anyone waited there to rescue her.

The heavy iron pan sitting on her stovetop caught her eye, much more appealing than the thin sandal in her hand. Another step took her closer, aware her boss echoed every one of her moves.

He was almost at her kitchen now. Another step and she casually placed the sandals on the island countertop. Her fingers itched to snatch the pan, but she bit hard on her lip to stem the impulse. Slow and easy. Don't freak out the demented psychopath holding a gun on her.

"Would you like a last moment, my dear? A final prayer, introspection, something of that sort?"

"That would be lovely." Ally swallowed her anger and struggled to be calm.

From the corner of her eye she swore she saw movement but forced herself to ignore it. Turning sideways to Chesterfield, she slid her lids almost closed and walked her fingertips over the cool granite until they touched the handle of the frying pan. Ally angled her body to block his view, wrapping her fingers firmly around the cold handle.

"Would you mind moving closer?" she asked, ever so polite. "I would prefer to die on impact. I'm sure you understand."

"Of course, my dear. There's no need for you to suffer."

He moved into the kitchen, stopped a few feet away and raised his pretty little gun.

Ally's muscles bunched and, before he had time to level the gun, she swung the heavy pan at his head with all her strength.

A dark shape rushed toward them from the hallway.

Chesterfield glanced to the side, in the direction of the dark shape.

Ally would forever remember the sensation of the cast-iron skillet connecting with his head. The dull, squishy thud. The warm drops raining on her.

Mr. Chesterfield dropped to the floor.

Buzzing started in her ears and numbness settled into her arms and legs, blanketing her emotions as she stared at his wide-open, sightless blue eyes. A dark puddle started beneath his head and slowly spread across her beautiful wide-plank floor.

Nike-shod feet came to stand at the edge of the ever-widening red.

Ally glanced up.

Greg looked up from his contemplation of the man at his feet.

"What are you doing here?" she asked.

"The mystery man in my jail cell finally admitted the truth. Once I knew he wasn't our man, I realized you were still in danger. The alarm going off helped." He rolled his shoulders and tilted his head to the side, as if easing an ache.

"So you rode to the rescue." Cynicism shot through her. Silly to think he'd come for her. To do what? Throw himself at her feet? Confess his undying love? Yeah, right. That was gonna happen.

Stepping over Chesterfield's prone legs, Ally set the skillet in the sink and turned the water to its hottest setting. From the side drawer, she retrieved a dishcloth and bottle of soap. Housework cured all ills, right? Willing the rampant trembling to subside, she set to work scrubbing the pan. She stuck the dishcloth under the water to wet it again but yanked her hand back with a gasp. The water was boiling hot.

Greg took her hand. Jerking free, she swung the heavy skillet out of the deep sink and spun to face him. He leapt back.

On any other day, she might have laughed at the wary expression on his face. Soapy washcloth dripping water all over her pristine floors—if one didn't count the pool of blood, she marched over and dropped the skillet in the garbage can. The burning in her cheek was almost a welcome distraction. Her head felt fuzzy and kinda numb. Ibuprofen, that was what she needed. She started to reach for the bottle of pills on her counter and froze.

A sea of blood separated her from the island. The world spun on its axis.

Greg grabbed her. "Deep breaths."

Ally allowed herself one sweet, blissful minute to rest against his reassuring strength. She breathed deep, savoring everything about the man she fiercely loved, despite herself. Then she stepped out of his arms. Shoved her emotions deep and faced him.

"If you don't mind, Detective, I'll wait in the other room. I'm sure your coworkers will be arriving soon. Please have them search the main floor and outside for Carl. He's in charge of patrolling the building tonight and I'm concerned that he may be injured."

Without looking at Chesterfield, she sidestepped Greg, snagged a kitchen towel off her counter to press against her cheek and walked into her living room. She curled up on her little couch. Mind blank, expression stoic.

The rest of the cavalry took forever, but better late than never.

An ambulance carted Ally back to the hospital, where the same doctor who'd operated on her gunshot greeted her. He was not happy to see her. All her powers of persuasion and cajoling were put to work to prevent him from admitting her, and the visit still took hours.

She was finally on her way out of the ER. In the waiting room, Greg read a magazine, lounging in a hard plastic chair. Pain and longing arrowed through her.

She stopped and crossed her arms. "You didn't have to wait. I can get a cab."

"No need." He dropped the magazine on the table and gave her a casual once over as he rose. "I see the doctor is letting you escape. How'd you manage that?"

Irritation flared. "It wasn't difficult."

"Might be better for all of us if you were kept under lock and key. I don't think I can handle any more surprises."

She drew back, buried the hurt and straightened her aching shoulders. "You know, I believe I will call that cab."

Not caring enough to wait for a response, she turned and walked away. There were pay phones in the entry.

"Wait."

She kept walking.

"Damnit, Ally. Wait."

Rigid, she stopped.

Greg circled to stand in front of her, his mask of lazy, casual carelessness gone. Tired, guilty and frustrated described him to a tee. While she could guess at the first two, she couldn't imagine why he was frustrated. Nor was she was going to ask.

"I waited for you so I could take you home. Or to a hotel. Wherever you'd like to go. I doubt you want to go back home after what happened."

"Is there still a mess in my kitchen?"

"No. I had a clean-up crew come in right after the crime scene guys finished. Your kitchen looks as good as new."

Ally shuddered. Crime scene. Her home had become a crime

scene. She squared her chin. It didn't matter. It was still her home. "Alright then. Let's go."

"Home?"

"Yes. Home." She skirted around him and made a beeline for the sliding exit doors.

"Are you sure you want to be alone tonight? After all that's happened?"

Un-freakin-believable. Ally glanced at him, her lips twisted in disdain. "I don't need your pity, Greg. I'm not some mercy-fuck."

Greg's jaw muscles twitched, but his mouth remained shut.

She continued out into the parking lot. She no longer cared if he followed. One more second in that hospital would be too long. If she had to walk home, she would.

A few seconds later, Greg appeared at her side. He ushered her to his car, held the passenger door, climbed in, started the car and drove her home—all in stoic silence. Seated in his Camaro, a slide show of memories hit Ally. The car roaring down the alley behind her house, Greg tossing her in, driving to his lakeside cottage.

When they arrived at her building, she bolted from the car. Greg stayed at her elbow all the way to the door. She wouldn't have thought she'd be able to, but she managed to turn and face him.

"Thank you for the ride."

"Do you want me to come in with you? Make sure your condo is empty and cleaned up good enough?" His face was impassive. He'd worn the same expression in the precinct. No clue as to whether he actually wanted to come in or not.

"No. That's okay. I'll be fine."

"Ally…" Greg paused and scrubbed a hand over his face. "I don't know how to do this."

"What?"

"You and me."

"There is no you and me, Greg. You've told me that often enough." Pain twisted her heart. Ally shut the door firmly on his inscrutable, stubborn, beautiful face.

Chapter Twenty-Two

A few days later, the pretty wingback chair in the corner of her living room caught Ally's eye. Yeah, it had to go. Now. She grabbed the side and started dragging. The feet scraped across her shiny hardwood and she winced. The marks would buff out. By the time she got it in the elevator, she was sweating.

The chair was *heavy*.

The elevator pinged, the door slid open and she tugged the chair out and down the hallway. Pushing open the back door, she shoved the chair through the doorway and it tumbled down the steps. Grabbing the chair again, she dragged it to the center of the back alleyway.

Ally jogged back upstairs, dug through her kitchen drawers and raced back outside with a grim smile. Striking a match on the box, she dropped the flame on the middle of the seat cushion. She settled on the back step to watch the show.

The chair went up faster than she'd expected. Flames leapt high and thick, black smoke choked the sky above the building. The heat of the fire warmed her face and the bare skin of her arms.

Before long, sirens wailed. She sighed. Couldn't a girl burn her chair without raising a ruckus? Weary, she stood and traipsed to the end of the narrow alley. Maybe she could hold them back long enough for the chair to burn down to a mere pile of ash.

A big red engine roared to a stop in front of her, followed by an unmarked police car, two black-and-white police cars and an ambulance. Greg climbed out of the unmarked car and she sighed again. His gaze zeroed-in on her and he bore down on her.

No doubt about it. He was one ticked-off man.

The firefighters rushed past, hauling a long hose into the alley.

"What the hell is going on, Ally?"

Going for nonchalance, she shrugged. "I was enjoying a little bonfire in the privacy of my own…alley." The excuse sounded better in her head. "I'm not the one who called the fire department."

"You didn't have to. I'm sure the neighbors were alarmed by the billowing black smoke." Was he grinding his teeth? Stubs would be all he had left by the time he turned fifty if he didn't get that nasty habit under control.

"I'll admit, I didn't expect quite so much smoke." She turned to look at the black cloud rising above the brick buildings. There seemed to be a lot less of it. The firefighters must have gotten the fire out. Pity.

"Ally." Greg scrubbed a hand over a day's worth of beard growth. It added to his rugged sexuality and the Surfer Dude appearance he worked so hard to foster. Unlike the bloodshot eyes and the muscle twitching in his jaw. He cleared his throat. "Ally, you can't light a bonfire in an alley. You're an intelligent woman. This isn't news to you."

Pleased he thought she was intelligent, she smiled. "Well, I suspected it might be a problem. However, I was hoping there wouldn't be enough smoke to be noticeable."

His eyes narrowed. "What exactly did you burn?"

Several firemen came around the corner, making a beeline for her.

"Oh, you know. Wood, fabric, that sort of thing."

The firemen were surprisingly intimidating in their thick yellow coats and pants, heavy boots and stern expressions.

"Ma'am," the older of the two addressed her. "Are you aware it's illegal to burn within the city limits? Especially a chair in an alley?"

"Ah, hell." Greg rubbed his face again. "Go on inside, sweetheart. I'll take care of this."

"Wait a second, Detective. You can't—"

"I can and I am."

Ally trailed inside, leaving the two men arguing on the sidewalk.

"Thank you, Jia Li." Ally accepted a steaming cup of coffee from her. The first cup of the morning got the whole day moving. "Did you get those forms sent off okay?"

"Yes, Miss Thompson. And I filed the copies."

"Good. I've asked you to call me Ally."

Jia Li ducked her head, a blush staining her porcelain cheeks. Between her and Celia, Ally felt like an awkward, bumbling Amazon. But she hadn't endured uncertainty and violence for naught. If nothing else, she'd secured a definite vision of who she was and her value. She smiled. And a whole new life.

"You're my boss. It doesn't seem right to be so informal." Jia Li's voice was lyrical.

In the time she'd been working for her and Celia, Jia Li's English had improved by leaps and bounds. Her ability to absorb information had ceased to amaze them several weeks into training. She was like a sponge.

"We aren't exactly running an international cooperation here. A little informality won't hurt."

Jia Li's head came up, a surprising fierceness shining in her blue eyes. "No, we offer much more important service than some huge company caring nothing for anything but their bottom line. We save women. We rescue them. You and Miss Marsing are doing remarkable things, reaching out and working so hard to help other women."

Tears sparkled in Jia Li's eyes. After a little up-and-down bob remarkably like a curtsy, she fled the room.

Ally stared after her. She'd known Jia Li thought a lot of what they were trying to do, but she'd had no idea.

Wow.

Celia strolled into her office and sat down in a chair across from her desk.

"What have you done to Jia Li now?" Humor lined her voice. "She about ran me down in the hallway."

Ally shook her head, picked up her coffee cup and took a sip. As usual, Jia Li had added the perfect amount of sugar and creamer. "I didn't do anything. She gave me a beautiful set down about what a wonderful thing we're doing for the women of this town and how we're a thousand-fold above some big corporation." She grinned. "I'm paraphrasing, but you get the idea."

"I'll say. Good for her." Celia smoothed her already-perfect blonde hair.

Ally caught a flash of sparkle on her left hand.

"Celia!" She bolted from her chair and rounded the desk to plop down in the other chair. Ally took Celia's hand and examined the lovely diamond solitaire. "Well?"

Celia smiled. "He proposed during lunch at our favorite restaurant, over a chilled bowl of chocolate mousse. When Lucas got down on one knee, the waitress gasped and clutched at her chest so dramatically I thought she might faint. Anyway, that's why I was late this afternoon. We took a detour on the way back."

"Had to run home and celebrate?"

She nodded and Ally hugged her tight. She was so happy for her. As they'd built their business, they'd grown as close as sisters and she knew Lucas meant everything to her.

A few minutes later, Celia left and Ally went back to work. Or tried. Resting her chin in her hand, she stared out the window.

Celia and Lucas were so in love. Watching the stern-faced Lucas love and care for Celia so tenderly made Ally realize how much she wanted the same thing. Someone to love her. Unbidden, Greg's face danced through her mind.

Even if she didn't find a special someone, she could, and would, be strong on her own two feet. Look how far she'd already come. The shelter was bustling. They'd received hundreds of thousands of dollars in donations from people throughout the city, and beyond. Celia's connections proved more and more valuable with each passing day.

Celia's connections included an older brother who owned the building they sat in. Or he had until Celia convinced him to sell it to them for a song. Ally suspected he was the reason she'd gotten such an amazing deal on her condo, but she refused to dwell on it.

The location made leaving work difficult—a fact in the forefront of her mind hours later. Her stomach growled, reminding her she'd missed lunch. She sat back and stretched, her muscles popping from being hunched over her computer too long.

One of the shelter's women needed a job, a special one. Still in transition, learning to trust people and to comport herself in a business environment, she was a tough case. She'd get there, though, and when she did, she'd need a job.

One of Ally's tasks involved finding the perfect job for each woman's individual strengths, while remembering their weaknesses. She loved the challenge, no matter how difficult. Like now.

Jia Li bustled in. "Your tickets will be waiting for you at the airline counter, Miss Thompson. I requested an aisle seat like you prefer and I confirmed your reservations. You're all set to go."

Jia Li handed her a sheet of paper with the information, stood back and beamed at her like a proud momma. Ally wriggled in her seat. "What?"

"You're such an inspiration to me. To all the women you bring here to help."

Ally flushed. Confronting her fears and daring to be adventurous had been hard. Especially alone. Celia occasionally went along on her weekend getaways, but Ally knew she preferred to stay close to Lucas. Even so, Ally didn't see herself as an inspiration to anyone. The women who arrived there had endured far worse than she had. If anything, they encouraged *her* to continue on her chosen path and not to give in to the heartbreak dogging her.

"You're sweet, Jia Li. All you've accomplished since coming to work for us has inspired *me* more than you'll ever know."

"You are too kind, Miss Thompson. It's time to go home now."

"Okay." Ally shuffled through some papers and glanced up.

Jia Li still stood there.

"Okay. I'm going, I'm going."

They walked to the front door together. Through a locked security door to the left was the main entry for the condos above, all of which had sold in the past six months.

Jia Li opened the front door, smiling. "Have a good trip, Miss Thompson. Don't do anything too dangerous. I expect to see you back here Monday morning."

"I'll be careful. I promise."

Ally smiled and waved, locking the door behind her. Celia had left early. More celebrating, she assumed. Plus, she had a wedding to plan.

Ally ignored the twinge of envy and climbed the stairs to her room. She had to be at the airport in an hour, toiletries still needed to be thrown into her carry-on and having something to eat before she was trapped aboard a plane would be nice.

Water splashed Ally's face, soaking her hair and clothes as the remote river tossed the big raft from side to side. Laughing, she clung to the side. She wasn't too concerned about getting thrown overboard, thanks to her trusty life jacket.

If she'd known "adventurers" took so many precautions, she would have joined them ages ago. Now she tried to find something new and exciting to fill each weekend. Might not be the best coping mechanism, but it worked for her.

The raft bucked in the air and a middle-aged man grabbed a-hold of her. She laughed and untangled herself from him.

"Mr. Brown, I told you to behave."

He grinned. They hit another crest. Too late, she reached for the rope handle, went airborne and landed hard in the cold water.

The swirling water closed over her head before the life jacket did its job and shot her to the surface. She coughed up water, only to swallow more. A strong arm wrapped around her chest and hauled her into the raft. Collapsing into the bottom, she gasped and coughed up muddy river water.

She stared at her rescuer.

"I can think of better places for a bath, sweetheart."

"Greg." She scrambled to her knees. "What are you doing here?"

"I was bored. Thought I'd take a weekend trip. Who knew I'd get to play hero and rescue you, just like old times."

Ally climbed onto the seat beside him and slapped him on the shoulder.

"Ow." He rubbed his shoulder. "You been working out?"

"Funny. I don't get into that much trouble."

"You've been trouble since the day I sat down in a roller coaster beside you."

"Hey. That wasn't my fault." She smacked him again, putting a little more muscle into it this time.

"Ouch. You have been working out." Greg rubbed his arm, grinning.

Like her puny little muscles could bruise him, even if she had been working out. Which she had. All her extra energy had to go somewhere. The man hadn't done her any favors by waking her libido. Granted, she could take care of the more pressing needs herself, but most of the time, it only made things worse. So, she'd borrowed a page from the testosterone handbook and hit the gym.

"So, you just happened to turn up on the same rafting trip? How did I miss you getting on the boat?"

"Yep. As for missing me, you were a little busy with chubby and balding up there." He gestured up front.

Mr. Brown stared forlornly back, his soulful brown eyes glazing over when he spotted her. She smiled and waved. He wasn't the first man on one of these trips who thought a single woman would be desperate to hook up with the first available male.

After all, the big 3-0 had hit last month. She glanced at Greg, sitting there looking so untouchable. Emotionally, at least. He'd made it clear he was open for a roll in the hay.

They hit another wave, almost throwing her out of the back of the raft. Greg anchored an arm around her waist, hugging her to his side.

"Careful there, Sugar Lips. We wouldn't want to lose you."

She pulled free of his arms and put some safe distance between them. "I'm supposed to believe this is all some big coincidence?"

He shrugged. "Twist of fate, nothing more."

She snorted. Fat chance. She wasn't the gullible girl she'd been when they first met.

Ally unlocked the door, dragging her carry-on behind her into her condo. She re-engaged all the locks and reactivated the alarm. Sleeping for a week sounded like heaven, and she didn't want any uninvited company disturbing her. Far too many people in her life could break in without so much as a by-your-leave.

Between staying in the raft, keeping Mr. Brown at bay and preventing Greg from strangling the amazingly persistent man—all while dealing with her own conflicting emotions about Celia and Lucas' engagement—the trip had exhausted her. She felt like she'd been through the wringer and strung up to dry.

Without even bothering to unpack, she dumped her luggage in the compact laundry room and headed into her bathroom. After a long, hot shower, she felt more human. A thorough rubdown with her favorite lemon-scented lotion further relaxed her, and she pulled on her knee-length robe.

Wandering into the living room, Ally curled up on the couch with a blanket, a glass of wine and a romance novel she'd picked up at one of her stopovers. She lost herself in historic Edwardian England until hammering on her door rudely jerked her back to reality.

"Of all the nerve." She twisted the door handle. "Interrupting me right in the middle of the first love scene."

"Do you always talk to yourself? Because that could be something of a problem." Greg lounged against her doorframe, grinning.

"Okaaay."

He stepped inside.

Ally crossed her arms and raised her brow. "What?"

"You smell incredible. Fresh."

"That happens when people take a shower." Interest darkened his eyes and she swallowed. "So, uhm, did you need something?"

He nodded. Even after so long, her body responded to the heated look in his eyes.

"Yes." One step brought him within arm's reach.

"I told you, I'm not available for a roll in the hay."

"You said you need more."

She tightened her arms defensively, trying to still her racing heart.

Greg trailed his fingers along her jaw. "What if I'm offering more?"

Was he offering more? She licked her lips.

His gaze dropped to her mouth.

"Well, I suppose that would depend on how much more."

He dropped down on one knee.

Ally was pretty sure her eyes bugged out of her head. For sure, her heart stopped beating for half a second.

"Ally, would you do me the incredible honor of becoming my wife?"

"What?" she whispered. Oh, no. She'd had too much wine and passed out on the couch dreaming. "Why?"

"You have to have it all, don't you?" Sighing, he shook his head. His blue-green gaze snagged hers. "I love your hazel eyes, your brown hair, and your sassiness. I love your bone-deep loyalty to your friends. I love the way you demand equality and protection in the same breath. I love you, sweetheart."

Her heart cracked open. Tears rolled down her cheeks.

Tugging on her hand, Greg pulled her down to sit on his bent knee. "I love you," he whispered against her lips. "Put me out of my misery. Say you'll be mine for the rest of our lives."

The girl she'd been, with no self-esteem, loomed in front of her, laughing. *Are you really buying all this? This guy doesn't love you. He's just looking to get laid again.* Ally trembled, trying to get back to the new woman she'd discovered inside and loved. She failed.

"But...I don't understand." Ally pulled away and stood. "All these weeks you've been gone, doing your own thing. I mean, sure, you've shown up on my trips a few times, but it never seemed like anything had changed. You still didn't want a relationship. I can't. I can't do this, Greg. I'm sorry. I just don't believe that out of the blue you realized you were in love with me."

Her heart was breaking all over again. "You need to leave," she said quietly.

He stood. For the longest minute of her life, he just stared at her with disbelief written across his handsome face.

Looking at him hurt. So she didn't.

The sound of her front door closing sounded more like the slamming of a jail cell on a life-long sentence of loneliness.

Chapter Twenty-Three

Ally stared at the back of some guy's white T-shirt. The sun beat down on her. Grease-scented air wafted past and the screams of people having fun filled her ears. Ah, the sounds and smells of an amusement park.

"Come on." Some guy grabbed her arm and she snapped her head around. Unbelievable. The same pushy park attendant from her first time dragged her along behind him. "You're a lucky lady. You get to ride in the special car."

Oh, joy. Facing the most pivotal moment of her life had *seemed* like a great idea. Well, the time when she was thirteen and Jimmy Boeze had singled her out had been pretty momentous, until he'd dumped a bowl of lukewarm chili in her lap. Walking around junior high with a stained lap had garnered all sorts of lovely commentary from her peers. Ah, memories.

Mr. Obnoxious pushed her into the last car. Seriously, if he laid one more finger on her, she'd remove it.

"Okay, let's get you buckled in." He grabbed the belt.

"Alright, that's it." Ally smacked his hand away, but when she turned to tear a piece off his hide, blue-green eyes the color of the Aegean Sea twinkled down at her. Greg hooked the back of Mr. Obnoxious' shirt collar and yanked him upright. His eyes widened when he spotted Greg.

She didn't blame him. Greg had beefed up. Those biceps…yum. A week ago, she hadn't noticed. A week. Seven of the most miserable nights spent tossing and turning, barely sleeping. Seven days of deliriously struggling to get through while deliveries arrived like clockwork. The daily dose of massive flower bouquets had turned her condo into a flower shop.

Greg climbed in beside her. Exactly where he'd sat the first time. With an uneasy smile, she started to slide over to the far seat. But somebody else was already climbing in. Drat.

"Need some help with your buckle?" Greg asked.

"Uh, nope. I've got it. Thanks."

"If you're sure."

"Yep." She forced a big smile and latched the belt. "See? I'm good."

The roller coaster started with a jerk and whine of gears. Five seconds later the ride whipped around a corner and threw her against Greg. She nearly whimpered aloud, he felt so good. All hard and muscular. Sitting up straight took more willpower than she cared to admit. Up and down, around a few more curves, and they careened inside the building.

Ally tensed. A big, warm hand settled at the nape of her neck and rubbed the tight muscles. Tingling erupted everywhere. She snagged her lower lip between her teeth and bit down against a moan.

"Ally," he whispered in her ear. "You're killing me, baby. I've never told a woman I loved her before. I think your response traumatized me for life."

She shook her head. "Greg…"

With his finger under her chin, he turned her to face him. The rumble of the car, their fellow passengers, all faded away. "I'm serious. It took me a while, but I get it now. For a long time I avoided a real relationship with you. With anyone. When my parents were killed and I had to take over raising my sister, it tore me up. I kept relationships simple and temporary after that.

I didn't want to risk the pain of loss again."

"I know."

"Even when I knew for a fact I cared for..." He frowned. "What do you mean you know?"

"I know you were afraid of having a relationship. Commitment, feelings, all that stuff." Ally patted his thigh. And if her hand lingered a little longer than absolutely necessary...well, what of it?

"Afraid? I wasn't afraid." The appalled expression on his face would've been priceless if it weren't for her muddled emotions. "Look, I love you. I want to marry you. I want to have babies with you. What more do you want?"

"I don't know." Confusion warred inside her. What did she want? "All those weeks I worked so hard to put you out of my mind. I laid down my pride for you, even when I knew you'd probably throw my love right back in my face. And you did. Maybe I'm just afraid you'll freak out and change your mind."

Right there on the roller coaster, flying through fog and darkness, Greg kissed her. Not a polite, we're-in-public sort of kiss. A curl-your-hair, haze-your-mind, dampen-your-panties kiss. And she kissed him back.

"Baby, I love you. I'll tell you I love you every hour, on the hour, if you need me to. I don't care. I need you. I'd be lucky to have a woman like you. Please. Marry me."

Lucky to have her—exactly. Sniffing, she pulled away and crossed her arms. The ride screeched to a stop, freeing her to climb out and stomp away from the big jerk.

"Ally, wait."

She didn't want to wait. Or stop either.

"Ally!"

The people around her stared. A woman giggled and pointed behind her. Curiosity got the better of Ally. She turned and her jaw dropped.

In the middle of the amusement-park concourse, surrounded by hundreds of people, Greg kneeled on the blacktop. The crowd had helpfully left a path open between the two of them. She couldn't believe it. Proud Greg was down on both knees, hands spread, staring at her.

"Please, Ally. I screwed up big time. I know that, but I'm willing to spend the rest of my life making it up to you. Please, sweetheart. I love you. Marry me."

Crossing her arms, she bit her lip. Everything she'd ever wanted was hers for the taking. And he was essentially groveling in public for her affection. Maybe, just maybe...

She strolled toward him. The people lining the path whispered and a few laughed.

"I don't know, Greg." She tapped her foot on the blacktop and arched her brow. "Where's my ring?"

Choking on a laugh, he surged to his feet and picked her up. His muscles flexed beneath her fingers as he swung her around. Her heart soared higher than any measly roller coaster and she laughed. The crowd cheered. He set her down and fumbled in his pants pocket. Cool metal slid onto her finger, but she was too busy kissing him senseless to care. How fast could they get out of there?

They tumbled backward through the door of her condo. Ally tugged at Greg's clothes and slammed the door shut with her heel. Two seconds later, they landed on the hardwood. Greg pulled his shirt over his head in that cool, one-handed guy-move. Straddling him, she sat up to admire the sight.

Even her best fantasies hadn't been this good. Muscles she'd enjoyed six months, two weeks and four days ago were harder and bigger. She ran her fingers across his pecs and down the sexiest trail of hair to his fly. Touching wasn't enough, so she leaned down to taste. Maybe all those months apart had changed his flavor.

Uhm...no. Greg groaned and reached for her, but she slapped his hands away. She wasn't finished making him pay for all her months of loneliness. Watching his face, the way his eyes glittered at her—she hoped those babies he'd mentioned had his eyes. She undid his pants, stood and pulled them off. Oh, my. He'd gone commando. Very nice. His six-pack bunched as he lifted off the floor.

"Uh-uh." She wagged her finger back and forth.

His head made a dull thud on the floor when he dropped back and she winced sympathetically. Didn't mean she was letting him up. Well...she eyed his impressive erection...he was definitely already up. Her fingers played with the ends of her sash. Once she had his attention, she slowly pulled it loose.

The wrap dress fell open, revealing a thin strip of bare skin from her collarbone to her thighs. Watching him, she trailed her fingers along her skin. His erection jumped. A little shimmy slid the dress down to her elbows as her fingers moved lower. Never in her wildest dreams had she imagined touching herself in front of someone. But this wasn't a dream. It was better. And this wasn't someone, it was Greg.

Gently, softly, how she liked to be touched at the beginning, she coasted her fingers over the smooth, soft skin of her pelvis. In her very personal attempt to gain control over her memories of what Victor had done to her, she kept herself waxed. From the fire in Greg's eyes, he liked it. Touching her clitoris, she circled the rapidly hardening little nub. Greg's gaze didn't waver. She moaned.

"Ally..."

He was getting there. Dipping her finger lower, she found the pool of arousal at her entrance and spread the moisture higher. Where she needed it most. A little more pressure, circling, skirting around, teasing herself. She licked her lips. His erection jerked harder. Bringing her other hand up, she fondled her breast. Rubbed back and forth across her nipple.

Greg's gaze darted back and forth. From her fingers between her legs to her breast. The poor man didn't know where he wanted to look. Perhaps she could help...more pressure built the fire of desire burning so hot inside. Making sure he could see, she slid her finger down, inserting the tip inside. She pressed her palm over her clit and rubbed. Her moan was louder this time.

"Ally, for the love of…please," he groaned.

"What, Greg?" she whispered. So hot for him her legs trembled, she worked her finger in and out.

"Let me touch you. I need you."

"Well, since you put it like that—"

He lunged up from the floor in one fluid movement. Gentle hands glided up the back of her legs. She moaned, pleased to discover she was very sensitive at the back of her knees.

"You're so beautiful, Ally. I'm the luckiest man in the world. I get to spend the rest of my life with you." His hands moved higher, discovering more sensitive skin. "I get to make love with you every night, wake up with you every morning, watch your belly swell with our child…" his fingers skimmed over her belly, which turned to molten lava at his touch "…see you nurse our child at your breast…" those too-clever fingers grazed the underside of her breasts and she struggled to stay focused "…and watch you grow old by my side." Back down his hands went, parting her folds to his gaze. Blue-green flashed up and held her gaze. "I love you so much, sweetheart. I'm sorry I hurt you. I'm sorry it took so long to pull my head out of my ass."

He set his mouth to her, circled her clit with his tongue, the same way she had with her finger. Sensation shot through her, weakening her knees. She clutched the wall for support. He sucked, ever so gently. An orgasm she hadn't known was building crashed through her.

As the last waves rippled through her, Greg pulled her down, thrust inside her and filled the empty ache deep inside that existed just for him. Hands on his chest, Ally opened her eyes and held his gaze as she rode him. Unbelievably, the tension of another climax built. Greg pulled her head down and kissed her, captured her cries when she came again and gave her his as he pumped his seed into her body.

Sometime later, she held up her hand to admire her engagement ring. The big diamond caught the late-afternoon sunshine from the window and cast sparkles through her room. They had made it to her bed at some point, although she couldn't quite remember how or when.

"Did I ever tell you I dreamt about you a few years ago?" She rolled over and rested her chin on Greg's bare chest.

"You did?"

"Yep. Only in the dream, you were kinda pudgy and balding. And short. Danny DeVito short."

He flipped her onto her back and tickled her until she begged for mercy. Breathless, he kissed her until she begged for something else entirely. Slow and sweet, he made love to her as the sun set, gilding the room in soft pinks and purples.

Epilogue

"Stop," she screamed. Desperation made her voice higher than she'd thought humanly possible. Silence reigned for all of three seconds before pandemonium resumed. She struggled to catch her breath.

"Uncle. Uncle!"

Gasping, she collapsed against the rug.

"Mamma, you gave up too soon." Lizzie planted her little fists on her hips and stuck out her little lip.

"Yeah, Mamma."

Ally rolled over and glared at Greg. "It's your fault."

"Oh, yeah?" He cocked a brow.

Uh-oh. She knew that look. She scrambled to escape, but he grabbed her and tickled her until tears of laughter ran down her cheeks.

Time to play dirty. She grabbed Greg's hair and pulled his head down. Locking his lips to hers, she swept her tongue into his mouth. His arms wrapped around her and he took over. With a sigh, she relaxed in his arms and lost herself in his kiss.

"Ewww!"

Greg pulled away, laughing, and tugged on Lizzie's blonde pigtails. "Don't knock it, munchkin. Kissing your mamma is the next best thing to breathing for Daddy."

Lizzie cocked her head, looking from Greg to her. Ally pushed off the floor and gathered her into her lap. "Don't pay any attention to your silly daddy, sweet pea."

"Okay."

Ally snorted on a laugh at her easy agreement and winked at Greg. "Aunt Celia and Uncle Lucas will be here soon."

Greg scooped up Lizzie and carried her to the kitchen. Ally rolled to her feet, following them. Lizzie looked at him with very solemn dark-green eyes, the picture of her own. "Are they bringing Henry and Alice?"

"Yep."

"Good."

Greg bounced her in his arms. Watching them together always brought an ache of happiness to Ally's heart. Life couldn't get any better. Well, except for the little surprise she had for Greg.

"And Suzy?" Greg asked.

Lizzie made a face, scrunching up her adorable little nose. "Suzy's a baby. She's no fun to play with."

"She's not a baby anymore. She'll be four soon. You have to be nice to her too. You're the hostess and it's your job to make sure everyone has a good time—even the guests who are a few years younger than you."

"Yes, Daddy."

"Good girl." Greg gave her a smacking kiss on her round little cheek and Lizzie giggled.

He set her down and she skipped down the hallway toward her bedroom. Greg circled the counter and wrapped Ally in his arms. She sank into him. Ten years of marriage hadn't lessened her response to him in the least. He still turned her on like nobody's business. Hard to believe they had a six-year-old little girl. Not to mention…oh, she hadn't mentioned.

She leaned back in his arms and smiled.

Greg eyed her suspiciously. The man knew her too well.

"Have I mentioned how much I love you today?"

He grinned. "Nope."

She resisted when he tried to pull her close. "Have I mentioned how much I love our daughter?"

Eyebrows drawn together and a quizzical look in his beautiful eyes, Greg nodded.

"Have I mentioned how much I love our life together?"

"Ally, what—"

"Have I mentioned we're going to have another baby?"

A big grin creased his cheeks. Greg picked her up and spun her around, laughing and kissing her until she was positive smoke was pouring from her ears. And other very important body parts.

Ally's legs wobbled when he released her. Oh yeah, they still had it.

Grinning, he steadied her. "I love you so much, sweetheart."

She ran her fingers over his cheeks and along his jaw, staring into his eyes. "I love you, too. So much."

"Do you know when? How far along? Any of that?"

"I'm two months. The baby is due December fourteenth."

He frowned.

She wouldn't have thought it possible to frown and grin at the same time, but he managed.

"You went to the doctor? Without me?" He sounded so offended. He was so adorable.

"Yes. I wanted to be sure before I told you."

The doorbell rang.

"I guess I'll have to forgive you."

She laughed and spun out of his arms but didn't escape fast enough to avoid his broad palm smacking her playfully across her bottom.

She skipped down the hallway, meeting Lizzie part way. Heart overflowing, she and Lizzie greeted their guests hand in hand.